MURDER AT EXIT 0

A CAPE MAY MYSTERY

MILES NELSON

Enjoy the tour of Cape May!

WS WORKING STIFF PRESS
www.MilesNelsonAuthor.com

WORKING STIFF PRESS
www.MilesNelsonAuthor.com

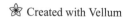 Created with Vellum

For all my Cape May friends - past, present, and future

INTRODUCTION

Friends, family, and fellow lovers of Cape May, I hope you enjoy this, my third novel. While my first two books, "The Privilege of The Dead," and "To Die No More," established a multi-part series, this Cape May murder mystery is entirely unrelated. Well, almost entirely, because if you've read either of those other books, you may notice a cameo appearance…

Those readers who are familiar with Cape May will notice that "Murder at Exit 0" takes place in a somewhat fictionalized version of the town. In order to tell the tale I wanted to tell, I needed Cape May to be a smaller and more isolated place than it really is. In this altered version of Cape May, the West Cape May Bridge, at Seashore Road, has never been built, and the one at the end of the Garden State Parkway is closed for several months for emergency repairs. The town truly has become an island that can only be reached by boat. I have changed the names and characteristics of some businesses and locations, and left others as you may know them. As far as street names, neighborhoods, and other physical aspects of the town, I have left almost all of it exactly as it really is. Many thanks to the owner and manager of the Ugly Mug Bar & Restaurant for allowing me to use "The Mug" as a major location—a character really—in my book.

For those readers not familiar with Cape May, New Jersey, the following is a very brief background, which I hope will enhance your enjoyment of the book. Cape May is a small city at the southern tip of New Jersey. Its position at the southern terminus of the Garden State Parkway has led to the popularization of the affectionate term "Exit Zero" as a name for the town. Cape May City, together with the towns of West Cape May, Cape May Point, and parts of Lower Township, make up what is frequently referred to as "Cape Island", which is in fact technically an island by virtue of the man-made canal that connects the Cape May harbor with the Delaware Bay. One can only get to Cape May by crossing over water. Cape May is considered one of the country's largest collections of standing Victorian Architecture, and the entire city is designated a National Historic Landmark. That architecture, along with several miles of beautiful beaches, and lots of great shopping and dining options, make the town a major east coast tourist destination. Among other things, Cape May bills itself as "The Nation's Oldest Seashore Resort", and is considered to be one of the "jewels" of New Jersey. Cape May is home to the United States Coast Guard Training Center Cape May, which is *the* training center for Coast Guard recruits. Everyone who joins the Coast Guard from anywhere in the country, goes to Cape May for their initial training. One prominent feature of the town that is mentioned in the book, is the popular Washington Street Mall. "The Mall", is a popular outdoor strolling, shopping, and dining destination, and was created in 1970 when the westernmost three blocks of Washington Street were closed to vehicular traffic and transformed into a landscaped pedestrian area. The wintertime population of Cape May is less than 5,000 people, while the summertime population is easily ten times that number.

Oh—and yes, that really is my old mug on the back cover, and yes, it was # 007.

1

W ith the first hints of dawn showing in the sky over the seawall to his left, Chickie Templeton switched on the right blinker and pulled up to the stop sign at the end of Madison Avenue. After checking that there were no other cars behind him or anywhere else in sight, he sat for a moment, sipping his coffee and admiring the way the red-orange fingers of morning light stretched upwards from somewhere out across the ocean to mingle with the endless expanse of dark blue above. From the low vantage point of the driver's seat in his old Chevy Impala, he could see only the cement face of the seawall with the sky above, but he knew the promenade and the beach were just there on the other side, with the edge of the Atlantic Ocean perhaps two-hundred yards beyond that.

With a smile and a nod to the morning sky, he made the turn onto Beach Avenue, the right-side tires crunching on some snow and ice that had been plowed over near the curb and left there after the last big snowfall. As he passed the several blocks of huge and mostly dark Victorian mansions, Convention Hall on the left, then the Lafayette on the right, Chickie was not surprised to see that almost everything looked deserted. The empty houses were illuminated only by street lights and by the odd floodlight that adorned every second or third closed-up property. Passing Ocean, Jackson, and Perry Streets, he cruised all the way down to where the road ended and had been widened to allow for turnarounds and increased parking, before slowing to a stop. The beach beyond the end of the road stretched out westward into the early darkness and towards the lighthouse and the small town of Cape May Point. Having grown up in town, he still thought of the area as "South Cape Beach," though he was aware that many people commonly referred to it as "The Cove."

He swung the car to the left and towards the ocean, pulling nose-up to the seawall in one of the end spots, and switched off the motor. Pulling the zipper of his parka up high, and taking a last slug of the lukewarm coffee, he pushed the car door open with a loud metallic groan, and stepped out into the cold.

The weather report had been accurate, and while it was seasonally cold for an early February morning in Cape May —somewhere in the mid-teens—the wind had died down to a light breeze from the north. An experienced winter fisher-man, Chickie was dressed the part, and made the adjustment from warm car to cold early morning ocean side without any fuss. After freeing his long surf rod from the cords that held it to the Impala's roof rack, he opened the trunk and got out his black plastic tackle box. He paused for a moment, looking at the pair of heavy rubberized waders, finally deciding that it was a morning best kept to dry land. An hour or two of casting into the surf from the beach should do it for today, he thought to himself, and with luck, he'd be driving home in the company of a few blues or stripers. He closed the trunk and walked the short distance to where he could cross over the base of the jetty and down onto the beach.

With no surfers, swimmers, or beach goers around to steer clear of, he only planned to walk a few hundred feet before setting up. That would put him far enough out to avoid casting into the rocks of the jetty, but still close enough into where he thought the stripers might be running. It was near low tide, and as he walked, the smooth expanse of sand, recently washed with the receding waves and then left exposed to the freezing air, made a crisp, crunching sound with each step.

In the dim light, he picked out a large piece of seaweed-covered driftwood maybe thirty or forty feet farther ahead, and decided that it marked a good spot to stop walking and start fishing. As he closed the distance, several seagulls noticed his approach and took flight in a sudden flurry of grey and white. As the pile came more into focus, he was struck by the way that two long pieces of the wood appeared to be splayed out towards the water, and he thought to himself that they looked almost like outstretched legs. Coming up closer, he stopped, looking carefully at the mass. Within a few seconds, he realized that the two long "branches" that pointed towards the water had bare feet attached to them, protruding from what looked a lot like some kind of dark slacks. Despite being steps from the Atlantic Ocean on an icy February morning, a further chill managed to find him and travel down his spine as his eyes moved up the legs, past a few inches of pale exposed belly, across some thick, grayish pullover, and on to a human neck and...

His hands opened, dropping the fishing gear onto the beach as his legs went wobbly. He dropped to his knees in the sand before finally allowing himself to look openly at the face.

Oh no. Oh no. He thought to himself, shaking his head from side to side. *This can't be real.* He looked around at the desolate landscape of beach and water, wishing for some practical joker to pop up and release him from his nightmare. *This can't be...* He looked back at the face. Dead, clearly, but not decomposed or banged up in any noticeable way. Recently dead. Eyes closed, thankfully, mouth closed also. A woman, he decided, with long brown hair. And not old enough to be dead.

Chickie felt the signal from his stomach as a mixture of coffee and bile tried to rise in his throat, and swallowed hard just in time to keep it down. He knew the sensation well, having been in war and having seen more than his share of lifeless bodies. Unlike some, he had never been able to become numb to it and always found it upsetting.

He looked away from the body, towards the surf, and made himself take deep breaths. After a moment, he stood up, testing his legs for steadiness, and started back towards his car. There still wasn't much wind, but what there was seemed to him to have suddenly gotten much colder.

2

Tate Saxby was running down the quiet street in front of his childhood home, trying to build momentum for a good flight. He'd been working at it for the past half-hour, running back and forth as fast as possible, but hadn't been able to get more than ten feet off the ground—and even then only for a half-block at a time.

Faster now, faster, breathing hard, and with the strongest jump he could muster, he held his arms out like the wings of a great bird and was lifted by the warm summer wind. Finally, everything worked and he was soaring free, higher even than the tops of the telephone poles. He could see over the houses now. He saw the new pool in the Brown's back yard, and over to the right was the shiny station wagon outside the Van Zandt's house on the next block. The open expanse of the apple orchard with the old white farmhouse in one corner was beyond that. The twin girls who had just moved into one of the houses in the cul-de-sac were walking their dog along the sidewalk below, and he could see the amazement on their faces as they watched him pass by overhead.

With arms outstretched, he rose to fifty feet above the road as he made a banking turn back towards his house. As he neared the landing strip that was his parent's driveway, a loud, jarring noise tore through the silence. The noise—like the tortured peel of some terrible bell—seemed to steal his power of flight, and suddenly he was coming down fast. At the last moment, he was able to turn just enough to miss the hard asphalt of the driveway, slamming instead into the freshly-mowed lawn.

He smelled the grass and dirt for an instant as his face smacked into the pillow, and he awoke with a yell that bounced off the walls of his bedroom. His eyes opened wide, trying to blink themselves into focus. The yard, the grass, and the summertime itself were all gone, but the ringing of the terrible bell was still with him, and was coming from the night stand.

He reached over to the small table and fumbled for the phone, getting it off its cradle with some effort. He brought it over to his ear slowly, needing a few deep breaths to help with the transition from sunny, childhood summer to the reality of cold winter morning.

"Tate here."

"That you Chief? I wake you up?" He immediately recognized the voice of Vicki Barstow, one of his four deputies. More than half awake now, he saw that the clock on the nightstand thought it was almost six.

"Yeah, yeah," he said. "Deep sleep, but it's okay. What's up? What's going on Vic?"

"Sorry to wake you with this, but I think we may have a floater. A body I mean. It's a woman, no ID on her, maybe thirties or forties, don't really know yet. A fisherman found her just at the high-tide line on South Cape Beach."

"Oh shit," Tate said. "Just wonderful. Shit. Okay, call Dr. Coyle up in Courthouse and see if he can get down here on the double. We'll have to get someone to bring him across the harbor. Dammit—don't need that hassle right now."

"Already on it Chief. And we're in luck. He spent the night at his aunt's house here in town. Why don't you call him and pick him up on your way here?"

"Fantastic idea Vic, I'll do that. That's a good break. You hold things down at the cove and I'll see you there in twenty or thirty."

Tate stood up and did a quick series of stretches before dialing the county medical examiner's number. Dr. Mark Coyle was a resident up at the hospital in Courthouse, and lived just off Route 9 near there, but frequently visited his aunt in Cape May. He and Tate were friends from way back in their teenage years. With Coyle's successful medical practice, along with his responsibilities as Cape May County Medical Examiner, he was a busy man. With that and with Tate's schedule as Cape May City Chief of Police, the two weren't able to get together for cold beers as often as they might have liked, but their friendship nevertheless remained strong.

"Morning Tate. What took you so long?"

"Very funny Mark, good morning to you too," Tate said.

"I guess Vic woke us both up. Tore me out of an especially good dream to boot."

"Oh, sorry to hear that," Coyle said. "Was it the one with the red-headed mermaid again?"

"No, I haven't had that one in a while," he said. "No, this morning I was flying. I'd just finally gotten into the air when the phone rang, dammit. You know, it doesn't always work. The wind has to be just right, and… Oh never mind. Anyway, needless to say, sorry to rouse you at this hour. Can I pick you up?"

"Sure. I'm at my aunt's house on Hughes Street. You know the one. Text me when you're on the way and I'll be out front. Give me at least ten minutes."

Skipping much of his normal morning routine, Tate went through the bathroom quickly, but paused for a moment to look in the mirror after washing his face with cold water. *Not bad at all for fifty-six*, he thought to himself. *Hell, I could still pass for late-forties. Well, on a good day maybe.* Generally not prone to wrinkles, he figured that he had earned the few lines around his eyes fairly. Likewise for the grey around the temples, and he was glad that hadn't yet spread upwards into the thick crop of sandy blonde hair. With only a modest ten extra pounds to his six feet and change, he was grateful for both the athletic physique and the boyish good looks his father had gifted to him so many years ago. Deciding that shaving would have to wait for another time, he dressed in his standard winter uniform of blue jeans, thick flannel shirt, and vibram-soled boots. His heavy gun belt, winter coat, and baseball-style 'CMPD' hat completed the ensemble, and he was out the door.

A few minutes later, Dr. Coyle jumped into Tate's police cruiser. His lanky frame was bundled up similarly to Tate, but with one of his standard Philadelphia Eagles knit caps on top. Even on an icy winter morning with bad news in the air, it seemed to Tate that Coyle's face smiled even when it wasn't trying to.

After a quick stop at the Wawa for coffee, they headed down along the beach towards the cove. When they pulled up and stopped next to Deputy Barstow's cruiser at the end of the road, it had been twenty-five minutes since Tate had been awakened by the ringing phone.

Tate saw his deputy coming up from the beach to meet them as they got out of the car.

"Hey Vic," he said, "you know Dr. Coyle. Whatta we got?"

"Chief, Dr. Coyle," Barstow nodded to both men in turn. She gestured to the old Chevy Impala parked nearby. Exhaust smoke could be seen coming from the tailpipe. "Fisherman—Chickie Templeton—came out early thinking to do some surf casting out here. Says he heard the stripers would be running. Walked out along the beach about two hundred feet and found the body. He said he first thought it was a pile of driftwood and seaweed or whatever, until he got close enough. Some seagulls took off when they saw him, but it doesn't look like they did anything much. That must have been about five-thirty, give or take. Just about an hour ago. Would have been substantially darker then."

"Okay, how's Chickie holding up? He all right?"

"Shook up a bit, but he'll be fine. What he told me sounded pretty simple. Parked there and got out his gear, walked out on the beach, coming up to the body from this side. Was there a minute, two at most. He didn't have his cell on him, so he hurried back to his car along roughly the same path and called it in. I picked up the call and got here five minutes later. I took a quick look before calling you, the doctor, and the EMTs." She pointed to the ambulance parked nearby, also running. "They confirmed that the lady was dead, but otherwise have waited for you and Doctor Coyle to show up. One of them's in their vehicle, and one stayed out there by the body to keep the gulls away. I got Three out of bed too and he should be here any minute."

As she finished speaking, a third police cruiser pulled up and stopped. Deputy Chase Conner III, who was simply called 'Three' by those who knew him well, got out and came over to them. They all exchanged nods and brief greetings.

"Vic, fill Three in on what we know so far please," Tate said. "Let me talk to Chickie for a sec and let him go for now. Then get the camera and we'll all go out on the beach."

Five minutes later, Tate and the two deputies, accompanied by Doctor Coyle and the second EMT, started the short walk down the beach to the body.

"Three," Tate said, gesturing for everyone to stop about ten feet short of the body. He waved to the other EMT, who was standing the same distance away but on the other side of the body, motioning for him to circle around towards the water and join them. "Get a series of pictures all around, from about this distance before any of us gets closer." The deputy nodded and started moving around in a wide circle, snapping away with a digital camera. It was not yet quite daylight, and the automatic flash went off for most of the shots as he moved around the area. "I want everybody to think carefully about where you've stepped already, and from this second on. We'll need to compare that to any other tracks we might find." Everyone in the party either nodded or gave a verbal acknowledgement.

"When I came up," Barstow said, pointing to a spot in the sand that looked like it had been recently disturbed and had a small branch sticking up. "I stuck that branch there as a marker for where Chickie had stopped. He walked pretty much straight up, stopped there for a minute or two, and then backtracked away. The rest of the area all around was very smooth, except that kind of trail there above the body. That could be tracks I guess, hard to tell."

Just then Deputy Conner called out that he was finished with taking pictures around the body. He moved back to take more of the potential tracks that Vic had pointed out, and the larger area higher behind and up closer to the marsh. The doctor moved in to kneel beside the body and start his preliminary exam. After working for a few minutes he took what looked like a household meat thermometer out of his bag and stuck the pointed shaft deep into the body's abdomen. There was a series of barely audible beeps, and a small display flashed a few times. He put the device into a plastic bag and dropped the bag into his case, coming back to stand with Tate and Vic. They both looked at him in silence while he rubbed his chin for a minute.

"Well," the doctor said, "I'll have to do an autopsy back at the lab of course, but just after this quick look, I'd say that it looks like she drowned, but it doesn't look like she was in the water for long. Extremities are mostly frozen through, but her core is still in the forties. Very strange."

"Strange how, doctor?" Barstow asked. "What are you thinking?"

"I'll really need to do some testing before I can say much more with any certainty, but I don't think she's been out here for more than a few hours, two, three, not much more."

Tate was looking around, studying the area. He glanced at his watch. "Six forty-five, which makes it low tide. Looking at the wave marks on the beach, and the bits of ice here and there, I'd say that she's laying right about at the high tide line. She could have floated in on a heavy wave, but that would have to have been six hours ago, maybe more." He turned and gestured to the sand above the corpse. "Or if she's only been here two or three hours, and if those are tracks, or were tracks, then what happened? Did she walk up from the trail back there, maybe from Mt. Vernon Avenue, suicidal maybe, go in the water, and then stumble out to die right here?" He turned to address the doctor. "Do you see anything offhand that indicates foul play?"

"Odd yes, foul play?" the doctor said. "I can't really say that yet." He looked down at the body and shook his head slowly before looking back at Tate. "But I can't rule it out either. Not yet."

"No shoes or socks," Tate said. "That seems pretty odd. They could have come off in the water, but I don't know.

Both shoes and both socks? Also it looks like she's wearing sweat pants or some kind of lounge pants. Like pajamas almost. And the sweatshirt. She looks like she's dressed for hanging around the house watching TV. I'd put on more than that just to take the trash out."

"Right," Dr. Coyle said, "like I said, definitely odd."

"As far as tracks," Barstow said, "you were probably both asleep—which I know because I woke you both up—but there was a gale that went over the island last night. I came on at four, and it was just dying out. My point is, it's very still now, but a few hours ago, it would have been very windy out here."

"I get you," Tate said. "So if we suppose for a moment that there was some kind of foul play—and I'm just imagining Doc, I know you haven't said that—then, whatever happened must have happened before four. Before the gale moved away. If there was activity here after that, we would probably be seeing footprints in the sand, or signs of a struggle."

"You're right," the doctor said, "that makes sense. But also, let's remember her core temperature. She couldn't have been out here since much before four. As early as three, tops, is my guess."

"All right, well, something to think about anyway," Tate said. "When will you have more for us?"

"My schedule's flexible at the moment," the doctor said. "Let's get her up to the hospital and I can work on her today. I'll have more for you later. As long as Three's taking enough pics, there's nothing more I need to see here. All this is contingent on the department buying me breakfast though. George's should be opening at seven. Sound good?"

"Sounds more than good," Tate said. "I'm frozen and my stomach is growling." He spoke to the two EMT guys, who were shivering but waiting patiently nearby. "Okay guys, she's all yours. Watch for anything coming off her or falling out of pockets. Get her up to the morgue and have a wonderful rest of your day. Thanks for your help." He turned and spoke to his two deputies. "Three, get a few more shots of them lifting and bagging the body, and check for anything that might be under her. One of you see if you can get Larson Finch to get up there ASAP and get her prints. After that, both of you get somewhere warm for a while. I'll see you at the station in an hour and we can start hashing it out. Hopefully the day gets better from here."

3

George's had been open no more than ten minutes when Tate and Dr. Coyle walked in. The small corner restaurant was warm and brightly lit, and filled with the comforting smells of breakfast cooking. They were the first customers. The man working the griddle looked up and gave them a friendly nod and a wave of a spatula. A young woman came up from behind him, dressed in blue jeans, fur boots, and a thick Cape May sweatshirt. The short apron tied around her waist was her only concession to any sort of server uniform. As it always did when he came in early on a cold morning, it seemed to Tate that her smile, while completely natural and unforced, did as much to warm the place up as the old oil burner in the rear corner of the historic building's basement.

"Good morning Chief," she said, "sit anywhere you like."

"Thanks Cassie, good morning to you too," Tate said. The two men walked halfway down the single aisle and settled into one of the booths along the window. Cassie brought mugs of coffee and a little round dish of creamers.

"Something going on down at the cove Chief?" she asked. "I saw the lights down at the end there when I turned off of Broadway on my way in."

Tate's eyes went quickly to the doctor, then back down to the menu before answering. "Not sure yet Cassie, just something we're looking into. Can't talk about it just yet, okay?"

"Yeah, sure Chief," she said. "Didn't mean to pry, just, you know, I hope everyone's okay. I'll be back in a minute to take your order." She went off to greet a few customers who had just come in, coming back shortly after to take their order and refresh their coffee.

"So what's your gut telling you Doc," Tate said, when they were alone again. "Now that we're warmed up and it's just you and me."

"What's my 'gut' telling me—you mean aside from two eggs, scrambled dry and well done bacon? Well, I'll answer you only because it's just us." Coyle thought for a minute as he tore the top off one of the little creamers and poured the contents into his coffee. He leaned in and spoke quietly.

"I've got some work to do when I get back up the road, but between you and me right now, it doesn't look like suicide. And I don't see how it can be an accident either." He put down his spoon and took a few sips from his mug, looking out the window and across the intersection of Perry Street and Beach. The pancake house across on the opposite corner was boarded up for the winter, and there were no more than a half-dozen cars in sight anywhere. "No, I think someone else must have been out there with her. Before, during, after—who knows? Look, that's really all I can say for now. I'll have more for you later. Hopefully I'm wrong and all we have here is some kind of freak accident."

"Fine, fine," Tate said. "I hope that's how it ends up too, though there sure have been a slew of freak accidents lately."

At that, Coyle threw him an exaggeratedly stern look, holding up a finger in a '*Don't start with me*' gesture.

"I know the ones you're thinking of Tate, and I get the frustration, but I did what I could with the evidence we had."

"I know Mark, I know you did. We don't have to rehash all that now. How about we change the topic to something nicer for breakfast? We can talk about all the snow, ice, and gloom of this unusually harsh winter."

They both laughed at that as breakfast arrived and Cassie topped off their coffee again. They turned their attention to their plates and ate quietly for a while. At one point, the doctor looked up and caught Tate laughing to himself as he took a bite of toast.

"What's so funny? Maybe I could use a laugh too."

"Oh, it's just a silly thing, but this toast and this little bowl of grape jelly thingies reminded me of something about my father."

"Hmmm, toast and jelly reminds you of your father," the doctor said. "That sounds like a good family memory. Don't keep me in suspense—let's hear the story."

"Okay, so, I don't know when it started," Tate said, "but going back as far as I can remember, my father loved guava jelly. As you might imagine, guava is probably not a very popular jelly flavor, and he couldn't get it at the Acme here in town. I think it must have been sometime in the mid-eighties, early nineties maybe, whatever, but he got tired of the Acme not carrying it. He contacted Smucker's and managed to get them to sell him a case of the stuff—shipped it right to him."

"You know I'm going to have to find some guava jelly now," the doctor said, "and give it a try. Must be some good stuff."

"Good luck finding it," Tate said. "I remember it as having a pleasant, mildly tropical flavor. Nothing dramatic. More like papaya than mango. Anyway, my father really went for it. I inherited a few jars but never got around to using them. Threw them out finally when I realized they were five years past expiration. I don't remember how many cases he bought. Maybe that one time satisfied his 'guava tooth'. But I remember that Smucker's box up on a high shelf in the kitchen.

"Anyway, around that time, he and my mother were still living just up behind this building on Atlantic Terrace, and he used to come down here a few days a week for breakfast. Sometimes I would join them, or him."

Tate twisted around in the booth to point towards a rack of shelves just to the side of the restaurant's door.

"It was George senior himself running the place back then, and he and my father were friendly. George let my father keep a jar of his guava jelly right up there on the top shelf. I don't know if you remember this about my father, but he liked to label everything, and there was a strip of masking tape across the Smucker's guava jelly jar, with 'Saxby' written on it in black sharpie. Whatever my father ordered for breakfast when he came in generally included whole wheat toast, and the waitress, who was usually one of George's daughters, would just know to bring over the 'Saxby jelly' from that top shelf."

"That's a great story," the doctor said. "You should really write that down some time. Tell me something—and be honest. Did you ever come in for breakfast without your father and ask for 'the Saxby jelly'? Like to impress a girl?"

"You know me too well," Tate said. "Yeah, once or twice, just for fun. I wasn't much for putting jelly on toast myself, but as I said, it did have a pleasant taste."

Just then the bell on the door announced a new customer and a tall man came in by himself. Tate was facing the rear of the restaurant, but could see the reflection of the man in the mirror that covered most of the back wall. He stood up to intercept the man as he walked by.

"Hey Earl," Tate said. "Good to see you—how are you doing?"

The man's face broke into an easy smile as he pulled off a glove and took Tate's outstretched hand. He was two or three inches taller than Tate's six feet and a solid thirty pounds heavier. His face was a well-weathered version of Hollywood-handsome, framed by a full head of hair that was now mostly grey but must have been closer to dirty blonde not too many years ago.

"I'm good Tate, no complaints. And you? Things going all right for you?"

"Oh yeah, I'm fine," Tate said. "Just, you know, trying

to solve crimes and keep the peace. Hey Earl, this is an old friend of mine from town, I don't know if you've met Dr. Mark Coyle. Mark, this is Earl Parrish." Tate gestured across to Mark, who reached out to shake hands.

"Actually I don't think we've ever met Doctor, though I've seen you in the papers more than once—you're the county medical examiner, right?"

"As a matter of fact I am, for the time being anyway, or at least until the next election. I've heard of you too, Mr. Parrish. It was generous of you to set up that little ferry across the harbor. I'll be using it to get across myself later this morning."

"Oh that's nothing," Parrish said, "I had the docks on both sides of the harbor and my company had the drive-on barge that we weren't using. A little tweaking here and there and it was up and running. Glad to be able to give back to the town."

"Well here, sit down and join us," Tate said, "or are you meeting someone?" At that moment something caught his eye and he realized that there was another single man in one of the rear booths waving towards them. Parrish returned the man's wave.

"There's Frank," Parrish said. "Thanks for the invite but we've gotta go over some business. You must know that we've got a small part of the bridge project, and there's just so much state paperwork it's hard to keep up with. But it was good seeing you, and finally meeting you Doctor."

"Sure Earl," Tate said, "good seeing you too. Hey, how's Buddy doing? He okay?"

"Oh he's doing good. Just fine," Parrish said." He's been

helping Angela over at the Ugly Mug. Cleaning up, some painting, it's good for him, you know. Thanks for asking— I'll tell him I ran into you. Take care guys. Stay warm." He walked off to join his friend in the other booth.

A few minutes later, after Cassie had cleared away the dishes, and Tate and the doctor had refused any more coffee, Tate settled the check, over tipped, and they stepped back out into the cold morning. The sun was up, if still mostly obscured by clouds, and the wind coming in from the ocean had resolved itself into breathtaking gusts that blasted across the beach and up into the streets every minute or so. Tate soon had the cruiser's heat running at full blast as they pulled away from the seawall.

"So that's Earl Parrish," the doctor said. "Kind of the 'Big Man in Town'. Strange that I've never actually met him until today."

"Yeah, that's the big guy all right," Tate said. "He seemed in a good mood just now, but he can be a prickly character. I don't know why you would know this, but he and I are actually distant cousins. I'm his second cousin, once removed, or something like that. A blood relative, but distant."

"No shit," the doctor said, "I had no idea. He looks more like he could be your uncle than a cousin. Isn't he old enough to be your father?"

"He's a little younger than that," Tate said. "I think he must be early seventies. But you're right—I've always thought of him as my uncle. He was double-cousins with my mother."

He looked over at the doctor, who gave him a look that said '*you better explain that one*'.

"My mother drew it out on a paper once to explain it to me," Tate said. "The couple that would be her parents, Stella Parrish and William Radley, married in 1940, and my mother, Jean Radley, an only child, was born soon after. Right after World War II ended—I actually think it was 1945—my grandparents had a big party to celebrate. His sister and her brother were there, and they met and hit it off —as they say—famously. That was Nathan Parrish and Angeline Radley. They married soon after meeting at the party and Earl was born a few years later. He was an only child too. So that's why he and my mother were 'double cousins'. They would have been cousins if either wedding had occurred. Pretty cool, huh?"

Tate pulled up outside the doctor's aunt's house on Hughes Street.

"Yeah, that's interesting," the doctor said. "You and Earl Parrish as second cousins, hmmm. Who is the Buddy person that you asked him about? Is that Earl's son?"

"Yes, he has one son, Buddy Parrish," Tate said. "I think the right term these days is 'special needs'. He's functional and he does all right, but he's only ever lived with Earl. There were major problems when he was born, and Earl's wife died within months. Earl takes great care of him. Buddy must be in his late thirties or early forties."

"Well, you are just full of interesting stories this morning," the doctor said, as he gathered himself to get out of the car. "I'll get it together and get across the harbor within about an hour. Give me a few more hours after that and I'll try to get back to you with whatever I can. And we'll get her prints scanned in and down to you first thing. Thanks for breakfast—next time someone finds a body on the beach, I'm buying."

As he drove away, Tate noted that the sun had apparently given up on its efforts to try to show itself and the sky had returned to a palette of greys.

4

By eleven o'clock, Tate Saxby had made a substantial dent in the pile of 'urgent this' and 'important that' that seemed to be a permanent part of his desk. Allowing himself a moment of satisfaction, he plopped the rest of the pile back into the wire basket that was his IN bin. Picking up the smaller stack of processed work, along with his empty coffee mug, he went out of his office and down the hall to the department's reception area, where Deputy Doreen Watson was at her desk.

Doreen had been a fixture in the department for more than thirty years, serving a half-dozen of Tate's predecessors, and knew the workings of the department—and probably all of city hall for that matter—better than any other single person. Though she was a full-fledged deputy, she rarely got involved in any action outside the office. She served as receptionist and dispatcher during the normal day shift, managed the schedules, and generally kept the office well supplied and running smoothly. She was only ten years older than Tate, but still managed to let a hint of 'mothering' slip into the relationship. It was never enough to annoy him, and in fact, Doreen was so smooth with it that, more often than not, Tate only realized that he had been the recipient of any 'mothering' well after it had occurred.

Tate set his pile of paperwork in the designated basket on the corner of her desk. "I'm finished with these. There's a few things to be mailed, others to be filed, one or two you might decide to shred. Any word from Dr. Coyle yet?"

"Not yet Chief," she said. "I'll find you if I hear anything. You know as well as I do that he'll probably call your cell, but if he doesn't, I'll let you know. That's so horrible about that poor woman. People seem to be dropping like flies around this town, isn't that the case?"

"I know," Tate said. "You're right, it is horrible, and not what people think of when they think of Cape May. Best thing we can do is for all of us, me included, to keep doing our jobs as well as we can. Try to keep people as safe as we can."

"You're right Tate—Chief," she said. "You can count on me. It's just strange…too many accidents to make much sense. Anyway, there's a fresh pot of coffee in the break room. You look like you need it."

"Thanks Doreen," Tate said, with a laugh. "I'll try not to take that too personally."

He walked back down the hall and turned into the squad room where Deputies Barstow and Connor were at their desks. As he walked in, both of them looked up from their computer screens to give him their attention. He pointed to Barstow.

"Are you still here?"

"Another hour Chief," she said. "Brody has the late shift this week."

"Good. And you?" Tate said, turning his attention to Connor. "You came in early, right?"

"Only by an hour Chief," Connor said "Do you want me to leave early?"

"No, no, that's fine," Tate said. "There's no problem with the overtime. I just want to make sure we're covered and everybody gets some sleep now and then. I know we're spread thin this winter and everyone's been great about it. We're all going to be due for a vacation come summer, which is exactly when we won't get it. Oh, Doreen made a fresh pot of coffee. I think it might be holiday blend or something like that—pretty good."

As Tate started to turn to go out of the room, he thought he caught a look between the two deputies.

"What?"

There was the look again, from Barstow to Connor. Tate recognized it as the 'should we say something or not' look.

"Okay, out with it," he said. "What are you guys up to? Is there something on my shirt? Do I have bed-head? Come on, spill it."

Deputy Barstow spoke up first. "It's no big deal Chief, it's just something we wanted to ask you." She looked over at Connor, who nodded to her as Tate came closer to her desk. "I took a few minutes to tidy up the conference room yesterday, and Three came in to help me move the table a little, and, well, we saw that you have a bunch of stuff up on one of the boards. You know, like we do for a project or an open investigation."

"Oh right," Tate said. "Those are three accident cases from the past few months. Yes, I've been kicking them around in my spare time."

"Right," Barstow said, "recent cases. We both remember them. What we wondered about though, is that, they're all closed cases right? Or have they been reopened?"

"No, you're right Vic," Tate said. "Those three cases are closed. I had concerns about each of them, and I brought it up, but the coroner ruled them accidental. The mayor didn't want to make waves, the families wanted closure, and that's that. I can't reopen them unless or until I find something really good."

He looked in turn at the two deputies, who stared back at him, waiting patiently for more.

"This stays here in the department," he said. "Let me get a little more of Doreen's good coffee, and I'll meet you in the conference room in a minute."

————

The police department, along with the mayor and other city offices, had for decades been in the old Cape May Elementary School building on Washington Street, and Tate's conference room was equipped with a huge, old style chalk board with a sliding panel. With the two deputies seated at the table with their notepads and fresh cups of coffee, Tate pushed the forward panel from one side to the other, revealing an equal sized board behind it. The rear board had several photographs taped in a row along the top, with an assortment of various sized bits of paper taped or stuck to the board below them. Chalk lines connected photos with notes, and comments were scribbled throughout.

Tate took a sip of coffee before setting his mug down on the conference table. He pointed to the row of photos along the top of the board. "I'm not sure how much statistics mean in the context of this very small town. And by 'very small town', I'm referring to Cape May in the dead of winter, and with this bridge construction going on. The winter population has generally been about ten percent of the summer population, but for obvious reasons it's a lot smaller this year. So—statistics. For a town this size, the average amount of accidental deaths is about three or four in a calendar year. Remember—I'm not talking about the high season, when there's ten times as many people here—I'm talking about the small winter town we're in right now."

"The population's about five-thousand in January and February," Connor said. "Isn't that about right?"

"Yes it is," Tate said. "Pretty close. Except that with the bridge construction going on, and all the hassle to get across the harbor, a lot of people who work up the road, in Court-house, or AC, near Philly, or whatever, have gone to stay with family or wherever they can find a place. I'm not about to do a census, but I'll bet you the town is more empty than usual by at least half, and maybe two thirds."

"I'd agree with that," Barstow said, "just based on what

I see around town and in the Acme. The few bars and restaurants I've been in have been mostly empty."

"Okay, so, in the latest twelve month period," Tate said, "we are now up to seven deaths that have been ruled accidental. That could happen, sure. Maybe we're just having a bad year." He paused and pointed again to the board. "I'm not going to officially contradict the decisions of the county coroner, but as you know, Dr. Coyle is a friend of mine, and we've talked about some of these cases quite a bit. Some of them are very clear. When that guy fell off the back of that scallop boat in the harbor and banged his head on the maintenance barge—no problem there—pretty clear cut. And remember Mrs. Jansen over on Stockton Street? Fell down her back stairs in the dark. Knocked herself out and tore up her leg to boot and her heart couldn't handle it. Again, no problem there. But these three up here are different. Or at least I think they deserve special attention." He moved closer to the board and pointed in turn to the three photos taped near the top. "Mary Ellen Barnes, sixty-four, slipped and fell on her bathroom floor, banging her head on the edge of the tub. Gerry Fisher, forty-four, tripped and fell down some stairs in a house he was working in, and broke his neck. Last is Augie Danforth, fifty-eight. He was puttering around his boathouse over on Yacht Avenue, when he tripped on a fishing rod and fell onto the pointed part of an old anchor. Those two sharp triangles stuck into his chest, you know that type of anchor? It was not a pretty picture."

"But… you thought there was something missing," Connor said. "Or something didn't smell right to you."

"Right Three," Tate said. "For better or worse, I thought something was a little off with all of these. Let's take them one at a time. Mary Ellen Barnes, older lady, sixty-four, comes into her upstairs bathroom late in November, apparently getting ready for bed, and steps in something slippery on the floor. Her legs go out from under her and her head comes down hard on the edge of the old cast iron bathtub. Dies almost instantly, according to the doc. So nothing out of line there on the face of it, right? We all know that the bathroom is one of the most dangerous places you can ever be. There was something very odd though. There was a small amount of something slippery on the floor under her, but it was dishwashing liquid from her kitchen. Or to be fair —from 'a' kitchen. Just a little bit, kind of smeared around an area of her floor less than about eight inches square."

"For certain kinds of stains," Barstow said, "dishwashing liquid can be the best. I use Dawn. Maybe she had been using it for a certain reason? I remember the case but I was never inside her house."

"That's a good point," Tate said, "but there was no sign of any stain or special cleaning project going on. And, like I have at home, she had a bucket—sort of like a cleaning kit —that she would move around the house on cleaning days. Toilet brush, cleaning solutions, few sponges, you know. It was in a closet down the hall along with the vacuum cleaner and the like. No dishwashing liquid in it. The stuff on the floor matched the stuff in the squeeze bottle that was sitting downstairs on her kitchen counter, but when I looked for it, it was sitting on the wrong counter, next to the stove. I mean, who doesn't keep their dishwashing liquid right beside the sink?"

"I remember that one Chief," Connor said. "I think Vic was off that day. That house was so neat it made me uncomfortable. Everything was in its place."

"I remember that too," Tate continued. "Another thing was that the smears didn't seem right. What I mean is, if you walk on a tile floor and slip on slippery liquid, you would expect to have a wide smear—like where your heel slid outwards, maybe even some toe marks if you fell forward. With Mrs. Barnes, the little puddle looked almost undisturbed, like someone had squirted it on the floor and just left it there to be found. Also, there wasn't much of the stuff on either of her feet, and no big smear anywhere. I thought that big smear was missing. Then there was the position of her body. I spent an hour in that bathroom, pretending to fall every which way, and I just couldn't see how she would end up laying the way she was laying. I couldn't shake the feeling that it had been staged. Larson thought it was strange too, but we didn't have much else to work with. Anyway, that's about what we had in the bathroom.

"The other main thing is that it looked like the door from the back yard into the kitchen may have been forced open. I say 'may have', because her nephew told us that when he was house sitting for Mrs. Barnes last summer, he forgot his key one night and ended up forcing in the door. He had done a patch-up job the next day. In the end, he couldn't be sure that what looked like damage to the door wasn't just the result, after several months, of his own poor carpentry skills. That's it."

"If I remember correctly," Connor said, "it was the house cleaner that found her the next morning. She had someone come in every week or two."

"That was a pretty sharp lady too," Tate said. "I asked her about the dishwashing liquid and she didn't know what to make of it either. So then, the lady's injuries were consistent with falling onto the edge of the bathtub, the bathroom is statistically the most dangerous place in the house, and I didn't have anything strong enough otherwise."

"Who's next," Barstow said, as Tate sipped his coffee.

"Let's look at the middle guy up here," Tate said, "Gerry Fisher. Brody was on that call first, and then I joined him. Middle of December. Pretty sure neither of you were there.

"Gerry Fisher was a contractor, carpenter mostly I think. He was working in one of the big houses up on the beachfront. I forget the name of the house, but it was one of those up near The Sea Mist and The Baronet. It was owned by an older couple from the Princeton area. They were out of the house for the season and Gerry was doing some fix-up work; spackling, painting, stuff like that. His girlfriend came by around noon to bring him some lunch and found him dead. There was a flight of stairs in the house that had a square landing in the middle, where it made a half turn and came down to the foyer. He had apparently tripped and fallen down the top section of stairs to the middle landing, where his head hit the wall just right and he broke his neck.

"So between Gerry and Mrs. Barnes, there you have the

two most dangerous things you can do in your house—be in the bathroom or walk down the stairs."

"So what bothered you about this case then Chief?" Connor asked.

"Only one thing Three," Tate said. "It could easily have looked on the up and up. Hell, maybe it is on the up and up. Gerry wouldn't be the first strong, physically fit man to take a fatal fall down some stairs, not by a long stretch. The thing that bothered me was something Dr. Coyle had said. He said that two of the upper cervical vertebrae were broken in several places."

"Which would seem to fit," Connor said, "with someone falling down to an almost horizontal position and then smacking into a wall, snapping the head up, right?"

"Exactly right," Tate said, "based on what the doc told me. But he also told me that the actual breaks made him think that Gerry had hit the wall with the *back of his head*. Like he fell, or stumbled down the steps *backwards* into the wall."

"Could he have tripped on something," Barstow asked, "at the top of the stairs, and then somehow twisted around as he started to fall, trying to recover? Was there a bannister that he could have grabbed?"

"The bannister had been taken down," Tate said, "because that was one of the things Gerry was working on there. Replacing the bannister was one of the reasons he was on the stairs a lot. It had been cut into a few pieces that were sitting around on the steps and the landing. That may even be what he tripped on, if that's what happened. Could he have turned around somehow, struggling to grab something maybe—I guess so, but I don't buy the idea myself. He was a few inches north of six feet tall, and there were only seven steps. I just don't think there was enough real estate there for a man that size to get turned around and still have enough room to get almost horizontal before hitting the landing wall. Oh—and the other thing was that he was found face down. Like he hit the wall face forward. What else comes to mind?"

"There must have been a dent in the wall," Connor said, "where his head slammed into it. In a modern house, he might have just torn through the sheetrock, but if the walls in that house are original, they're probably lathe and plaster —pretty hard stuff."

"You're on the right track," Tate said, "but there the plot thickens. The walls in the foyer of this house had stained oak wainscoting all around, and that followed up the staircase. You're right that the walls were plaster and lathe, but with oak paneling up to about waist height, with a decorative cap all along the top. Not unlike a chair rail. So however he hit that wall—if he did at all—it looks like he hit the oak paneling or the cap, which was also oak. The point is, there was a mark on the wood, but it was indistinct. Something about the size of his head had hit that area, but it could have been a long time ago. As far as the body, there was some evidence that he had banged his forehead into something, but there was also some evidence that he banged the back of his head. Dr. Coyle told me that the lack of bleeding or clearly developed bruises was consistent with him having died very quickly."

"So what's your theory Chief?" Barstow said "Your secret theory that is. Between the three of us."

"I don't know Vic," Tate said. He rubbed the back of his neck and stretched. "I'm not claiming to be some great detective, but it's like with Mrs. Barnes. Maybe there isn't anything there, but it just didn't all add up right for me. The scene looked like he had stumbled or tripped, maybe on a chunk of the old bannister, and started out of control down the stairs. Maybe he flailed away trying to get hold of something, maybe he got turned around. He hit the landing, falling out almost flat, but the landing wasn't big enough for him. His head hit the wall and snapped backwards with great force. Or did it snap forward?

"Maybe I'm nuts, but my vision of what happened is different. I think there was someone else there. Someone very strong. At or near the top of the stairs, that person grabbed Gerry and slammed his head forward, breaking his neck and killing him. He then posed the body on the landing in order to make it look like he had fallen down into the wall face first. That's it. That's all I've got on Gerry Fisher."

"So Chief," Connor said, "your...ah...uneasiness with the case is based on what Dr. Coyle said about how his vertebrae had broken, right? Unless I missed something else."

"No, you haven't missed anything," Tate said. "That's it. I know it isn't much to go on. Maybe it's just an oddity. Anyway, at this point it isn't enough to reopen the case."

"Got ya Chief," Barstow said, "both those cases do seem a little weird. What about the last one—Augie Danforth? I was on that call with you."

"Why don't you start then Vic," Tate said. "Sum up what you remember about it."

"Sure thing," Barstow said. "That was just last month and I remember it pretty well. His wife was away—visiting family in Pennsylvania for the weekend I think it was. They had one of those ritzy houses over on Yacht Avenue that has the attached boathouse, which is where the neighbor found him that morning. He had a small power boat—a Boston Whaler I think—and the place was done up like a work shop with all kinds of nautical decorations, like a shark jaw on the wall and that kind of thing."

"Good, that's how I remember it too," Tate said. "What else?"

"It was the neighbor from a few houses down that found him in the morning—guy named Davis, can't think of his first name at the moment. He had a habit of coming over with his morning coffee to hang out and shoot the breeze. At the front of the shop, nearest the harbor, there were two or three steep steps down to a kind of walkway that attached to his dock. Danforth tripped over a fishing pole that was laying on the floor along the top step, and had gone crashing down to the lower level, where he fell on some old anchor that had the sharp points sticking up. I think one went into his upper chest and one went into his throat. I almost lost my breakfast when I saw that."

"Good memory Vic," Tate said. "It was pretty gruesome, but all in all, it had the look of a terrible but normal accident that could happen on a dock or in a cluttered workshop. Just like Mrs. Barnes though, I couldn't put my finger on enough to raise a serious objection to the accidental death ruling.

But also like her case, there were a few things that didn't seem quite right to me.

"The neighbor who found him was a guy named Mitchell Davis, also retired. He and Augie were close, and he told me that they spent a lot of time hanging out in that boathouse. One thing he pointed out to me was that the fishing rod in question was a fly rod, and wouldn't likely be used for any fishing that goes on around here—at least not that Augie would have done. He said that Augie had done fly fishing years ago when he lived out in Colorado. Davis said that rod was there only as memorabilia—a decoration, and it should have been on a set of hooks high up on one of the walls. In fact, I saw myself that it was very dusty. He didn't see any reason that it would be off the wall, or if it was, knowing Augie, there's no way that it would have been just laying across the floor.

"That's one—odd but very circumstantial I'll admit. The other thing Davis told me that morning had to do with the anchor. Vic, I think you were checking out the rest of the house when I was talking with him, so you probably didn't get this. The thing about the anchor, Davis said, is that it wasn't in use either. It was an old anchor from a sailboat that Augie no longer had. Like the fishing rod, it was just around as a keepsake, but there's something else about it, and you're going to like this. As Vic already mentioned, the boathouse did double duty as a workshop. There were shelves full of carpentry tools, paint brushes, screws and nails, all that. There was a long work table that was built along one of the walls. Davis told me how, a few years ago, one of the underside supports had worn out, and one of the outer corners of the shelf had started to sag. That anchor was leaning against the wall and Augie had grabbed it one day and put it under the corner of the table, like a makeshift table leg. Davis said that he and Augie had both got a laugh out of the way the anchor stood at the perfect height to prop up the table, and they liked the look of it, and had just left it there. The only thing Augie had done was to carve out a groove on the underside of the table, so the top edge of the anchor kind of snapped into place."

"But if someone had grabbed that anchor," Connor said, "to use as a weapon maybe, wouldn't the table have fallen down?"

"No, that's the trick," Tate said. "The table had only ever been a little wobbly, but with the anchor standing under it, felt completely solid. I tested it myself. Anyone with a little strength could yank out that anchor and the corner of the table would sag by an inch or two at most. They might not even notice it. But the thing is, Davis told me, that anchor had been there for years, quietly doing its job. There's no reason that Augie—or his wife, who was rarely out there anyway—would move it. Before you ask, it did occur to me that maybe Augie had finally decided to do a real fix to the table, but there was no evidence in the shop that he was working on anything like that."

"You think that maybe somebody attacked Augie," Barstow said, "grabbing that anchor as a weapon of opportunity? Then staged the scene to look like an accident?"

"They could have looked around," Connor said, "seen the fishing rods on the wall, and laid one across the step to make it look like he had tripped. I'm assuming that Augie couldn't have been moved very much, because with wounds like what Vic described, there would have been lots of blood."

"Right," Tate said. "That's my thought too. In my alternate version of the story, somebody grabbed the anchor from under the table, maybe just for its appeal as a blunt instrument, and then waited for Augie, maybe sneaking up on him, and wailed that thing into his chest. Might have even been surprised when the points tilted out and stuck into the poor guy. Then yes, placed the fishing rod to look like Augie had tripped. There were no signs of a struggle, and nothing to say definitively that the body had been arranged."

"And the scene looked like an obvious accident had occurred," Barstow said. "Just like with Mrs. Barnes and Gerry Fisher. Neatly wrapped up and case closed. This is giving me the creeps Chief."

"That's pretty much it," Tate said. "And all of them tripped or slipped and fell to their deaths. If you wanted to fake an accident, it would be hard to think of something more obvious than making it look like someone tripped and fell, right? Which is not to suggest that falling in the house is not a deadly thing that doesn't happen all day long across the country. And maybe that's exactly what happened to all three of them. They tripped and fell. Or slipped. Anyway, now you know the secret of my notes on the chalkboard."

At that moment, Doreen poked her head through the door.

"Dr. Coyle called Chief, and wants you to call him back

as soon as you can about the lady on the beach. He says he has some preliminary findings for you."

———

With reheated coffee beside him, Tate leaned against his desk and used his office phone to call Doctor Coyle. His friend answered on the third ring.

"I gotta say Doc, you work fast. What have you found?"

"I'm not finished yet—there's a lot more to do, but I wanted to share a few things that I think you'll be interested in."

"Okay, I'll take what I can get," Tate said. "Lay it on me. Did she drown?"

"Well, first things first. When I started working, just moving the body around, several times I thought I noticed a scent on her. I called over an assistant who noticed it too. We finally figured out that it was lavender."

"Lavender? Really? I didn't notice that out on the beach," Tate said. "But maybe it was just too windy. If she was wearing Lavender perfume, she really must have poured it on heavy to still be noticeable after everything she went through."

"Really now Tate," the doctor said, "no woman her age would wear lavender perfume. No, it wasn't on her. It was *in* her. In her lungs, specifically. I also found traces of sodium laureth sulfate, which is a common surfactant."

"I don't know what a surfactant is Doc, can you dumb it down a little for me? What is this sodium stuff?"

"It's like a detergent, or a soap," the doctor said.

"Sodium laureth sulfate is used as a sudsing agent. It makes bubbles in water."

"Bubbles? I don't get it—stop playing with me Mark. Did she drown or not?"

"Oh yeah, her lungs were full of water," the doctor said. "Bubbly, lavender scented water. She drowned all right.

"In a bathtub."

5

A fter the impromptu briefing session with Tate and Barstow in the conference room, Deputy Connor had gone out for a routine patrol around town. On a hunch, he did a slow cruise through the few residential blocks closest to South Cape Beach. As expected for the off-season, and especially for the current situation in town, the area showed few signs of human activity. As he drove past the dozen homes along the short block of Second Avenue that dead-ended at the marsh, some movement off to the left caught his eye, and he realized that a screen door on the side of one of the houses was flapping open in the wind. A sign from a local realtor was attached to the front of the house, advertising apartments for rent and giving a phone number to call. There was a car in the driveway that ran along the side of the house. After parking the cruiser and zipping up his parka, he started up the driveway, intending to secure the door and give the property a once-over. As he climbed the four wooden steps to reach for the loose door, he saw that the inner door to the house was also ajar. *That's not good*, he thought to himself. *It's twenty degrees out here.* On the outside wall next to the door was a small plaque on which '1-A' had been professionally painted, and he realized that he must be at the door to a rental apartment that had been carved out of the larger house.

Conner knocked on the door, calling out to the interior and announcing himself as a police officer. Getting no reply, he did the same again, and then a third time, pushing the door open a little farther each time. Finding a switch plate on the wall beside the door, he flicked on the light and entered what looked like a small living room. Off to one side was a similarly sized eat-in kitchen, separated from the living room by a half-wall that supported a row of healthy-looking potted plants. He pushed the door closed and called out once more, again getting no answer.

With a hand resting on the butt of his holstered pistol, he went down the short hallway to explore the rest of the apart-ment. There was a bedroom with a king-sized bed and the expected dresser and other related furniture. The covers on the bed had been pulled back as though someone had been planning to get in soon, but otherwise the bed was neatly made. Directly across the hall was a spacious bathroom that also appeared neatly kept and had a clean smell. Connor noted that the bathtub was half-filled with water and that more water had been splashed around on the floor. The third and last door off the short hallway took him into a smaller second bedroom that appeared to be doing double duty as extra storage space and as an office or crafting room, with a large work table along one wall. Walking back out towards the front door, passing the half-wall with the potted plants, he noticed a framed photograph of two women and picked it up for a closer look. It looked to him like a classic picture of mother and daughter during a happy brunch at some fancy restaurant, probably taken by a friend or a waiter. The older lady looked to be about sixty or maybe sixty-five, but it was the younger woman, with a strong family resemblance, that he couldn't look away from. An electric shiver spread through his body as he realized that he had seen her just six or seven hours earlier, lying dead and mostly frozen on the beach just a few blocks away.

Pieces of the puzzle began to fall into place quickly after that.

The local realtor whose sign was on the front of the house confirmed that the only one of the four available apartments currently occupied was rented to a single woman, one Alaine Sawyer. A check with the motor vehicle division confirmed that the car in the driveway belonged to a person by that name. The dead woman's fingerprints had been entered into the system a few hours earlier as a Jane Doe, but now with a name to go on, a search quickly turned up a positive match. Alaine Sawyer, at thirty-four years old, did not have an arrest record, but her prints were on file because she had applied for the gaming license needed to seek a position as a blackjack dealer at one of the Atlantic City casinos six years earlier.

———

After Larson Finch retired from running the crime scene unit of the Trenton Municipal Police Department, he and his wife had moved into a small but comfortable house in the Village Green section of Cape May. Experienced in all aspects of crime scene investigation, and with an expertise in fingerprint collection and processing, he had agreed to an on-call arrangement with the City. The occasional call to assist Cape May's finest added a little extra to his retirement income, and perhaps more important to him, got him out of the house with work that he found to be interesting and meaningful.

His left knee made a distinct snap-crackle-pop sound as he stood up from the bathroom floor, bracing himself on the edge of the bathtub. He picked up his crime scene case and went out of the room to look for Tate and the two deputies. It was nine-thirty in the evening of the day that the body of Alaine Sawyer had been found on the beach.

He found Tate and deputies Brody and Connor in the kitchen of the small apartment.

"Three brought an extra coffee for you if you'd like it," Tate said, gesturing to a Wawa cup on the counter. "Cream and sugar and it might still be hot."

"Thanks, it's a little late for caffeine but I'll take it," Finch said. He pulled the plastic cap off the coffee cup, and after looking down at the contents, took a careful sip. With a nod of approval, he took a larger sip before snapping the cap back on. "Well, I think I'm done here for now. Not much to see but what there is to see is pretty clear. How long did this lady live here?"

"Just short of a year," Connor said, "about eleven months."

"And how about men?" Finch said. "Do we think she had male visitors—friends, lovers, whatever?"

"Hard to say yet," Tate said. "We've only gotten to speak to her boss at the insurance office, and two of her co-workers, both female. But the picture we get so far is that she was a private and quiet person, but normal—nothing weird. Both friends thought she was taking a break from men for a while."

"Okay, that makes sense," Finch said. "It's clear looking at this place that she kept to herself a lot. Nothing odd about that in itself—quiet town, dead of winter, great time to catch up on reading or whatever you're into." He paused for a minute, apparently in deep thought. He took another slug of the coffee. "Most of this place has been wiped down. Out here, you've got the kitchen counters, faucet, refrigerator door, stove top, all that. The only good prints I see are partials on the faucet and the fridge handle. My guess is that she was a very clean person who probably had just wiped up after cooking and doing the dishes. The dishes in the dish rack, the clean pan on the stove, the slight smell of sautéed food. Bits of food in the trash. It all tells me that she made dinner for herself last night and then cleaned it all up.

"But then it gets interesting. Maybe she read for a while, maybe she watched TV. There are a few prints on the coffee table and on the TV remote that appear to be hers."

"Mr. Finch, with respect," Deputy Brody said, "I didn't think we could tell so much about prints so fast. Do I have that wrong?"

"Ah, let me show you a new toy." Finch said. He reached into his case and pulled out what looked like some sort of large, mutated camera. "This is a NikorScan 2000. Made by a division of Nikon. A friend up at the crime lab in Trenton liberated it for me when they decided to go to a different model. The things the newer ones can do are things I don't care about, so I'm happy with this one. What I do is, I enter a good reference set of prints, I can then use this lens here on the side to scan a new print, and it will instantly do a compare. Earlier today I scanned in Miss Sawyer's prints. Here, let me show you."

He reached into his case and pulled out what looked like a common household cleaning rag and used it to wipe a few square inches of the shiny black stove top between two of the burners near the front. He gestured to Brody.

"Now, Roy, give us a nice neat thumbprint there please."

Brody pressed his right thumb into the center of the freshly-wiped area as directed.

Larson reached into his case again and pulled out a large aerosol can, using it to spray a short burst at the stove top. Against the shiny black of the stove, the spray left only a slight haze. He set the can back into his case and picked up the NikorScan 2000. As he pressed a switch on one side of the device, the men gathered around could all see that the display screen lit up brightly, going through what appeared to be a start-up process, before settling into a mostly dark screen framed by thin green lines, not unlike that of a typical digital camera.

"Now watch the screen as I move the scanner lens over the stovetop. I don't have to know where the print is—this beauty will find it." He first positioned the device at the rear of the stovetop, and slowly moved it towards the front. As soon as the lens was fully over the fingerprint, there was a series of beeps and the screen flashed with the clear image of a fingerprint. Within two or three seconds, the words "NO MATCH" appeared in bright red lettering at the bottom of the display.

"That is fantastic," Tate said. "So just to be clear, this thing's not online right? I mean, it isn't doing any kind of database search, it's just doing a comparison to the reference set that you loaded."

"That's right Chief," Finch said. He gestured to Deputy Brody. "I'll assume that your prints are in the system because you're a police officer. Note that the machine didn't find that. All it 'knows' about at the moment is Miss Sawyer's prints.

"So, moving on to the bathroom then, she went in and started to fill up the bathtub, adding some bubble bath or bath soak or whatever you call it. Dr. Coyle mentioned lavender scent, and there's a bottle of lavender scented bath stuff in there. The room has been mostly wiped down, but not completely—hastily maybe. Her prints were all over the sink and the sink faucet, as expected, as well as the tub faucet, but the edge of the tub had nothing. With a big old tub like that, a petite woman getting in and out—there should be prints on the edge."

"Yeah, that makes sense all right," Tate said. "And there was that black smudge on the floor near the door. She had a lot of shoes, but the only pair we found that look like they could have done that were way at the back of her closet. As clean as she kept the place, she wouldn't have left a smudge like that."

"Couldn't it be a kind of smudge that's just really hard to get off?" Connor said. "Like, pretty much permanent?"

"Good thought," Finch said, "but no. I tried wiping a corner of it and it came right up. I think the Chief is on the right track with that one. That smudge came from some unknown visitor, or intruder more likely, and very recently.

"I've seen a hell of a lot of crime scenes, and what this one tells me is a simple story. Some amount of time after dinner last night, when she was getting ready to get into the bath, someone came in through the unlocked door, overpowered her, and killed her by holding her down in the bathwater. Most likely it was a large and powerful man, but certainly it was someone bigger and stronger than her. Dr. Coyle told me there was a serious contusion on the back of her skull, which fits with being slammed back against the edge of the tub."

"Cause of death was drowning," Tate said, "but that could have knocked her out or at least stunned her enough to make the drowning easier."

"Precisely," Finch said. "Between any struggle there was, and then dragging her out of the tub, a lot of the water got splashed all over the floor. My guess is that the killer laid her down on the floor for long enough to wipe down most of the tub and the door knobs, and then picked her up and carried her out. Maybe he thought he closed the door all the way, maybe he didn't care. It's just a half-block to Mt. Vernon, then there's that pathway through the corner of the marsh out to the beach."

"And in this part of town," Brody said, shaking his head, "nobody would notice someone carrying a body down the street for a block or two. It's crazy but it makes sense. A lot of people in town leave their doors unlocked during the day. She might have forgotten, or who knows, she might have been on her way to lock the door when someone burst in. No one would hear a scream out here."

"Other than that smudge," Tate said, "there's no sign of a struggle, and no sign that anyone has tidied up after a struggle. It's a small apartment. He—I'll assume it's a 'he' for now—came in easily, grabbed her, saw the full bathtub, and took advantage of it. She wasn't raped, and the few hundred bucks in cash that she had between her purse and her nightstand wasn't touched. He carries her out to the beach in freezing weather but then doesn't bother to throw her in the ocean. Doesn't add up right to me."

"You're right Chief," Finch said. "It's a fishy one, but it's hard to say what people do in a situation like this. It could have been an intended robbery, but then he ended up fighting with her, and was freaked out when he realized she was dead, and did a half-assed job of trying to make it look like a drowning. You've got some work to do there. And I'm out of steam for the day, gentlemen. If you'll seal the place up, I'd like to come back in the morning and do some more poking around."

"Thanks Larson," Tate said. "Call the station when you want to come back and we'll make sure one of us is here to let you in."

Handshakes and thanks went around amongst the men,

and Larson took his case out the door and walked off towards his car.

"Brody, Three," Tate said, as they zipped up coats and gathered their things, "a lot of good work today, and we've come a long way fast, but it's going to be a busy week." He looked around at the apartment as he moved to follow the other two men out the door. "As unlikely as it sounds, it looks like we have a real murder on our hands. Which means, that somewhere in this pretty little town, we have a real murderer."

6

Tate arrived at the police department by nine the next morning, grateful that nobody had woken him at dawn again with news of a dead body found somewhere.

"Vic is out at that Sawyer woman's apartment with Larson Finch." Doreen said. Tate had fixed himself a cup of coffee and parked on the bench across from her desk. "He called early and wanted to spend some more time there— said you knew about it already. Three was here too and he went out right before you came in. He had a list of people to talk to about the deceased, friends and co-workers I gather."

"All right then," Tate said. "We're off to a good start. What else?"

"Three messages," Doreen said, picking up a few sheets of memo paper. "The mayor wants you to stop by when you have a minute to give him an update on the case, that's one. Three found out that the deceased lady, Miss Sawyer, had worked part time at the Harbor House last year. He was hoping that, since you know Earl Parrish, you wouldn't mind asking him about her."

"Hmmm, okay," Tate said. "Not much to tell the mayor yet, but I'll track him down before I call Parrish. You said there was a third message?"

"Someone called for you just after I got in," Doreen said. "He said he was an old friend of yours but didn't have your cell number. If I heard him right, he said his name was Boudreau."

Tate sat up a little straighter, his surprised face full of a question. "Boudreau? Dean Boudreau? Is that who it was?"

"That's what he said Chief." Doreen was reading one of the slips of paper. "He said he was coming to town for a few days and hoped to get together. He left a phone number —here."

Tate got up off the bench and took the paper from her, reading the message with a laugh. "Old friend is right— haven't seen him in years. Okay, if that's it for now, I'll go find the mayor. After that I'll see if I can find Earl Parrish, so you can tell Three I'm on that.

"Oh, and Doreen," Tate said, "I'd like to get everyone together this afternoon for a brief status meeting on the Sawyer case. Who's working on what, where we stand, that kind of thing. Let's say two o'clock in the conference room with whoever can get here. Brody, Three, and see if you can get Vic and Larson Finch to come in too. Maybe we can get Dr. Coyle on a conference call."

———

At age sixty-two, Jack Torrance was in the middle of his second term as Mayor of Cape May and was well liked and respected in town. Though the age difference meant that they had not gone to school together, he and Tate had known each other for years and had a friendly working relationship. Torrance was no pushover, but Tate considered him to be fair. When Tate entered the mayor's outer office, Mrs. Davis, long-time secretary and Guardian of The Mayor's Office, waved him through. He found the mayor putting on a heavy winter coat. He greeted Tate with a quick smile.

"I'm glad you caught me Tate," Torrance said, "but I only have a few minutes. I've got to get over to Wildwood for another meeting about those damn parking meters. If I had known that fifty percent of this job was dealing with the parking situation in this town, I don't think I ever would have run."

"Yep, that is the puzzle that can't be solved and probably won't ever go away," Tate said, with a laugh.

"I'm afraid you're right about that," Torrance said. He picked up a briefcase and took a look around his desk before moving towards Tate and the office door. "Can you walk me to my car?" As they left the office and started down the hall, he leaned his head towards Tate and spoke quietly. "So it's really a murder then, huh? Am I hearing that right?"

"I'm afraid so Jack," Tate said, matching the other man's lower volume. "Dr. Coyle and Larson Finch are in agreement on that. She had an apartment in one of the big houses on Second Avenue. Looks like someone drowned her in her bathtub, then carried her up the Mt. Vernon beach path and laid her out at the water's edge. Doesn't look like a robbery, but it could have started out as one. That does happen."

"Shit, shit, and triple shit," Torrance said. The cold hit them both in the face as they pushed open the door to the rear parking area. "Good thing we've got Finch on our team. Do you have everything else you need?"

"For the moment, I think so, yes," Tate said. "Yesterday I called your friend Gavin Paige up at the State Police barracks, and he offered to help however he can. They can't send people here to town just yet, but he's working on that. They can help with lab work or state and federal database searches if we need it. We'll see."

The two men had reached the sedan that the city provided for the mayor's use, and Torrance loaded his brief-case onto the back seat. After closing the door, he turned back towards Tate and looked down at the pavement for a moment before raising his eyes again.

"I can't believe we have a real murder here in this beautiful little town. It's incredible. This person may still be out there. You and Vic, Three—your whole team, be careful as hell, and let me know if there's some way I can help. We need to find this guy, or find out that he's gone."

"We'll get it done Jack," Tate said. "Let me get to work and we'll get it done."

As the mayor drove away, Tate walked along the side of the building to where his own car was parked on the street. A few minutes later he heard the familiar tire buzz as he drove over the short steel grate bridge that connected Cape Island to Schellenger's Landing. Driving through the marina area, and then making the turn into the Harbor House complex, Tate pulled up in front and walked towards the main entrance.

The huge restaurant was closed for the season, and he could see workmen installing new carpeting inside as he passed the foyer. Tate knew that the receptionist would be stationed right there in high season, ready to astound hungry customers with news of a ninety minute wait for dinner. He walked through and out along the dock, passing several tied-up fishing trawlers, until he came to the business entrance of Harbor House Fisheries. The office looked much like any other modern office, with modular wall sections, desks, and cabinetry making up a half-dozen work areas. Tate saw two casually dressed young women peering at computer screens as someone else on the other side of a cubicle wall held a loud phone conversation that seemed to be about a delivery of scallops to a restaurant in Philadelphia. A tall woman in red lipstick and a tailored tweed skirt suit appeared from around a corner, and Tate immediately recognized her as Earl Parrish's long time secretary and assistant, Velma Fontaine. He thought that she was allowing a little more grey to show in her light brown hair since the last time he had seen her, and it suited her.

"Chief Saxby," Velma said, with the mischievous look that she usually gave him. "What a nice surprise."

"And a nice surprise for me as well Velma," Tate said. "As always you look like a fancy dame from a Bogart film, sent here to the future just to make the rest of us look bad."

"Oh Chief, there you go again," Velma said, as she smoothed an imaginary crease in her skirt, before wagging a finger at him. "You know you're my favorite Cape May Police Chief. But I hope you're not looking for Earl, he's up on the bridge."

"Oh, I see," Tate said. "Well, that's what I get for stopping by without calling first. How long ago did he leave—maybe I can catch him up there."

"He just left right before you came in," Velma said. "I'm almost surprised you didn't bump into each other."

"Probably because I came in from the dock," Tate said. "I like to walk along the dock and look at the boats. It's the next best thing to having one. I'll look for him up there. Say Velma, before I go, you may have heard about the young lady that was found on the beach yesterday morning…"

"Yes, I did," Velma said, turning serious and cutting him off. "What a terrible thing. Joanie, the office manager over at the insurance agency is a friend of mine. She dropped by when we opened the office this morning and told me about it. She told me that your people had been in talking to everyone that knew her, Sawyer—wasn't that her name?"

"Yes, Alaine Sawyer," Tate said. "And it looks like she also worked here for a while up to about a year ago, but I don't know if it was here in the office, at one of the restaurants, or even the fish market."

"I already looked it up Chief," Velma said, "right after Joanie was here. She worked for us, but at the Ugly Mug over on the mall—not here in the office. She was there for almost a full year, ending last April. You should talk to the manager there. Do you know Angela?"

"Oh yes, I've known Angela for years," Tate said. "Thanks much Velma, I appreciate it. I'd better get up the bridge to find Earl before he goes off somewhere else. I'll hit the Mug after."

"Well then Chief," Velma said, "you'd better leave before you distract me from my work any further."

With that, Tate and Velma exchanged exaggerated winks, and he left the office via the hallway towards the front of the building and the parking lot.

Leaving the Harbor House complex, he turned to drive up the bridge that normally would lead to the beginning of the Parkway and points north. Not wanting to get in the way of any of the workers, he stopped the car halfway to the peak of the bridge to get out and walk the rest of the way up. He passed a pickup truck with the insignia of the Army Corps of Engineers, along with other trucks and vans from several different contractors and consultants, noting that two of them were from Janus Construction, a company that he knew to be owned by Earl Parrish. The whole area was a controlled mess of interesting looking tools and palettes and piles of construction materials. He stepped around two huge spools of shiny metal cable, and several coiled pyramids of thick hemp rope.

As he approached the array of bright orange signs and cones that warned of the danger of falling off the edge, a tall man gave him a wave and separated himself from a group of other men to come over and greet him.

"Good to see you again so soon Tate," Parrish said. "Here, come over and let me show you my company's small contribution to this project. You okay with heights?"

"I don't like to fall from them," Tate said, "but I'll make do. Sure, I'd like to see that."

Parrish laughed and gestured to him to step over a simple barrier consisting of a length of rope stretched between two stacks of ordinary cinderblocks. Orange plastic ribbons were tied to the rope at about every foot, and blew back and forth in the breeze like small flags. On the other side of the rope, the two men walked to within several feet of where the road surface dropped away into empty space, revealing a view of the rocky canal shoreline below. Looking across at where the bridge surface resumed on the other side, Tate figured that the gap must have been about twenty feet. Fighting a slight feeling of dizziness as he looked down, he saw that heavy steel beams extended two or three feet out from under the roadbed on each side, about six feet apart. It looked to him like the main span of each beam had been cut away, leaving huge rusty stubs reaching out towards their mates on the other side.

"As you can see," Parrish said, pointing to one of the remaining steel sections, "the compromised parts of these beams have been cut away, leaving this gap of about twenty-two feet. I'm told that the root of the problem was that there was a defective seal between sections of the roadbed at the highest point of the bridge. That allowed too much water to sit in the crotch of those girders, and, over time, well, you know what happens when water sits on steel for a long time. So now they need to fit new supports in there—new girders."

Tate followed along, looking where Parrish pointed to. "But they can't just stick a new section of girder in the middle there and weld both ends, right? That doesn't seem like it would be strong enough."

"No, you're right," Parrish said, pointing again. "A girder like that wouldn't have enough linear integrity. They're going to use a sort of saddle—see they test fitted one on the end there—that will allow for a final joint that the engineers think will actually be stronger than the original beam. I'm part owner of the company in Somers Point that's going to fabricate those saddles."

"Right, I knew that," Tate said. "Janus. I saw a couple of the trucks down there."

"Yes, that's them. Hey Tate, you're looking a little green there. Here, let's get away from the edge. Did you want to see me about something, or are you just checking up on the project?"

"I did want to see you, yes," Tate said. "Just a courtesy call really. You must have heard about the woman on the beach yesterday. Alaine Sawyer was her name. She worked at the Brookstone Agency—you know, the insurance company—so we've been talking to people over there. But we found out that she also worked for one of your properties about a year ago. I saw Velma in the office for a minute before I came up here and she dug up for me that this Sawyer lady worked at the Ugly Mug. I know Angela and I'll talk to her, but I just wanted to check in with you first to let you know I was going to be asking around."

"Of course Tate, of course," Parrish said. "Do whatever you need to do. Just let Velma know if you need employee records or anything like that. And let me know if anyone gives you anything less than full cooperation."

"I will Earl, thanks," Tate said. "It's all routine really, what was she like, did she have close friends, did she fight with anybody, that kind of thing. It was last year that she was here, so we're just fleshing out the story. Thanks for your help."

They shook hands and Tate turned to walk back down the bridge to his car. Earl called after him before he got very far.

"Hey, Angela's been using Buddy for some painting and other odds and ends—I'm sure he'd love it if you said hi to him if you see him."

"Of course, I sure will," Tate said, turning back to Parrish. With a last wave, he got in his car and drove back across town to park a half-block from the Ugly Mug, which sat on one of the inside corners of the popular Washington Street Mall—the shopping and strolling mecca of Cape May. Before getting out of the car, he dug out the slip of paper Doreen had given him, with the message from his old friend. He remembered Dean, but hadn't seen much of him for several years. The last he'd heard of the guy was when it was all over the news that he had killed a bunch of armed intruders who had broken into his house in the middle of the night in the Philadelphia suburbs. Apparently they'd really botched it—breaking into the wrong house looking for some drug dealer or something like that. *Jeez,* Tate thought, shaking his head, *talk about a mega screw up. They certainly had gotten more than they'd bargained for that night. A hail of hot lead.* He picked up his phone and dialed the number on the paper. A man's voice answered, vaguely familiar.

"Hmmm, a six-oh-nine area code. Could this be the Chief of Police of Cape May calling me?"

"It sure is, you old fraud," Tate said. "And this must be the long lost Mr. Boudreau himself. Good to hear your voice Dean. A real blast from the past."

"I don't know Tate," Dean said. "Some of these cold mornings I feel more like a gust out of the dust."

"That's just the winter—that and middle age," Tate said. "Happens to the best of us, including me. So what's up man —you coming to town any time soon?"

"As a matter of fact I am," Dean said. "I'm up in the city for a few more days, then I'll come down there for a while. We'll need to get together more than once, if you have time."

"That sounds fantastic," Tate said, "do you have a place to stay yet? I have a guest room if you don't mind a twin bed. Yours if you want it."

"Appreciate the offer Chief," Dean said, "thanks. But I like to stay at the Carolina when I'm in town. Is this your cell number? I'll text you in a day or so when I know what I'm doing."

"Yeah, this is my cell, so let me know," Tate said. "I'm a half block down the street at The Tides, so that'll work out just fine. Looking forward to catching up."

Tate told his friend about the situation with the bridge construction and pointed him towards how to get across the harbor on the temporary ferry. They chatted for a few more minutes before signing off.

As Tate got out of the car and into the cold again, his breath making miniature clouds that rose upwards and faded away above him, he realized he was smiling. *And I'm going to make him tell me all about that night.*

With a shake of his head and a deep breath of cold air, he snapped back to the matter at hand. Knowing that the restaurant didn't open for another hour, he went around back, passing the dumpster and the storage shed, and went in through the unlocked kitchen door. Inside, two workers in kitchen whites looked up from their prep work and nodded his way. Cumin-scented steam from a huge simmering pot of the restaurant's signature Texas-style chili permeated the room, mingling with the aroma of fresh baked rolls cooling on a nearby counter. An almost audible growl from Tate's stomach reminded him that all he had managed for breakfast was a slice of peanut butter toast.

"Smells good guys," Tate said. "I'm looking for Angela. She around?"

"Out at the bar Chief," one of the men said. "Go ahead on out."

Tate gave a wave of thanks and left the kitchen through the double swinging doors.

The Ugly Mug Tavern was a popular hangout for locals and visitors alike. They offered a full menu of lunch and dinner items, but were probably best known for the several hundred beer mugs hanging from hooks mounted in rows all over the ceiling. Tate knew the tradition went back to well before he was born. Regular customers could buy a mug and get their name printed on it, and it would hang there, available for use whenever they came in. Over time, as the amount of mugs went from ten to twenty, and then from fifty and onwards to hundreds, the unspoken rule was that, if you could find your mug and reach it, the bartender would be happy to rinse off the dust and use it to serve you. Otherwise, they were decorations and conversation pieces. One of the most important things about the mugs, that few non-locals would have known, was the importance of which direction they were pointing. The vast majority of the mugs hung from the ceiling with their open ends pointed inland, while the mugs that were pointed the other way—towards the sea—were those of deceased people. As Tate's eyes made the adjustment from the brightly lit kitchen to the darker bar he thought the ceiling looked different than he remembered. Cleaner perhaps? Brighter somehow?

"Well if it isn't Chief Saxby in the flesh," A woman's voice said, from the near end of the bar. The woman got off her stool as Tate came over, enveloping him in a tight hug.

"Whoo-wee," Tate said, as they separated. "It's about twenty-five degrees outside, but between you and the chili smell in the kitchen, I'm suddenly all warm and toasty."

"I'll put it on your tab," Angela said. "Can I get you a drink, or something to eat?"

"Nothing for me, thanks Ang," Tate said. He gestured to her to sit down and she returned to her barstool. He took the one beside her for himself. "I know you're getting ready to open so I won't take more than a few minutes."

"You're here about the woman on the beach, right?" Angela said. "I had to go over to the office a few minutes ago and I ran into Velma. She told me I might be hearing from you. So yeah, Alaine Sawyer. She waitressed here for almost a year. I think she was taking classes for data processing or something like that. Left last April for Brook-stone Insurance. She was a good worker and I was sorry to see her go, but you know, I was happy for her."

"Do you remember if she had a lot of friends," Tate said, "or was she a loner? How did she fit in?"

"I wasn't personal friends with her," Angela said, "but she was friendly. I don't remember her as Miss Personality, but she was outgoing enough. No fights, no problems. She chatted with the other girls, usual girl stuff. She was a successful waitress, you know. You can't do that job if you don't have decent social skills. Working in a restaurant can be a high stress job, but she handled it pretty well."

"How about men," Tate said. "Anything or anyone special come to mind?"

"Not particularly," Angela said, after thinking for a moment. "At least not that I saw. There was a little bit of standard flirting with some of the guys, but nothing serious that I ever noticed. I don't know why I know this, but I had the feeling that she was taking a break, which is something women do sometimes."

"Yeah, we got that sense from some people who knew her over at Brookstone too," Tate said. "Well, I'll keep plugging…"

Just then they were interrupted when a man appeared from out of the basement door. Fortyish, tall, and solidly built, dark hair just starting to show flecks of grey, he had a boyish face that easily looked twenty years younger than the rest of him. He stopped when he saw Tate, his face breaking into a smile. Tate got up and walked over to Buddy Parrish with an outstretched hand. "Hi Buddy, I heard you were doing some work here. How are you?"

"I'm good Tate, good Tate," Buddy said, nodding vigorously. "Are you good?"

"I am Buddy, thank you for asking," Tate said. "I just saw your father on the bridge, that work is very exciting, but too high up for me."

Buddy seemed to delight at that and laughed out loud. "I don't mind it Tate. Just don't look down!"

"Buddy's been helping out here for a few months now," Angela said. She gestured to the ceiling. "Right after they shut down the bridge, we closed here for a week and Buddy cleaned and painted the ceiling. He did a really good job, didn't he?"

"He sure did," Tate said. He looked over at Buddy and was surprised to see that the boyish face was clouded, as if with some suddenly remembered worry. "You do good work Buddy. Next time I need some painting done, you're the first person I'm going to call."

"Thanks Tate, thanks Tate," Buddy said, brightening. "Have to go now. I'll be back tomorrow Miss Angela. Bye Tate." Buddy picked up his heavy coat from where it was laying in one of the booths, put it on quickly, and went out through the kitchen door as Tate and Angela watched.

"I guess he doesn't take praise very well," Tate said, turning back to Angela. "I hope I didn't make him uncomfortable."

"Oh, he's fine, don't worry about him," Angela said, "It's always a bit of a balancing act with him, but he's a good guy. He's forty-one or forty-two, but mentally he's more like twelve. There's a limit to how much interaction with other people he can take, but he's friendly and highly functional as long as you give him clear instructions."

"Yeah, I'm sure you're right," Tate said. "Okay, well, I'd

better get going and leave you to your paperwork. "Thanks for your thoughts on the Sawyer lady, and let me know if anything else comes to mind. By the way, do you remember my friend Dean Boudreau, or does that go back to before your time? He grew up in town."

"That name isn't familiar," Angela said. "I've been here about twenty-five years, so I guess I would only know him if he was here and you introduced us. Is he as good looking as you?"

"Oh now I wouldn't go that far," Tate said, "but people did mix us up once or twice, back in the day. Anyway, he says he'll be coming to town in a few days, and I know he's going to want to hang out here. I'll make sure you get to meet him. So I'll see you within a few days, in off-duty mode. Maybe you'll be able to join us for a drink."

"Can't wait Chief," Angela said. "Come back soon."

7

It was shortly after two in the afternoon when Deputy Brody made final adjustments to the video conference software on his laptop, and the picture of Dr. Coyle sitting in an office up at the hospital came clearly into focus on the big flat screen at the end of the room. Brody looked up at the small camera mounted atop the screen and saw that the blue light was blinking slowly, telling him the camera was live. Satisfied that the system was working as expected, he nodded across the table to Tate.

"Thanks for joining us Doctor," Tate said, directing his voice to the large conference phone in the middle of the big table. "Can you hear us and see us okay?"

"Coming in loud and clear Chief," the doctor said. "Picture is a little distorted as usual, but I see you."

"Fantastic, thanks for joining," Tate said. "And Larson, appreciate your time also. I don't see that this needs to be a long meeting, but I wanted to get us all together for the first time to see where we stand. Vic, would you please start us off with a basic bio on the deceased woman?"

"Sure Chief," Barstow said, shuffling a few sheets of paper on the table in front of her. "The deceased, Alaine Sawyer, was thirty-four years old. Born in Mapleshade in 1984, she graduated from Cherry Hill High School in 2002. Her father died from a heart attack in 2006, her mother lives with a sister in Bucks County. Alaine had an older brother, Jason, who's lived in Arizona for about ten years. Everything looks like a normal nuclear family. Summer vacations at the shore almost every year, mostly Ocean City, but occasionally Wildwood and then Cape May in later years. So far I've spoken with the aunt, the brother, and one neighbor, all by phone. Everyone is stunned of course but I haven't heard about anything out of the ordinary. No known enemies, no threats, good grades in high school, no big fights with boyfriends, nothing. She lived in Ocean City for a year, with friends, but I haven't gotten those details yet. Been in the Second Avenue apartment here in town for eleven months, a place on Eldredge Avenue for the year prior. Worked at Brookstone Agency recently, and the Ugly Mug Tavern on the mall before that. Her prints were in the system because she applied for a gaming license six years ago. The license was approved, but if she ever actually applied for a job, nobody I've spoken with yet seems to know about it. That's about it for the basic bio, unless there's any questions."

Tate looked around the table, allowing a chance for anyone to chime in, but nobody did.

"Good work Vic," Tate said. "Three, you're next. What have you been working on?"

"Okay, well, yesterday," Connor said, "after we confirmed that the Second Avenue apartment was hers, I spent almost an hour walking between there and the beach path, thinking that she may have been carried along that way. It seemed to me that if somebody was worrying about being seen, they would cut through those four back yards to Mt. Vernon, and there aren't any fences in the way. The ground is all frozen so there aren't any tracks that I can see. If someone was worried about going through the yards and went along the sidewalk, there wouldn't be any tracks anyway, because there wasn't anything wet or slushy around. There is a jumble of tracks where the sand starts at the end of Mt. Vernon, but with all the wind yesterday and the night before, nothing really stands out. I walked the path all the way out to where she was found and filmed it for the file anyway. No ATMs or banks anywhere in that part of town, so no camera footage to look at.

"Between yesterday and earlier today, I've spoken with her manager at the Brookstone Agency, along with most of her co-workers. Everyone seemed genuinely stunned and saddened—I didn't get anything strange. By all accounts she was good at her job and was well liked. No boyfriend or girlfriend that anyone was aware of. Accepted the invitation to the after-work happy hour every third or fourth time and seemed to have fun. Nobody I spoke with could think of any reason someone would want to hurt her. I went back over to her apartment this morning with Mr. Finch, and while I was there, I went over the outside of the house and the yard again—nothing out of the ordinary."

"What about her car," Tate said. "Did anyone check that out?"

"Sure did Chief," Connor said. "Brody and I went through it with a magnifying glass. Like her apartment, the car was pretty clean. Insurance and registration were both up to date and the car seems well maintained. There was a small make-up kit in the console, pens, a notepad, some change, but otherwise not much in the way of personal belongings."

Tate looked around the table when Connor finished, nodding to Larson Finch after a pause.

"When I was back over there with Three this morning," Finch said, "I found one partial print that I hadn't seen last night. It was on the underside of the edge of the bathtub—you know how those old tubs curl over at the top? I ran it through the system and didn't get a hit, but that could be just because it wasn't clear enough. I don't know if I'd swear to it in court, but my best guess is that it's from either thumb of an unknown male, and it's probably not more than a few weeks old. Since it was in an area that wouldn't collect much dust or other dirt, and also could easily be overlooked during cleaning, I have to admit that it could have been there a lot longer.

"When we were over there last night," Tate said, "you said that it looked to you that the place had been wiped down, at least in part. Did you see anything new today that would change your mind about that?"

Larson thought for a minute, shaking his head slowly, before answering.

"No, I'll stick with that. Knowing that the lady kept a

clean house, I found a few areas that still should have been full of her prints, but didn't have any, or had some that seemed like they'd been partly wiped away."

"Off the record for now then," Tate said. "What's your best guess as to what happened to her?"

"At the moment," Finch said, "my off the record is probably the same as my on the record would be. Sometime late the other night, for reason's unknown, a powerful man—though it could have been a woman—entered through her unlocked door and surprised her getting ready to take a bath. I don't think there was much of a struggle. The assailant hit her or caused her to hit the back of her head on something, most likely the rounded edge of the bathtub, and then killed her by holding her down in the water. I'll let Dr. Coyle speak to any injuries and cause of death, of course. At some point after that, this person transported her out to the beach. I suspect that Three's idea is correct, and she was carried the block or so up to the beach path and put out there near the water." Larson looked around the table and shrugged. "It's pretty clear to me that is what happened."

Tate turned towards the camera over the monitor that showed Dr. Coyle.

"Does that fit with your findings, Doctor?"

"Yes, it does," the doctor said. "Larson and I have gone over it a few times and I believe his description of what happened is solid. She took a serious blow to the back of the head that's consistent with her being shoved roughly in the tub in such a way that her head hit the rear edge. She didn't live long enough after that for there to be much of a bruise, but it had to be a forceful blow. I don't see any other recent cuts or bruises, and no other signs of a struggle. Cause of death was drowning in her bathwater. Not that it makes any difference to her at this point, but my guess would be that the blow to the back of the head probably rendered her unconscious. A small mercy I suppose. It's also possible that she was hit from behind with some sort of club-like object and then put into the tub. If that's what happened I would still say it was likely that such a blow would have knocked her out.

"As to time of death, that's a little trickier than usual because she was half frozen, obviously, by virtue of the fact that she was left outside. Best I can do for you on that is that she probably died between about 11:00 p.m. and 2:00 a.m. the other night. That could be give or take as much as an hour in either direction."

"That's interesting Doctor," Tate said, "and brings up some questions. With what we know about the tides and the storm that passed through, and where her body was found, it seems like she must have been put there on the far late side of your estimate—like maybe two or three in the morning. Thing is though, I don't think it's very likely that she was getting ready to take a bath at two in the morning. I mean, she could have I suppose, but it was Sunday night, she had work in the morning, and by all accounts was a reliable and together person."

"Isn't it possible," Connor said, "that she could have taken a bath before bed, say nine or ten o'clock, but left the water in the tub when she got out?"

"That's certainly possible," Brody said, "but I doubt it. My wife likes to take baths now and then, and she always pulls the plug as she gets out. You don't want to come back later and have to do that because then you get your arm all wet again."

"I can't speak for all women," Barstow said, "but I know it's common for women to put lotion on all over when they get out of a shower or bathtub, so I have to agree with Brody that she would probably have pulled the plug right as she was getting out."

"So she took a bath," Connor said, "at nine or ten, then someone broke in later and knocked her out. He saw that the bathtub was wet or that the room was steamy, and got an idea. He fills up the tub again and holds her underwater. How about that?"

"No, that couldn't be it," Finch said, "want to chime in on that Doctor?"

"Right, well, the problem with that idea Three," the doctor said, "is that the water in her lungs had some of her lavender scented bubble bath in it. If the killer had refilled the tub in order to drown her, it's hard to imagine that they would have poured in some of her bath stuff. I mean, why would they?"

"So then, how it seems to be shaping up," Tate said, "is that she had a quiet night at home, prepared to take a bath before bed, and was probably killed as the tub was filling or soon after. Then it looks like a few hours may have passed before she was carried out to the beach. Doctor, is there any indication that she might have been left in the tub water for several hours?"

"I don't think so," the doctor said. "Maybe an hour at the outside."

"Maybe the killer was freaked out," Barstow said, "and didn't know what to do. Maybe he left her but came back after a few hours to clean up the mess he made."

"I like that," Finch said, "that happens quite often with homicides. The crime is committed and the perpetrator runs away, only to come back later after they've calmed down. As you say—to clean up their mess. That's a reasonable explanation for the gap of several hours."

"Agreed," Tate said. "For me at the moment, that sounds likely. Brody—last but not least—what've you been working on?"

"Okay Chief," Brody said, "after Three found the apartment yesterday, we went through every inch of the place, including her car, like he said. I took over a hundred pictures for the file. There was nothing that jumped out at us as being very different from a typical well-kept apartment for a single young woman. Fresh groceries, evidence of recent cooking, good sized wardrobe, small collection of movies and music. Looks like she was a non-smoker, and we didn't find any evidence of pot or any other illegal drug. She had a typical assortment of over-the-counter medicines—allergy, headache, cold and flu—same stuff I have at home. The wallet in her purse had eighty dollars and change, and there was a banking envelope at the bottom of her night-stand with an even three hundred. There was a checkbook that shows a balance of almost two thousand. Last two checks looked like normal amounts for rent and a car payment."

"Doesn't look like robbery was the motive then,"

Barstow said. "Even if they didn't look in her night stand, they would surely have taken the money in her purse."

"Unless they were interrupted—or freaked out," Connor said. "Someone could have come in thinking she was easy pickings, only occupied place on the block, but got scared after killing her."

"Which is another thing that happens," Finch said. "Robbery becomes murder in the heat of the moment, killer panics and loses focus."

"But then again," Connor said, "if that's what happened, and they came back later, why not at least look around for some money?"

"All right folks," Tate said, holding his hands in the air for attention. "Let me sum it up as I think it stands right now. We've got a quiet but well liked young woman, smart and hard-working as far as we can tell. No known recent fights, feuds, or enemies. Making a living but not wealthy or flashy enough to be any kind of target. No drugs and no police record. Somebody who appears to have done a decent job going through life and avoiding trouble. Whoever killed her didn't take her cash, jewelry, credit cards, or anything else. Even though there was privacy and she wasn't wearing much, she wasn't raped. Carried out to the beach afterwards for reasons unknown. Almost all murders are committed for one of three reasons, right? Money, love or passion, and these days—drugs. I don't see any of them fitting here."

"Keep in mind another thing about murder Chief," Finch said. "Not everyone who gets killed is killed because of who they are. A lot of people get killed because of where they are, or even what they are. Something to keep in mind. I'm just saying it's possible that she wasn't killed for any personal reason."

"You're right Larson," Tate said. "We do need to keep that in mind. So what am I missing people? What do you think of my summary?"

"I think that's pretty much where we stand Chief," Brody said. Both Vic and Connor nodded their agreement.

"I concur also," Finch said. "She was murdered, probably by a man, and apparently not for any of the most common reasons. As to carrying her out to the beach, well, I don't see anything ritualistic about it. My guess would be that was just a half-assed effort to cover up the crime."

"Anything Doc?" Tate asked the TV screen.

"Nothing to add at the moment," the doctor said. "I'll let you know when the toxicology tests come back, but I'm not expecting anything. I think you've summed up what happened as well as can be at the moment. If you're done with me I've got some rounds to make."

"Of course Doctor," Tate said. He gave his friend on the monitor a wave. "Thanks a lot for your time and help."

They could see the doctor reach across his desk and then the screen went dark. Brody hit some keys on the laptop and the blue light on the camera went out.

"I'll be off too," Finch said, "if you're done with me. I'll be going over my notes and looking at the pictures again at home tonight. If I come up with anything else I'll call you."

Thanks and goodbyes were said all around and Larson went out, leaving Tate alone with the deputies. Tate rubbed his temples.

"Whoever did this may have left, but we've got to

assume that they haven't. This person could be in Cape May, West Cape May, the Point, or anywhere in between. Hell, they could be on a boat in the harbor for all we know. Brody, keep going door to door, working your way outwards from her house, talk to anyone you find to see if they've seen or heard anything. Strangers, idling cars—you know the drill."

"Will do Chief," Brody said. "I started that this morning and I'll pick it up again right away."

"Three, and Vic when you come back on duty tomorrow," Tate said, "make your normal rounds through town, but I also want you to start checking with any hotels or guest houses that might be open. Get a feel for who's staying with them, or was the other night. Also, for the closed places, take a careful look around to see if anyone may have broken in recently. Is anyone camped out in a closed up B and B or rental house for example.

"One thing we have on our side is that this is a small town. With this bridge work going on, it's even smaller now. A lot of people know each other, if only to say hi in the Acme. It's more likely than ever that strangers would be noticed.

"I'm going to go over to the Coast Guard base to see if I can get them to do a check of any live aboards in the harbor. Not that I think there would be many of them in this weather, but who knows. Some of those boat people are pretty strange. I'll also see if the ferry people have been keeping records of who they've taken across. Another long shot but I'll try."

"What's your gut telling you Chief?" Connor asked. "Anything yet?"

"Not yet Three, not yet," Tate said. He was gathering the papers in front of him into a neat pile. "So far, my gut is drawing a big damn blank, and I don't like it."

8

T he next day passed with no substantial developments in the case.

The Coast Guard had been very happy to help out the town, and within hours, had determined that, of the approximately thirty-five boats anchored in the harbor that could reasonably be called "live aboards," none showed any evidence of recent human activity.

While the crew that was running the temporary cross-harbor car ferry had not been keeping records beyond a count of vehicles moved, they were able to say that both Sunday and Monday had been very slow days, and they had not seen anyone use the service that they hadn't known at least to say hello to. At Tate's request, they had agreed to start taking down names and license plate information going forward.

Early afternoon on the following day found Tate sitting in his office poring over the reports from Doctor Coyle and Larson Finch for what seemed like the tenth time, and thinking about lunch. At first he didn't notice that Doreen had come in.

"Earth to Chief Saxby, Earth to Chief Saxby…"

"Oh, I'm sorry Doreen," Tate said, looking up from the papers gratefully. "I didn't even hear you come in. I was lost in all this stuff again."

"That's okay Chief," Doreen said, "but there's someone here to see you. That Mr. Boudreau who called the other morning. Want me to tell him you're too busy?"

"Mr. Boudreau…what?" Tate said "No, no, that's fine, I'll come out—where is he?"

Doreen stood aside to avoid being plowed over as Tate rushed out of the office and towards the reception area.

A tall man turned away from browsing the old framed photos on the wall as Tate burst in. They looked across the room at each other for a moment before laughing out loud in unison.

"Dean, you bum," Tate said, "I thought you were going to call?" The two men grabbed each other in a bear hug. Doreen came into the room as they separated and noted that they were very close in height and weight, even if the visitor seemed somehow more tightly put together. His medium-brown hair was short, but stylishly cut, and the well-trimmed goatee was generously flecked with grey. Doreen briefly entertained the idea that the men might be related, but quickly dismissed it, aware that Tate had told her they were friends from way back.

"Yeah, I'm sorry," the man said. "I kept thinking to call as I was putting my bag together, and then as I was going to the car, next thing I know I'm taking the exit from the expressway, then here I am. But I know you're working—I can make myself scarce if this is a bad time."

"Oh no, forget about that," Tate said. "I need a break, and I need lunch, so you've come at a good time. Dean Boudreau, this is one of our deputies here, Doreen Watson. She runs the office and keeps me on track."

"It's a pleasure to meet you, Mr. Boudreau," Doreen said. "The Chief has said so little about you. We're on a first name basis around here, so please call me Doreen. His first name is 'Chief'."

"Nice to meet you Doreen," Dean said, taking her hand and smiling broadly at her sense of humor. "Please call me Dean, and I hope the Chief will allow me to call him Tate. So, to lunch we go then, right? Is the C-View still open? I've been thinking about their cheesesteaks ever since I decided I was coming to town."

Tate was already pulling on his coat. "We'll be at the C-View Doreen. I have my phone if anything comes up."

The drive to the C-View at the north end of Washington Street took five minutes, and the two men started catching up right away. By the time they were seated at a table along the window, Tate knew that Dean was working with a small department of Homeland Security. By the time they had ordered lunch, he had gotten the sense that his friend wasn't able to talk much about it.

"You know, I've always read that when someone gets hired at the CIA," Tate said, "they're supposed to tell their friends and family that they got a job with the State Department, or something innocuous like that. You know it's against the law to lie to a police officer in this state, don't you?" He said it with a smile and exaggerated finger wave.

Dean laughed at that and dug a wallet out of his left front pocket, pulling out an embossed ID card and pushing it across the table to Tate. "I wouldn't lie to you Chief, see, I really am with Homeland Security. It's mostly routine stuff —you know—tracking down people that shouldn't be in the country is a big part of it. Lots of surveillance. Investigations are always ongoing and some of it's classified, so that's why I can't talk much about it. Nothing very exciting, really."

"Good enough for me," Tate said, handing back the ID card. "Long as we're both on the same side, I won't pry. Are you off-duty? Vacation?"

"Off duty, yes," Dean said, "that is, to the extent that I'm ever really off-duty. I've been back and forth around the country a lot in the past year and I was overdue for a break. I have a condo on Rittenhouse Square and I was there for a few days. Thought it would be a great time to pop down here to exit zero, catch up with you and a few others, if they're still around."

Lunch arrived, and Dean asked the waitress for a second beer.

"You ready for a refill Chief?" she said, gesturing to Tate's glass. "On your iced tea?"

"You know what Terri," Tate said, "since I'm celebrating the arrival of my old friend here, and it's freezing outside, I'll have a beer. A winter lager if you have it."

As the waitress laughed and went over to the service bar

to get their beers, Dean pointed to his almost empty glass. "Are you sure you can do that? I mean, on duty?"

"I'm the Chief of Police," Tate said. "I can do anything."

"There you go," Dean said. "That's the Tate Saxby I remember."

After a few bites of lunch, and the arrival of fresh beers, they continued their conversation. Tate filled his friend in on the status of the bridge work and the situation in town.

"It all started with a routine inspection by the Army Corps of Engineers back in July. After they assessed the damage they decided that repairs would need to be started by the end of the year. The town put out a lot of communications to make sure everybody knew it was coming up. Full pages in The Star and Wave, Atlantic City Press, all of that. There was plenty of bitching and moaning from local businesses—the hotels and the B and Bs mostly—but in the end, whatta you gonna do? The bridge had to be fixed and there was money for it available in some federal infrastructure fund. They closed it to traffic on November 1st."

"But what about all the people that live in town," Dean said, "and work up in Courthouse, or A.C.? People taking classes up at Stockton? Must be a hell of a hassle for them."

"Yeah, no doubt," Tate said. "But at least people had a few months to get ready for it. Almost everybody who seriously needed to get up the road every day found a friend or a relative to stay with for a few months. I know a couple guys who went in together on an apartment in Marmora. The town really emptied out at the end of October. The work is scheduled to be complete by the end of this month, and as far as what I'm told, things are roughly on track."

"And that little ferry I came across on this morning," Dean said, "is that something the town put together, or did the Coast Guard help out with that?"

"No, that's private," Tate said. "A local businessman set that up on his own dime to help out. Do you remember Earl Parrish?"

"Yeah, sure I do," Dean said. "Parrish goes way back. He owned the Harbor House, and most of the fishing fleet. Am I thinking of the right guy? Was always sort of the 'big man' in town."

"Yep, that's him," Tate said. "He still has the Harbor House and the fishery operation, along with the Beach View Motel and pieces of a few other things. He owns most of a construction company that's got a slice of the bridge work. I'm sure we'll get over to the Ugly Mug while you're here. That's his too, though he's mostly hands-off now and lets someone else run it. He's a good guy. I'll introduce you if we run into him."

"And isn't he actually related to you?" Dean said. "You're uncle, right?"

"No, but that's what a lot of people think," Tate said. "He was my mother's cousin, so he's my second cousin. He has a grown son too, Buddy, who still lives with him here in town."

"That was good of him to set up that little car ferry," Dean said, "but that can't help much for people who need to get across the harbor in a hurry."

"The whole thing is a pain in the neck, to be sure," Tate

said. "But it's almost over. Three or four more weeks, with luck and minimal blizzards. A lot of people in town have boats, so they can zip across without too much trouble. No collisions in the harbor yet, as far as I know. The department has its own Boston Whaler, but I haven't bothered with that lately. I've used the car ferry a few times and it's no big deal as long as you have an extra twenty minutes or so."

After the remnants of lunch were cleared away and Tate had assured Dean that he wasn't in any hurry, they both ordered coffee. Dean took a minute to look around at all the sports memorabilia mounted on the walls and ceiling.

"Somebody's a big Eagles fan," he said. "And I remember there used to be a pool table back there against the wall, right?"

Tate turned around in his seat to look across at the other end of the restaurant, near the kitchen. "Oh yeah, it used to be over there at that end, but that's been gone a long time. Funny, now that you remind me, it was right up against that old fireplace—like too close. They had one cue stick that had been cut off really short, in case you needed to make a shot from that side. My father saw that once and he said 'that must be the flue-cue'. Yeah, go ahead and groan. He liked those corny jokes."

"No, that's good," Dean said. "I like corny jokes. Hey, I just remembered something else I wanted to ask you. When I came over earlier, I thought I heard the ferry guys say something about a murder. Did you have a real murder in town recently?"

"Unfortunately, yes we did," Tate said. Lowering his voice and leaning into the table. "A fisherman found a woman's body on the beach early just this Monday morning, and it's pretty clear that it's murder. Haven't had a murder in town—that we know of anyway—for years."

Tate gave his friend a five minute summary of the case and where they stood with the investigation while they finished their coffee. Dean asked for the check and was pulling bills out of his pocket when Tate's phone rang and he stepped outside to take the call.

"Hey Vic, what's up?"

"I hope you're finished with your lunch Chief," Barstow said. "We've got another body, looks like an accident. Homeowner trying to knock some ice off the eaves fell off a ladder and whacked his head on the stone path."

"Dammit," Tate said. He had not failed to notice a slight change in the deputy's voice when she had said the word 'accident'. "What the hell is happening in this town? Where is it and where are you?"

"I'm here at the house with Three," Barstow said. "It's 458 Columbia, right near the monument across from the Abbey. It's the only white house for most of the block. I think you might know the guy Chief, Dan Kershaw, according to the neighbor who found him."

"Oh crap, yeah, I know Dan," Tate said. "Okay, I'll be right there; I'm just here at the C-View. See if you can get Doctor Coyle and call the wagon."

"On it Chief," Barstow said, "see you in a few."

As Tate ended the call, shivering, Dean came out through the door and handed him his coat. "Something going on I guess? Bank robbery?"

"I wish it was just that," Tate said. "No, accidental death

it looks like, guy fell off a ladder and hit something harder than him. It's just down on Columbia, I'll drop you at your car."

"Okay if I tag along?" Dean asked, "if I stay out of your way? I am a licensed law enforcement officer, sort of. Maybe I can help somehow."

"I don't know why you'd want to," Tate said, "but sure, that'll help me get there faster."

———

"You might know this guy too," Tate said, after a minute in the car. "Dan Kershaw. Do you remember him from around town?"

"Dan Kershaw," Dean repeated the name to himself, thinking. "Yeah, I think I do. His wife used to run the ice cream shop next to the Beach Theater, right? But that memory's gotta be thirty years old. Can't imagine the last time I would've seen him. Did we go to school with him?"

"No, pretty sure he went to Wildwood Catholic," Tate said. "But you're right about the wife and the ice cream place. She died a while ago…ten years maybe. Some kind of cancer."

As they pulled up and parked behind the other two cruisers and an ambulance, Tate noticed Larson Finch's car pull up also behind them. Finch came up to the two men as they got out of Tate's car. He saw the quizzical look on Tate's face.

"Vic called me after she couldn't get Doctor Coyle," Finch said. "Nobody's said anything about any crime, but my wife had some friends over and I liked the idea of getting out of the house. Maybe I can help."

"That's fine Larson," Tate said. He gestured to Dean, who held out a hand to Finch. "Larson Finch, meet my friend Dean Boudreau. He's from Cape May too."

As Deputy Barstow had remarked earlier, 458 Columbia was a mostly white house amidst a row of other homes that wore a variety of shades of blues, greens, reds, and browns. Several of the houses in the row had clearly been built from the same plans, and the side yards that separated them were narrow strips of lawn or garden no more than twenty feet wide. As they approached the house, Deputy Barstow stepped through an opening in a black cast iron fence to wave them into the yard. A fire department SUV pulled up on the street and two men got out. Barstow went over to talk to them while Tate, Dean, and Larson Finch went off towards Deputy Connor in the side yard. He was standing several feet away from where a man's body lay flat out on the frozen ground, a uniformed EMT kneeling over it. A second EMT stood nearby, writing on a clipboard. A twelve-foot aluminum ladder lay across the yard nearby, slanting away from the house. A small shovel lay on the ground close to the house, and a neat pile of various hand tools was arranged on a portable wooden work table that stood nearby. Tate and Connor exchanged nods. Tate gave the EMT a look and pointed to the body with his eyes. The man shook his head back and forth several times.

"Whatta we got here folks?" Tate said. "Please tell me this is a simple accident."

"Looks like it Chief," Connor said. "Dan Kershaw—I

think you knew him—fifty-six, widower who lived here alone. His ID was in a wallet in his pocket, and Doreen ran a quick check on him. This is his house."

Tate nodded to Connor and turned to the EMT by the body. "How about you Gerry, what're you seeing? Yard work accident?"

"I don't see anything that says otherwise Chief," the EMT said, standing up and coming closer. We aren't authorized to pronounce, but he's dead all right. Based on his temperature, I don't see how he could have died more than an hour ago."

"I'd say not more than a half hour," said a voice from behind them, and they realized that a woman had approached from farther back in the yard.

"Oh Chief," Connor said, "this is Mrs. Caplan. That's her house right across there, which faces on Hughes Street. She found the deceased."

"That's Dr. Caplan, actually," she said, "retired for some years now. I was doing some cleaning in our back guest bedroom—it's that window right up there—and I happened to look out and saw him laying out like this, and I knew something must be wrong. I called the police right away and I remember the time on my phone as just after one-thirty."

Tate looked at his watch. "Ten after two now. All right Dr. Caplan, so you must have looked out your window right after he fell then."

"Yes, that has to be the case," she said. "As soon as I called it in, I grabbed my coat and ran down here, and I could see right away that he was gone. I must have gotten to him three or four minutes after the call, and, not being a medical examiner mind you—I would have to say that he died very quickly, and no more than about ten minutes before I got to him. It was me that pulled off his hat so I could check the back of his head. That's all I touched, aside from checking for a pulse at both his neck and his wrist."

"Thank you Doctor," Tate said. "Understanding that this isn't official, are you willing to give your opinion as to cause of death?"

"I think it's fairly clear that when he fell," she said, "the back of his head impacted one of those paving stones with great force. Maybe that one there that's sticking up more than the others." She pointed to one of the paving stones that made up the rough garden path onto which the man had fallen. The shape of the off-white stone was not unlike a brick, but larger by a third and very roughly cut. "I'd be surprised if the autopsy doesn't show a skull fracture. Anyway, that'll be up to the medical examiner. That's still Dr. Coyle, isn't it?"

"Yes it is," Tate said. "Doctor Mark Coyle."

"I've met him," she said, "he's welcome to call me if he likes. There's one more thing though Chief—when I first rushed out here after I saw him, I half expected to find someone else here, like someone had been helping him or maybe just stopping by, because a few minutes before I saw him, I really thought I heard him talking with somebody."

"You mean through the window," Tate said, "or had you opened the window?"

"No, I never opened the upstairs window," she said. "But right before I was in that room, I was in the room just below it, and I had opened that window for just a few seconds. It was then that I thought I heard two men talking, but from that window I couldn't see anything past my own yard."

"So what did you hear?" Tate asked. "Did you recognize Mr. Kershaw's voice?"

"I can't say for sure that I recognized his voice," she said, "it's more like, I made the unconscious connection that it was him based on what he said. It's freezing cold out and I only had the window open for a few seconds—to make sure it was moving freely—so I just heard a few words. There was a comment, something like 'hey, what are you working on...' or something close to that, and then another voice answered with something I didn't catch, and then '... getting this ice off the roof...' See, that's what made me think the second voice was him—Kershaw. Because from what he said he must have been the homeowner."

"What do you remember about the other voice?" Tate said.

"Just that it was a deep man's voice," she said. "Not a kid. I'm afraid that's about it. What little I heard, it sounded like a normal friendly conversation. I guess it could have been anyone walking by and seeing him up on the ladder. There's hardly anyone in the neighborhood right now, but it could have been someone walking a dog. Mailman maybe. When I got down here, I looked around quickly and didn't see anyone else, but my focus was on Mr. Kershaw by then. Wish I could tell you more."

Tate motioned to Deputy Barstow to come closer. "Dr. Caplan, this is Deputy Vicki Barstow. Would you please take her into your house and show her the areas you've described to us and give her a recap? And Vic, get the doctor's information and make arrangements for her to come into the station to give a statement, okay? That be okay with you Doctor, later today or tomorrow?"

"That'll be fine Chief," she said. She motioned to Barstow and the two of them went back towards the door in the fence at the rear of the yard.

Tate turned his attention back to the dead man and the rest of the group. Deputy Connor caught Tate's eye with a questioning look and gestured towards Dean.

"Right Three," Tate said, motioning for Dean to come over from where he had apparently been conducting a close inspection of the paving stones. "This is an old friend of mine, Dean Boudreau. We had just finished lunch together when I got the call. Dean is with Homeland Security."

"Homeland Security?" Larson Finch said, getting up suddenly from his own inspection of the walkway. "Is there something else going on here?"

"No, no," Dean said, holding up his hands to tamp down any possible excitement. "I am off duty and on vacation. Just visiting Chief Saxby and the old home town. Don't let me get in the way."

"Can we bag up yet Chief?" asked one of the EMTs. He and his partner had brought up a stretcher but had not yet moved the body onto it.

"Almost guys, give me just a few more minutes," Tate said, holding up a hand showing all five outstretched fingers. "Three, let's go through it. What happened here?"

"Looks like he was working his way along the eaves, knocking down some of the built up ice and snow." Connor walked towards the front of the house where he pointed to what looked like a long trail of broken ice and crusted snow along the ground. He picked up a thick two-foot icicle that he displayed to the group. "You can see the impressions from the ladder where he started up front, and the icicles and other junk that fell all along here. He must have made it about halfway there when the ladder slipped and he fell. Or maybe he lost his balance and took the ladder down with him as he fell. Smashed his head into one of those pavers."

"Why would somebody do that?" the EMT asked. "Why did he need to be out here in the cold whacking ice off the roof?"

"I think that's common around here," Tate said. "Most of these houses in the center of town were built in the late 1800's, and people are always working on the porches. He was probably concerned about all the extra weight sitting up there for weeks."

"When my family had the house on Jackson Street," Dean said, "we would get outside and do that sometimes when there had been a heavy snow, or when there was a ton of ice stuck up there. That part of the roof could easily be a hundred years old."

"Okay, learn something new every day," the EMT man said with a shrug.

"I don't want to make trouble here," Finch said, "but I'm just looking at where the ladder fell, and why he ended up on the pavers this far out from the house. Anyone else think that looks odd?"

"I can imagine someone starting to fall," Connor said, "and kind of pushing off from the house, like maybe trying to get a better jump down away from the ladder. That could put him farther out."

"Okay, okay," Finch said, nodding slowly. "I can buy that. Like the ladder starts to slide sideways, your adrenaline kicks in, and you try to jump free. Not a crazy idea."

"You get enough pictures Three?" Tate said. "Make sure you get the whole yard, the ladder, tools, all of that. Soon as he's done, you guys can bag up and get outta here." He turned from Connor and the EMTs to look around the yard and noticed Dean looking at something behind a bush at the rear corner of the house. "You find something interesting? I think we're about done here."

"Sure, sure, I'm starting to freeze anyway," Dean said. "This might be interesting—I don't know. Maybe have your guy get a few pictures. I was just following along the path to back here—see how there's no grass between the pavers? I mean, everything's frozen now, but there should be little bits of grass trying to grow up through the cracks and spaces, right?"

"Yeah, that makes sense," Tate said. "Our old yard had a brick walkway, and there was always grass and weeds trying to come up between. So it's a fairly new pathway, is that what you're getting at?"

"That's what I was thinking, yes," Dean said. "I'd say this path was laid down last fall after the grass growing season." He motioned for Tate to step over to the bush at the corner. It was a thick evergreen of some type, and had a lingering coat of snow and ice over most of the flattened top. He pointed to a pile of paver stones that had been stacked against the brickwork behind the bush. "He worked on the pathway last fall, say, October or November, after the grass had stopped growing and before it got too cold to work outside. I figure this is the pile of leftover stones."

"Yeah, okay," Tate said. "There's always leftovers when you do a project like that, so he piled them here near the end of the project."

"Exactly," Dean said. He gestured to Tate to look closely at one side of the pile. "But look here, one of them has been removed sometime after the last snow. See how the ice is here? One's been lifted off. Watch this." To illustrate, he pulled one of the big stones up from the other end of the stack, and it came away with a crack of breaking ice. The ice that was left behind clearly showed the outline of the missing stone. Tate straightened up and started to look around the area.

"There's one right there against the fence," Tate said. They both walked to the fence separating the yard from the one next door. Tate bent over to pick up the stone, holding it carefully by the ends. "This one's longer and skinnier than the others. That might be why he didn't use it." He carried it over to where the others were piled, and test fitted it into the empty spot. "Hasn't been warm enough for days for anything to thaw, and this part of the yard wouldn't get much sun. I'd say this is the stone that was yanked out of there. Maybe today, maybe not, but recently. Why?" He called across to Larson Finch to join them and described their findings after he came over.

"Are you thinking maybe he didn't fall off the ladder at all," Finch said, "but was coshed on the head with that paver?"

"No, not really Larson," Tate said, shaking his head. "Just something Dean here saw and I'm trying to cover the bases. You know whenever someone dies we have to cross all the Ts."

"I'm just a bystander," Dean said. "But it's something that looked out of place to me. If you look at his tools, and you look around at the yard, the job he did on the pathway —he was a neat guy. The kind of guy who puts everything in its place. Why was that one stone over there?"

"That one is relatively long and thin," Finch said. "If I came over to this pile looking for a good weapon to hit someone with, that's the one I'd grab. I suggest you get a few pictures and send that stone up to the lab with him. No harm in checking it out. Of course, the neighbor lady—the doctor—said he was still wearing his hat, so if he was hit with that, there wouldn't be any blood or skin on it. Could be threads from the hat I suppose. Bag it up."

Tate went over to speak with Connor, leaving Dean alone with Larson Finch.

"It's not a nutty idea, overall," Finch said. "Remember my remark about the ladder earlier. I can't rule out that he didn't fall off the ladder at all, but maybe he was taking a break or something, getting organized. The neighbor lady thought she heard someone else out here. Could be that someone grabs that stone from the pile and whacks him on the head, then looks around and gets the idea to move him another few feet so it looks like he fell on the stone path. I've seen worse."

"Yeah, I could see that happening," Dean said. "He could have been dragged over from closer to the house and this frozen ground wouldn't show anything. I don't know though. The more I think of it, the more it doesn't add up. The shovel's laying right there. Why grab a paver stone off the pile when there's a perfectly good shovel right there? A deadly weapon and a lot easier to handle."

Tate had re-joined the men as they were talking. "It's been a hell of a week, but I hope we don't start seeing ghosts—or worse—killers, everywhere we look. That would be terrible for the tourist industry."

9

From the front window of the attic bedroom of the house on Howard Street, Frederick Lee Herrington watched the last police car leave. He had recognized Chief Saxby, but didn't know the other man who got into the car with him. The volunteer firemen, along with the two other police cars and some car he didn't know were already gone. The ambulance had been the first to go, and Herrington had noted that it had driven away with no sirens or flashing lights. *That Kershaw Bastard had it coming to him*, he thought to himself. *Wouldn't even come down off that damn ladder to talk to me. Well, he won't be giving me any more trouble.*

The old window at the other end of the attic room rattled in a sudden breeze, breaking him out of his reverie. Looking at his watch, he remembered that he had four more houses to check out before his bi-weekly rounds were complete. Recent breakthroughs in all kinds of fancy internet-connected cameras and lighting controllers had cut into his small business, but the extra income was still welcome. There were still plenty of old-school folks in town who didn't mind paying a real person to stop in and check out their big old expensive house every few days. This winter, Herrington had contracts for sixteen houses, most of which he checked on twice a week. In the evenings on his "house sitting days," part of his routine was to sit down at his desktop computer to send out brief emails to the homeowners, telling them that he had been through their property and reporting on any problems or developments.

Back on the first floor, he sat down on a couch in the living room for a few minutes to fill out his standard inspection form on a clipboard he carried with him. When he was finished writing, he leaned back and closed his eyes. Letting his thoughts wander, they soon came around—as they usually did—to bitter memories of some of the twists and turns of his life. It had been almost twenty-five years ago that he had lost his fishing boat to Earl Parrish. A ninety-foot stern trawler, it was a fine boat, but he had always struggled with the finances of trying to run his small fishing operation. When, three years into the business, he had needed cash for some critical repairs, Parrish had loaned him the money. Another repair had led to a further loan, and that debt had led to more debt. In the end, he had no choice but to sell out to Parrish, and his 'Suzy Q' was rechristened the 'Bonnie Marie' as part of the growing Harbor House fishing fleet. Even though he knew Parrish had given him a good deal, he had never been able to shake the idea that his dream had been stolen out from under him by someone who didn't need another dollar or another boat. After some back and forth with Parrish regarding Herrington being able to stay on as captain of the Bonnie Marie, that position had been given to another of Parrish's friends—Dan Kershaw. A disappointed and somewhat beaten Herrington had accepted an offer from Parrish to take on the newly-created position of Director of Fleet Maintenance.

He had hid his bitterness towards both Parrish and Kershaw as well as he could, and done well with the maintenance position until tiring of it after twenty years. His savings, and a small family inheritance, along with the income from his part-time house sitting business, afforded him a reasonably comfortable life in Cape May, if not the life he had originally planned for himself.

Since leaving the Harbor House fleet, he and Dan Kershaw had maintained a somewhat volatile friendship. Their occasional arguments were invariably rooted in Herrington lobbying the other man to invest with him in a new fishing boat that they could run themselves. There had been several times over the past few years that it seemed to him Kershaw had warmed to the idea, but then each time the talks had fallen through, with the other man coming back to his base position that they had both simply gotten too old to dip back into the life of a commercial fisherman. Eventually, Herrington had accepted that, yes, they were probably too old for the whole idea, and in any case, it was clear that Kershaw and his money weren't going to help him resurrect his old dream.

A sudden series of loud seagull squawks from the roof of a house across the street reminded him that he had a few more properties to get to. Donning his heavy winter coat and picking up his clipboard, he left the house, locking the door carefully on his way out.

10

I t was almost ten o'clock that night when Tate finally made it over to the Ugly Mug. A handful of the tables were occupied, and he counted six people spread out around the bar, watching a replay of an earlier basketball game and sipping beers. A movement caught his eye and he saw his friend Dean waving him over to one of the booths along the wall.

"Evening Chief," the bartender said, from behind the bar as Tate walked towards the booth. "Let me know whatever you want and I'll bring it over. Waitresses are done for the night."

"Got it Cody," Tate said. "Be up in a minute."

He shook off his heavy coat and hung it on the pole beside Dean's booth. "Sorry to keep you so late. As you saw, sometimes the day can really get away from you."

"Don't worry about it at all," Dean said. "I only came out after I got your text and I just got here ten minutes ago. I waited for you for the first drink of the day too, so you should be greatly honored."

"Honored and flattered, yes," Tate said. "I'm thinking the day calls for something strong—how about you?"

"I'm a big fan of bourbon," Dean said. "I see they've got a bottle of Knob Creek. That suit you? An even hundred proof."

"Fantastic," Tate said. "Light ice, make it a double."

Dean went over to the bar, coming back with two large fistfuls of glass, ice, and whiskey. He set one down in front of Tate and settled himself back into his side of the booth.

"Old friends and old times," Tate said, raising his glass in a toast before taking the first pull. As the powerful amber liquid hit his taste buds, he involuntarily gritted his teeth and closed one eye. "Whew—oh yeah. That's the ticket."

"Guy I knew once—a bartender," Dean said, with a chuckle, "had a name for that face you just made. He called it the 'whiskey face'. Not very creative, but accurate. Happens to me too. So, long day. Were you working on that same case since you dropped me off? Dan Kershaw?"

"Pretty much, yeah," Tate said. "It was after five before I made it up to Courthouse to meet with the medical examiner. I took Larson Finch with me—you met him today, remember? He pulled up right behind us. He's retired from thirty or so years in the Trenton crime lab, but he lives in town and does freelance for us when we need him. Anyway, he went up with me to meet with Dr. Coyle…"

"Dr. Coyle," Dean said, "that rings a bell. Mark, right? Mark Coyle. I remember he was going to medical school. Good for him."

"Right, that's him," Tate said. "He's really good at what he does but also is a regular guy who works well with us. No complaints about my little small-town force, but I'll tell you, I'm damn lucky to have him and Larson Finch around."

"Sorry man, I interrupted you," Dean said. "You and Finch went up to Courthouse to meet with Dr. Coyle, who I presume had already had a look at Kershaw?"

"Right, yeah, that's right," Tate said. "We showed him all the pictures and kicked around the ideas we had talked about this afternoon. Larson had measured the ladder and everything else in the yard. Preliminary conclusion is that it happened just like it looked. He lost his balance at some point and fell out and down, landing on the stone path and smacking the back of his head on one of those pavers. It may be that the ladder slipped along the edge of the roof that was particularly icy, with the same result."

"Okay, well, that makes sense," Dean said. "No doubt that sort of thing is a typical kind of accident that happens all the time. Did you bring up the idea of maybe someone hitting him on the back of the head with that odd paver stone we found?"

"I did, yes," Tate said. "We talked about that for a while. We got the stone out of the bag right while we were there and the doc took a look at it under a giant microscope thing he has. He said there were some fibers on it that looked like they could have come from the hat Kershaw was wearing— you know, like someone hit him on the back of the head while he was wearing that hat. It all sounded very inter-esting until Larson pointed out that the hat was the same material that made up part of the gloves he was wearing. And the labels of the hat and his gloves matched exactly. Same maker—Chinese of course—and same material. Finch said he had seen a hat and glove set just like it last time he was in Swain's. He said it was in a display along with other yard-work stuff last fall. Giant paper bags, rakes and such. Anyway, the point is, that if he wore those gloves last fall when he was working on the pathway, it would make sense that any number of those stones could have fibers on them that would look the same as fibers from the hat."

"Hmm, all right then," Dean said. "That's probably a dead end, but it seemed like something that was worth looking at."

"I agree," Tate said. "It was something that needed a hard look. The doc's going to be looking at the head wound and the shape of the stones, but he didn't see anything substantial that suggested anything other than your basic fall-off-the-ladder accident. The only other odd thing is what the neighbor lady—that doctor—said about how she thought he'd been talking to someone."

"That's right," Dean said. "A man with a very deep voice I think she said. I don't remember her saying anything about a heated argument, right? She thought it was more like standard chat. Could have been someone walking by and stopping to say hello."

"Actually, we think that's exactly what it was," Tate said. "Two of my deputies went door to door through the area. More than half of the houses are closed up for the winter, so there weren't many people to talk to, but there was one woman across the street and about a block up who thought she might have seen someone. She was reading a book and happened to look out the window and saw someone coming out of one of those yards. From what she said, it could have been Kershaw's yard, but she wasn't sure."

"Was she able to give much of a description?" Dean said.

"Unfortunately not," Tate said. "About all she could say was that it was a tall slim man with light hair. She only had her reading glasses with her at the moment, so that's all we get. She did say that the person she saw didn't appear to be hurrying in any way. Just walking normally."

"Which would fit with the idea that maybe it was just someone walking by," Dean said. "Cold winter day, hardly anyone around, you're walking down the street and you see someone you know in their yard. It would be normal to stop and chat for a minute. And if that person had then whacked the other guy on the head, it seems likely that he might have run away, or at least been hurrying."

"Yeah, that's about the size of it," Tate said. "I'd like to find that guy and have a talk with him, that's for sure. So, that's how I spent my day. How about you? Did you find any of the people you wanted to check in on?"

"So far, you're the only old fart I've been able to locate," Dean said. "You know how it is. A lot of people flew the coop a long time ago and went off to wherever their job took them. Well, like me I guess, come to think of it. I plan to get over to Wildwood tomorrow, just to look around, see what I remember."

"Pretty desolate I would imagine," Tate said. "The

Dragon House might be open. Hmmm, maybe I'll have you bring us some takeout."

"I think our glasses are empty," Dean said. "How in the hell did that happen?" He was able to catch the eye of the bartender and signaled for another round. The bartender in turn signaled that he would bring the drinks over. Just then, a door on the other side of the bar opened and a woman came out, carrying some papers that she set down on the bar. Looking around and taking a casual inventory of the customers, she saw Tate and Dean, gave a wave, and started around the bar to their booth. Dean watched her approach with approval, figuring that she must know Tate. Her thick mane of light brown hair cascaded over an off-white cable knit sweater as though it was thrilled to have just been released from a bun or a tight pony tail after a long day's work. She smiled broadly as she came up to them, flashing a row of good, white teeth.

"Well hello again Chief Saxby," she said, arriving at the booth. "How nice to see you so soon."

"Hello to you Angela," Tate said, returning the smile. "And how many times do I have to tell you to call me Tate?"

"Probably as many times as I have to tell you to call me at all," Angela said.

"Whew, I think it's getting warmer in here all of a sudden," Dean said. He held out his hand. "Hi, Dean Boudreau, and I take it you're Angela. Nice to meet you."

"Angela Andrews," she said. "Nice to meet you too, and don't worry about Tate and me, we go way back."

The bartender arrived with fresh drinks and set them down in front of the two men.

"Are you off work Ang?" Tate asked. "Can you join us?"

"I'd like that," Angela said. "If I'm not interrupting anything." She looked at both of them in turn and then spoke to the bartender. "A Stoli and cranberry please Cody. A big one."

As Cody went off to fix her drink she slid into the booth beside Tate. They chatted for a few minutes, with Dean saying as little as possible about his work, but that he was on leave and in town to relax and catch up with old friends. Cody arrived with a huge drink for Angela, in a pint beer glass, and they talked more about the bridge work, who hadn't left town, and what businesses were still open.

"Word's going around that there was an accident earlier today, and someone died," Angela said. "Over on Columbia. Is it true that it was Dan Kershaw?"

"My, how word gets around," Tate said, with a sigh. He took a look around the bar, noting that it was mostly empty. "You're right, unfortunately someone was killed, and yes, it was Dan, but please try not to talk about it if anyone brings it up. We still need to contact the family. That is, if he still had any."

The three of them took a drink together in an unspoken toast. As Dean took a good slug from his glass, his eyes wandered up to the ceiling and the rows of hanging mugs. He set the glass down and listened distantly to Tate and Angela talking, breaking in when they stopped for a moment.

"Angela," Dean said, "I think I already know a lot of it, but if you don't mind, would you explain the mugs for me please?"

"Uh, sure, okay," Angela said. "I guess it all started a long time ago—like in the fifties or sixties. There was a "Secret Order of the Mug" or something like that. There was a big annual party and it was always at a time when only locals would be around, you know, like a weekday way off-season. You could pay to buy a mug, and the money went to charity. You could use the mug when you came in. Just a fun thing but the tourists love to hear about it. When someone died, their mug got turned around so it faced the ocean."

"Right, okay," Dean said. "That's pretty much how I've always understood it. And who keeps track of them? Like if someone dies, who would be in charge of finding their mug and turning it around?"

"That would be me," Angela said. "I'm the manager and the manager has always done that, but I'll tell you, I haven't done anything about it since early last year. When we had the ceiling cleaned and painted last fall, there was so much other stuff going on that I didn't have the time to get involved with updating the status of the mugs."

"So there may be people," Dean said, "mug owners obviously, who've died in the past year or so, whose mug is still facing inland?"

"That's exactly right," Angela said. "But updating them is on my to-do list."

"What are you getting at?" Tate said. "Why all the sudden interest in the mugs and which way they're facing?"

"Correct me if I'm wrong Chief," Dean said, "but Dan Kershaw had a nickname from the time he was a little kid. He had big front teeth and an overbite. You remember that?"

"Yeah, I remember that," Tate said. "Bucky. I remember that he didn't mind it. He would answer to it—he thought it was kind of funny. Bucky Kershaw."

"Right, Bucky Kershaw," Dean said. He pointed to a spot on the ceiling a few feet away from the booth. He kept pointing as he stood up, reaching to the ceiling until his hand was a few inches away from one of the mugs that was hanging with the open end pointing towards the ocean. Tate and Angela watched him intently as he unhooked the mug, looked closely at it, and set it down on the table facing them. "Bucky K. Hard to miss."

"Yeah, I'd say that's him all right," Tate said. "Though that is damn morbid. And you didn't move it Ang, right?"

"No, I haven't touched it," Angela said. "I mean, I only heard about him maybe three hours ago. It was the girlfriend of one of the firemen who had been there. She came in with a few friends. I haven't touched any mugs today. In months, actually." She stood up and went over to the bar, where she spoke briefly with the bartender before coming back. "Cody's been doing a double today so he's been here since we opened. He says he hasn't seen anyone at all touching or using the mugs."

"Somebody who knew about Dan must have turned that mug today," Tate said. "Somebody who probably meant well. Could it have been anyone else Ang? A waitress maybe? One of the kitchen crew who thought he was doing the right thing?"

"I can't rule it out," Angela said. "But Cody's been here and he doesn't miss much. Like I said, I heard about Dan only a few hours ago, but I guess other people could have heard about him earlier today. It must be what you said—somebody who knew came in and meant well."

"You're probably right," Tate said. "No harm done, it's just a weird thing. Another round? Last one for me I think."

"Wait a minute," Angela said, "I just remembered something—let me get my phone from the office." She went across the bar and back through the door that she'd emerged from earlier.

"She's pretty cool," Dean said. "And obviously nuts about you. You guys are…?"

"On again, off again," Tate said. "We keep it on the down-low, but if you asked me why, I don't think I'd have a good answer."

"That's great, good for you," Dean said. "You know, it's just strange about the mug. It doesn't even matter really, but I do like a good puzzle. Somebody knew he had died less than twelve hours ago, and also knew he had a mug here, and knew exactly where it was. And by the way, knew what his nickname was thirty years ago. Very interesting, but no doubt there's some simple explanation."

Angela came back and sat down, recent model iPhone in hand. "You guys know how everybody's always taking selfies these days, right? Well every once in a while someone wants one with their mug. Sometimes they like to take them looking up at the ceiling, you know, to show the whole idea." As she talked, she had started scrolling through screens on her phone. "A friend of mine from Wildwood came in last weekend. I heard he was here and I came out and we talked for a while. Well, he has a mug here, and was taking a few selfies, and wanted one with me, and I took a few with my phone. His name's Bobby D'angelo, but everyone calls him 'Bobby D.' See right there? Two, no, three over from the mug you took down." She pointed up at the ceiling and Dean got up and took down a mug. He looked at it and held it up so they could all see that the lettering on it read 'Bobby D', before returning it to the hook.

"Now," Angela continued, "if you look around at all the mugs, you can see that most of them are off-white, like a cream color, but some, maybe one out of ten, are darker. See what I mean over there? It's more like a tan or a light brown."

"Okay, yeah," Tate said. He was nodding up at the mugs. "I see that. Those two right by where Kershaw's mug was are the darker color."

"Exactly," Angela said. "This table where we're sitting is table number six. The same table where my friend Bobby D was sitting last weekend. Look up at those mugs again." She was pointing at the ceiling. "You see how the two molding strips meet right there where that row of mugs starts? Now look at this picture." She held the phone up so both men could see the screen as she pointed to the picture. "Here's me with my friend Bobby D. You can see he's holding his mug in front of him, but wanted to show the ceiling. There are the two strips of molding, then Bobby's empty hook, two of the darker mugs, and then the next one. Look."

She handed the phone to Tate who looked back and forth between it and the ceiling several times before passing it to Dean, who then proceeded to do the same.

"All right," Dean said. "That looks like the spot, but the mugs on the ceiling are out of focus."

"The camera in my phone has a mind of its own sometimes," Angela said. "Swipe left to the next picture."

Dean followed her instructions and looked at the next picture, which appeared to be the same shot at first glance, until he realized that Angela and her friend were now a bit blurry while the mugs on the ceiling were in sharp focus. He used his fingers on the touch screen to zoom in on the mugs.

"Holy shit," he said, as he handed the phone back to Tate. "I think the hairs on the back of my neck all just stood up at once."

Tate was looking at the picture closely, while Angela had moved in next to him so she could look at it at the same time. "That's a lot easier to see…there's the junction in the molding, and there's the empty hook for your friend Bobby, then the two darker ones, then Kershaw's. I can see the 'cky K' anyway. So this was taken almost a week ago?"

"And it's pointed the other way," Dean said. "Towards the ocean."

11

The three of them sat looking at each other across the table. Tate drummed his fingers on the polished wooden surface. Dean started to say something, pointing at the ceiling, but stopped himself with a shake of his head and took a pull from his glass instead.

"This is very creepy," Angela said.

"Well look," Tate said. "We know there's got to be an explanation. Probably just some innocent mistake which, because of the timing, looks creepy as hell. Ang, you told me that Buddy Parrish did the ceiling for you, and we know he did a good job, but he must have put the mug back the wrong way, that's all. That must be it."

Dean got up and started a slow tour around the bar, stopping here and there to look closely at the few mugs that were hanging in the opposite direction from the majority. Realizing that the last of the other customers had left, Angela went up to the bar to tell the bartender that he could leave and that she would close up.

Dean came back around from the other side of the bar and spoke to Tate. "That case you told me about at lunch—the lady someone found on the beach—didn't you say her name was 'Laine' or 'Alaine" or something like that?"

"Yeah, that's right," Tate said. "Alaine Sawyer was her name. Why?"

"There's a mug over there," Dean said, "near the kitchen door, that says 'Alaine S', and it's pointed to the ocean. Could that be her?"

"Angela," Tate said, as she set down a round of fresh drinks, "don't you have some kind of master list for all the mugs? Like with all the real names and what's actually written on it?"

"We have a pretty good list, yes," Angela said. "Let me run up to the office and get it. Be right back."

She came back shortly with a standard manila folder in hand, opening it at the table to reveal a small pile of printed pages. After briefly looking through the dozen or so papers, she pulled one out and handed it to Dean. "Would you take a quick look around at some of the mugs pointing the other way, you know, the 'deceased' ones. See if you find these names. There's the number, and then the person's real name, and the third column is what should actually be written on the mug, like a nickname or whatever they wanted." He took the paper from her and went around to look at mugs again.

"I have an idea about what might have happened," She said to Tate. "Let's see what he finds and then I'll explain.

"Your friend almost looks like he could be your brother. Kind of mysterious guy, but nice. I like him."

"He has to play it close to the chest," Tate said, "with his Homeland Security job. Secret clearance and all that. He's a solid guy though, and as sharp as they come. He spent some time in the navy, and then the Special Forces. That's what took him out of town ages ago. I think he's been shot up a few times, but you can't even tell." They sipped their drinks and talked for a few more minutes before Dean came back with the paper.

"All right, I didn't search the entire ceiling," Dean said, "but of the twelve names on this list, I found nine of them. Here, I stole a pen from behind the bar and made a little mark next to the ones I found. I guess you know that there are other mugs pointing that direction that aren't on this list."

"Yes, right. Those would be for known deceased people from a year or more back," Angela said.

"Let me see that list," Tate said. Dean handed him the paper and he studied it for a minute, reading names out loud to himself and repeating several of them while shaking his head slowly back and forth. "This is nuts. Ang, you said you haven't updated the 'deceased mugs' for almost a year, right? And Buddy Parrish did the ceiling right after the bridge closed—early November?"

"That's right," Angela said. "It was the first week or two of November. I'm remembering the twelfth. It had to be done by that day because we were reopening. Nobody's touched the mugs since then, except for the occasional person actually using theirs to drink from. Or taking a selfie."

"Yeah, that's what's nuts," Tate said. "I see four people

on this list who have died since then. Two were ruled to be accidents, and another probably will be—Dan Kershaw. Alaine Sawyer we know to be murder. Of the other eight, I see a few I know. I just talked to Milt at the ferry the other day. And I saw Bo Gibbons in the Acme. The rest of them don't ring a bell, but I don't know everybody in town."

"Shannon Simpson was here with her husband two or three nights ago," Angela said. "And I'm pretty sure Skylar's still working at the C-View."

"Help me understand this then," Dean said. "The ceiling is redone at the beginning of November, by this guy you know, and at that time, the people on this list were all alive? What is this list anyway?"

"I can explain the list," Angela said. "But that's about the only thing I can explain. Let me give you some background.

"The town had really emptied out when the bridge shut down to traffic on November first, so it seemed like a good time for us to close down to get some work done. One of the things we wanted to do was to take down all the mugs to clean them and put them back in order, and also repaint the whole ceiling before hanging them back up. The owner of the Harbor House and this place, Earl Parrish, had asked me to keep his son in mind for certain types of work that he might be able to do. Buddy is developmentally challenged, if that's the right term, but he's well behaved and polite, and physically coordinated. It seemed like the ceiling job would be a good fit for him and he was thrilled no end when I asked him. I know that his father told him to do exactly what I tell him."

"I know that the mugs are numbered," Tate said. "I think mine is ninety something. You said 'put them back in order'. Were they not always in order?"

"They all have a three-digit number," Angela said, "and were originally in order. Over the years though, it became something of a mess. People would take theirs down to use and then put them back in the wrong spot, or friends were using them together and switched spots, or even one might break and the owner isn't around anymore, and a new mug takes its place. Like look at the first page here, this guy, 'Miles' something—his last name is all smudged out, actually had number 007, fancy that. Note here says that he took his mug home because he didn't get to town as often as he used to and he didn't want it to get lost. So that left an empty hook between 006 and 008, which got filled in with some new mug with a much higher number."

"I think I knew that guy Miles," Dean said "He worked at the Merion Inn, for like, forever."

"Right, I think that's him, Hollywood handsome. So anyway, that kind of thing happened a lot," Angela said. "The point is that, over the years, the numbers have gotten all jumbled up. Now hold that thought a minute. Early last year, late May I think it was, we needed to replace one of the ceiling fans. To clear room for the electrician to work, we had to take down a few mugs."

"The twelve mugs on that list," Tate said.

"Exactly," Angela said. "I copied the information from the master list in the folder here, and put it in a box with the mugs. The thing is, the job took longer than we thought, and we rushed to open that day. The next day was hectic, and then the next, and then the season was going and we just forgot about it. It didn't help that the dishwasher had shoved the box way under a table in the office where I never saw it. Now fast forward to last November.

"After the ceiling was painted, Buddy put the mugs back on the hooks in the proper sequence. I think he thought it was a fun numbers game. Because the twelve missing mugs were still on the master list I had given him, he left an empty hook where that number should be. He had mugs spread out all over the tables, so who knows, he probably figured he would find so and so mug later and put it up. Which is pretty much what happened, because I finally found the box of mugs in my office, and brought it down to him just as he was finishing up. I know I checked against the master list and it showed all the owners as living, but it looks like when I listed out the twelve, I didn't indicate that on the new sheet. In any case it looks like for some reason, he took my instructions to mean that they should be hung up towards the ocean.

"And within, what—three months," Tate said "four of those twelve people are dead. At least one by murder."

"Kind of makes you want to warn the other eight, doesn't it," Dean said. "This is really strange. Are you sure Agatha Christie isn't living in town?"

"This has got to be coincidence," Tate said. "Or there's some kind of logical explanation. But I will certainly have my department check up on those other eight people. Of course if they're here in town, and alive and well, I don't know what we could say to them that wouldn't sound looney. I guess we'll cross that bridge when we come to it.

Ang, you have a copier here don't you? Can you make me a copy of that list please?"

While they waited for her to come back, the two men drained the last of their drinks.

"It has to be coincidence," Dean said. "It must be. Well, I hope it is. I have seen some shit though. There is evil to spare out there in the world. Maybe there's some in your little town."

Angela came back and gave Tate the paper. "I remembered something on my way upstairs. The day we were re-opening after all the work was done, was a Saturday. I was running late for some reason and came rushing in to open up for lunch. I remember seeing Buddy just starting to set up a step stool right in the middle of the aisle. I asked him what he was doing and he said he had to 'fix the mugs' or something like that. I told him the mugs were fine, we needed to open, and to put the stool away. He started to disagree with me—which is not like him at all—and I had to tell him very firmly to stop what he was doing. He looked very upset for a minute and I had to keep reassuring him that he had done a good job. He left after that and I didn't see him again for a few days. He must have realized his mistake with the twelve mugs, and then I came along and stopped him from fixing it. Poor guy probably felt terrible. Anyway, I just wanted to mention that."

"Aha, now I see it," Tate said. "That's why he seemed uncomfortable the other day when I brought up the job he did on the ceiling."

"Anyway, this has spurred me into action," Angela said. "In the next day or two, I will check my master list against all the mugs here and which direction they're facing. I'll let you know what I find." She gave Tate a kiss on the cheek and herded the men to the door and out.

"I mentioned before that two of the people on that list had died by accident," Tate said to Dean as they walked to their cars. "I'm less and less sure. Can you meet me at my office tomorrow morning? I want to show you a few things."

12

Doreen was already at her desk the next morning when Tate got in and stopped for mail and messages.

"Three's in the interview room with a possible witness," she said. "A man who might have seen something near the Kershaw house on Columbia yesterday. Vic knows more about it, she's probably at her desk. I just made a pot of your favorite hazelnut coffee."

"Mmmm, that sounds good," Tate said. "I'll definitely grab some of that. Oh, you met my friend Dean yesterday. He should be here anytime, please send him on into my office. Maybe point him towards the coffee first."

Doreen nodded and Tate went off towards the squad room. As he passed the window of the interview room, he caught a glimpse of Deputy Connor talking across the table with an older man who he thought looked familiar. Continuing down the hall he found Deputy Barstow at her desk.

"Morning Vic," Tate said. "Is that Frederick Herrington I see in there with Three? What do you know about that?"

"Good morning to you Chief," Barstow said. "Remember the lady who lives a block down from Dan Kershaw's place, told us yesterday that she had seen a man on the sidewalk? She called after you left last night. Brody took the call. She remembered that she had also seen Herrington's van out on the street nearby around that time, and thought we should know about that."

"Okay, good," Tate said. He looked down at his watch. "So did Three roust him out of bed this morning or what? It's only a quarter after eight."

"No, Brody set it up last night," Barstow said. "He contacted Herrington and asked him to come in this morning to help us with anything he might have seen in the area, you know, just routine. After that, Brody ran a check on him. Aside from parking tickets, Herrington was clean except for one thing. Three years ago, he was tossed out of the Rio Station Bar one night for fighting with another man. I take it they shook hands and it ended up that there were no charges, but would you care to guess who the other man was?"

"I'm tempted to say the suspense is killing me," Tate said, "except that I'm sure it was Dan Kershaw. I knew them both, but wasn't what you'd call friends with either. People who knew them also knew they had old baggage. Herrington always thought that Kershaw had stolen the job he wanted with Earl Parrish, and then later, they would go at it over whether or not to get a boat together. It got heated sometimes and I'll bet you anything that's what got them thrown out of the Rio Station."

"Does any of that change your thinking about what happened yesterday with Kershaw?" Barstow said. "Accident?"

"Accident, yes," Tate said. "I spent a lot of time with Larson Finch and Dr. Coyle yesterday and that's what it looks like. Heaven knows I don't need anything more added to the blackboard in the conference room. It's interesting though. We shouldn't dismiss any idea too quickly. You and Three met my friend Dean yesterday. We were hanging at the Ugly Mug with Angela last night and stumbled on something really interesting, and he was a big help. I want to fill the two of you in on that, and also, I want to show him all that stuff on the blackboard."

"I'll be right here Chief, unless there's a robbery or something" Barstow said.

"Great," Tate said, turning to leave the room. "I'll look for you after he gets here."

Tate was working at his desk fifteen minutes later when Dean knocked on the open office door.

"Ah, I thought I heard Doreen talking with someone," Tate said. "Did she hook you up with some coffee?"

"Yes, got it," Dean said. He held up a white box that he had pulled out of a plastic bag. "And I brought Donuts. Entenmanns. Chocolate."

"You brought donuts, did you," Tate said. "Is that supposed to be some kind of police joke?"

"I am shocked and offended at that thoughtless remark," Dean said.

"Let's take them into the conference room," Tate said. "And I want to grab my Deputies. They need to hear about what we found last night."

Having just finished his interview with Frederick Herrington, who had left the office, Deputy Connor met Tate in the hallway outside the conference room.

"Ah, morning Three," Tate said, "I want to hear details a little later, but how did your meeting with Mr. Herrington go?"

"It went well Chief," Connor said, "and I've got a few interesting things to report. Maybe even a lead."

"Good work," Tate said, as they all took seats. "I look forward to hearing all of it. Three, Vic, you met my friend here yesterday when we were all freezing our asses off out in Dan Kershaw's yard. I asked Dean to sit in on this because of something we found out last night, and I'll get to that shortly. He's with the Department of Homeland Security, but is here in town this week just visiting friends."

"Can I say something Tate...ah...Chief?" Dean said. Tate nodded. "As the Chief said, I am off duty and just here to catch up with him and hopefully a few other friends. This is your department and your investigation, but if I can help in any way while I'm here, I'll be happy to. If the Chief tells me to shut up and go away, I can do that too. Please call me Dean."

"All right then," Tate said. He moved one of the blackboard panels out of the way to expose all the notes he had gone over with the two deputies earlier in the week. "You two already saw this the other day. Bear with me for a few minutes while I run through the gist of it for our guest." He turned his attention to Dean. "You could call this sort of a pet project. These three people all died in the past several months, and the coroner has ruled all three of them to be accidental. As it stands right now, the cases are closed." Over the next fifteen minutes he summarized the circumstances of the deaths of Mary Ellen Barnes, Gerry Fisher, and Augie Danforth, as well as his concerns about each case.

"Now," Tate said, looking at Dean, "you're up to speed with Vic and Three on these cases, but hold your comments for now, while we tell them about what we found last night at the Ugly Mug." He then spent another fifteen minutes explaining to the deputies about the ceiling work, and how the box of twelve mugs had been almost forgotten, eventually to be hung up in the wrong direction as though the owners were deceased. He explained how Buddy Parrish had done the work and apparently made an innocent mistake. "Exactly why that mistake was made, we don't know, but next thing is that they were hurrying to re-open for business and it never got fixed."

"Sounds like a simple mistake Chief," Barstow said. "Why does the police department care about this?"

"The reason we care about this," Tate said, "is that since then, mid-November, four of those people are now dead."

Tate took a drink of his coffee while the others sat silently. He took several papers out of a folder on the table and handed one to each of the two deputies. Connor and Barstow looked at the list of names on the paper:

1. Gerry Fisher (d. 12/17)

2. Augie Danforth (d. 1/08)
3. Alaine Sawyer (d. 2/4)
4. Dan Kershaw (d. 2/7)
5. Shannon Simpson
6. Narina Delray
7. Skylar Park
8. Ed Gideon
9. Frank Ketchum
10. Milt Madden
11. Bo Gibbons
12. Rich Davis

"Those are the twelve people whose mugs were hung up wrong," Tate said. "With the four deceased at the top. Of those four, two of them are right up here on the blackboard. Gerry Fisher died December seventeenth, then Augie Danforth on the eighth of January. We just found Alaine Sawyer out on the beach this past Monday, and then yesterday, Dan Kershaw fell off a ladder in his yard. We know that Alaine Sawyer was murdered. These two on the board have been ruled accidental, and it looks like Dan Kershaw probably will be too."

"That all seems weird Chief," Connor said. "But I don't know—it's got to be some kind of coincidence, right? I mean, couldn't somebody just be turning the mugs around as the people die?"

"Angela has a picture, a selfie with a friend of hers,"

Tate said, "that shows Kershaw's mug pointing towards the ocean several days before he died. For the other three, we can't prove at the moment that what you suggest isn't what happened—sure, that could be the case. As for the eight other people on that list, I want the two of you to see what you can find out about them today. Don't contact them directly, unless you know them or can think of some reason to chat with them, but let's nail down their status. I've seen Milt and Bo myself within the past week or so, but check them anyway. Angela told us she's seen Shannon Simpson and Skylar Park, but same for them. If they're still here in town, or anywhere in Cape May County, I want to know that they've all been seen alive within the past 24 hours. You know what? You might try Facebook. See if any of them are out there and if they've posted recently. Just a thought."

"Do you think these mugs could be the basis for some kind of serial killer situation?" Barstow asked.

"I'm not ready to go that far, Vic," Tate said. "But I think it would be irresponsible to not consider the possibility that there could be a connection between them and the strangely large amount of recent deaths."

"What's your take on this Mr...sorry—Dean?" Vic asked. "Coincidence?"

"I think that...well, I'm not a big believer in coincidence," Dean said, slowly. "But all this is just odd enough that it could be. My two cents is that we should try to stay open to some logical explanation that we just haven't thought of yet."

"I think this might be a good place to tell you about my

meeting with Mr. Herrington this morning," Connor said. "That okay Chief?"

"Sure Three, go ahead," Tate said, sitting down at the table.

"When we finished up at the Kershaw place yesterday," Connor said, "Vic and I went door to door to see what anyone might have seen or heard. More than half the houses were empty, but one person we spoke with, Mrs. Wilson, about a block down towards Madison Avenue, told us that she had seen a man on the sidewalk near Kershaw's house. She thought he had come out of Kershaw's gate, but admitted that it could have been one of the other houses. She wasn't able to give any kind of meaningful description. Seems she only had her reading glasses with her at the moment. Anyway, that was that until she called back later to say that she had remembered seeing Herrington's van parked a few houses away on Howard Street at about the same time. You may know that he runs a small business where people pay him to winterize their house and then check up on it every week or few days. He has a white van with one of those big magnetic signs on the sides. Mrs. Wilson couldn't read the lettering on the sign, but recognized the van as his.

"So after Brody took the call with Mrs. Wilson, he called Mr. Herrington and got him to agree to come in this morning. He told me about his business and the houses he had checked on that day, but insisted that he had not been around the area of Columbia where Mrs. Wilson had seen someone. He did readily admit to knowing Kershaw and to having argued with him on more than one occasion. Something that went way back about Kershaw reneging on the idea of them buying a fishing boat together."

"Three, pardon the interruption, but let me add something here," Tate said. He proceeded to repeat what he had told Barstow earlier about the antagonistic history between Herrington and Kershaw.

"Right, thanks Chief," Connor said. "And no charges were filed for the Rio Station thing, but there was definitely some hot blood between those two. Anyway, Herrington says that he didn't see anything from the house he was checking on Howard Street, and that he had not gone near Kershaw's house. So if that's true, Mrs. Wilson must have seen someone else."

"That's if Mrs. Wilson really saw anybody at all," Barstow said. "With all due respect of course."

"Anyway, there's another interesting thing," Connor said. "You know how banks and other companies are always giving away pens and other stuff with their logo on them? Well, while I was meeting with him, I noticed that he had a pen in his pocket from the Brookstone Agency—the insurance company that Alaine Sawyer worked for. It's a bright green pen with blue lettering. I know it because that's my insurance company and I've liberated a few of their pens myself. When I asked him if he had known Miss Sawyer, he told me that he had dealt with her for his business insurance, and that their last conversation had ended with him raising his voice, as he put it, and hanging up on her."

"Now that's interesting," Tate said. "So he didn't try to hide that. Did he explain why they had argued?"

"He did Chief," Connor said. "He said it was because

she was unable to give him some kind of local business discount that he felt he was entitled to, but he couldn't remember the reason she had given. He said that later, he had realized that she had been a 'nice young lady', and that he had felt bad about yelling at her. He'd been meaning to call back and apologize until he heard about her being found on the beach. He told me that he had never run into her or seen her anywhere apart from that, and had no idea where she had lived. I told him I'd call if we had any further questions, but that's all."

"Okay, good work then Three," Tate said. "His connection to her is a thin one but let's keep it in mind. I imagine almost anyone who's worked customer service for an insurance company has probably been yelled at a few times."

"That's what I have for now," Tate said. "I'll get Brody up to speed on all this when he gets in later. In the meantime, Three and Vic, work on those other eight people. I need to track down the mayor and then I've got a few appointments after that."

The two deputies gathered their papers and went out, leaving Tate and Dean alone in the conference room.

"Do you really think the mug thing could be coincidence?" Tate said.

"If it was," Dean said, "it would be one hell of a whopper. I'm going to be thinking about it hard. I'll let you know if I come up with anything. Hey, I'll let you get to work. Look me up later if you want to do drinks again."

After Dean left, Tate leaned back in his chair for several minutes, studying the blackboard and thinking about mugs hanging from a ceiling.

13

Frederick Herrington sat in his van a block down from the police station, the engine idling and the heater working hard to keep out the cold.

That damn nosy cop thought he was clever, he thought to himself. *Somebody thought they might have seen me around Dan's house. Isn't that what he said? I wasn't anywhere near there yesterday. Or was I? I was on Columbia, and I know I spoke with someone, but was it Kershaw?*

And that girl from the insurance agency, I shouldn't have done that to her. That wasn't nice at all. I should have controlled myself better, but it's so hard sometimes. Sawyer was her name. Linda or Leanne or something like that. No…Alaine, that's it. Alaine Sawyer.

Saying her name silently to himself reminded him of something. Pulling his phone out of a pocket, he scrolled through his recent photos until he saw her. There she was, just getting out of her car in the driveway of the house on

Second Avenue. There was one of her getting some kind of black bag out of the back seat and then one of her slinging it over her shoulder. Finally, there she was just turning the knob to open her apartment door.

After another slow look at all four pictures, he deleted them.

I've got to get to work. I need to see who's next on the list and I've got to get to work. I hope I can sleep tonight. I'm so tired and I'm so sick of all these dreams.

He set his phone on top of the clipboard that was laying on the passenger seat, checked his seatbelt, and moved the shifter to put the van into gear. As he was about to pull out onto Washington Street, his foot brushed across the floor mat and made a rasping sound.

Why is there so much sand in here? I know, it must be from when I followed Chickie Templeton down to the cove the other morning.

14

Thirty minutes after the meeting in the conference room with the Chief and his friend, Deputy Connor was enjoying his second Entenmann's donut while doing some online research. Deputy Barstow rolled her chair over to his desk.

"What do you think of the Chief's friend?" Barstow said. "This Boudreau guy."

"He seems okay to me," Connor said. "I'm not sure why the Chief asked him to sit in with us, but I guess they go back a long way. He seems about right as far as not butting in too much. Pretty cool guy as far as I see. Why? I thought I might have to start fanning you with a notepad when we were in the conference room."

"Oh stop," Barstow said "It was just warm in there. I'm not that bad. Am I that bad? I'm not that bad." She looked away in an unsuccessful effort to hide the color rushing into her cheeks.

"Don't worry about it Vic," Connor said, with a chuckle.

"Your secret's safe with me and it's been a long winter for all of us."

"Thanks," Barstow said, "I appreciate it. I guess it has been a hell of a dry spell. Hey, but what I wanted to tell you, is that, remember about two years ago, up in Montgomery County somewhere, there was that big home invasion, and it was all mistaken identity? Five or six members of some drug gang broke into the wrong house? Remember what I'm talking about?"

"Yeah, I remember," Connor said. "Can't imagine what cop in the country wouldn't have been talking about that. It was five. Five armed men broke into a house and the home-owner killed them all in about two minutes. He was hurt too —shot I think, but not seriously. What about it? Are you saying…"

"Yes, that's what I'm saying. He's that guy," Barstow said. "The homeowner. The Chief's friend Dean is him. I did some searches on him and read all about it. So that was all public information, in all the papers, you know, but aside from that, there's almost nothing out there about him at all. The DOD file says he did ten years in the navy with an honorable discharge twenty-six years ago, but then the file just stops, like it's been wiped."

"Or locked down, more likely," Connor said. "If the Chief says he's with Homeland Security, I believe that. He's probably in some classified position where they wanted to lock down his file."

"You're probably right," Barstow said. "Whoever 'they' are. About the only other thing I found is that he does have a national firearms permit, which I guess is something that would need to be public. All right, well, I'm sure if the Chief thinks he's okay then he probably is. You ready to talk about that list of people, or do you need more time?"

"Sure, we can compare notes," Connor said. "When we're done I'll print it up for the Chief."

Barstow rolled her chair over to her desk, retrieved a notepad, and rolled back. "I saw Skylar Park at the Wawa early this morning. I only know her to say hello, but I'm sure it was her, so that's one we can check off. The Chief's idea about Facebook was a good one, because both Shannon Simpson and Narina Delray are on it. Shannon posted a picture of her dinner at Finn's last night and it really looked good—blackened mako. Narina commented on someone else's post late last night. They both have current New Jersey driver's licenses, and I compared their pictures to ones on their Facebook profile and I'm comfortable that it's them. For my four, that just leaves Ed Gideon, and it looks like he moved away years ago. A Jersey license in that name and with a North Cape May address expired two years ago. I don't see him on any of the area tax rolls, and I don't see anyone that's clearly him on Facebook. Next thing I plan to do is to check all the area schools for any record of him. How about yours—how far did you get?"

"Looks like I'm three out of four also," Connor said. "I know Bo Gibbons from seeing him around town. The Chief said he saw him in the Acme, and I saw him crossing Carpenter's lane yesterday when I was cruising around the mall. I went to school with Frank Ketchum and I know he lives somewhere up in the Philadelphia suburbs. I found a PA license and the picture looks like the guy I remember. I haven't proved that he's alive yet, but at least that he doesn't seem to live here anymore. I don't see him on Facebook. Next is Rich Davis. There's one on Facebook who clearly states that he's from Cape May and went to Lower Regional. Several of his friends are also from Cape May, so I figure that's him. He's happily living in Switzerland and working at some fancy bank in Geneva."

"Okay then, good for him," Barstow said. "What about your last guy—Milt Madden? The Chief said he was working at the little ferry."

"Yeah, my plan was to just drive over," Connor said, "and check in with the guys working there. I don't know Milt but I know some of the others. Shouldn't be too hard to figure out who's who."

"Pending a few more checks then," Barstow said, "it looks like our eight people are either still alive or living somewhere other than here. I think the Chief will see all that as a good thing. You'll get something together for him, after you check on Milt over at the ferry?"

"Sure will," Connor said. "As a matter of fact, I have an errand to do anyway so I'll take care of that and the ferry stop right now."

"And I'll go out on patrol for my last couple hours," Barstow said. "I think I'll take a walk around some of those big houses up on Beach and New Jersey—make sure they're all buttoned up tight. I'll check in with you before I'm off."

15

F rederick Herrington pulled up on the north side of New Jersey Avenue and looked across at the group of mansions filling the block that used to be home to the Christian Admiral Hotel. The enormous red-brick building that had stood for much of the 1900s was long gone, but he could still remember sneaking into the hotel's pool as a teenager on hot summer nights. The Admiral's last profitable days having faded into the distant past, it had finally yielded to the wrecking ball. The dozen modern homes that now stood in its place were huge, beautiful, and usually empty.

Taking his clipboard with him, he climbed the wooden steps to his client's house on the other side of the street and let himself in. Twenty minutes later, having checked off all the items in the 'Home Interior' section of his form, he locked up the house and spent another ten minutes walking around the outside. Back at the van after finishing up, he stood at the open driver's door for a moment while he filled out the rest of the inspection form. Rays of sun had unexpectedly found their way through a wall of grey clouds, and he enjoyed the warmth on his back. As he reached into the van to drop the clipboard onto the passenger seat, he heard a sharp noise. Looking up, a flash of motion at the side of the house next door to the one that he had just come from caught his eye, and he saw the figure of a person disappear around the corner of the house and into the back yard. He closed the door of the van and went around to step back up onto the sidewalk, looking towards the house. A colorfully painted oval sign hung from chains between two wooden poles in the lawn, proclaiming 'Springside Guesthouse & Apartments' in shiny gold lettering. A wood-framed screen door on the near side stood slightly ajar, and he figured that must have been the source of the sound he'd heard. *Someone just came out of there, and hurried off around the house and into the back yard.* Which didn't make sense to him because the big old house looked as empty and closed up for the winter as the one he'd just inspected. No cars, awnings put away, blinds and curtains closed. And the snow and ice that the last two storms had dropped onto the steps and walkway had never been cleared.

Walking back between the houses, he passed the side screen door, following some tracks that led farther on to the back yard. He reached the back corner of the house in time to see someone disappear into the wooded strip that ran along the rear border of the block, adding a degree of visual privacy between where he stood and the backs of the houses over on the next street. Herrington knew that those houses would likely be empty also.

I think I know who that was, he thought to himself. *Could that have been who I think? But why would he be here? Is he watching me right now—from the woods?* He remembered the feeling that someone had been watching him when he had been down at the cove the other night. *Is someone always watching me?*

He walked back to the side of the house, pulling the screen door open and cupping his hands to look through one of the glass panels of the inner door. Just inside was what he knew many people would call a 'mud room', with coat racks and storage shelves along the wall. To one side a stairway led up and away, and on the other side, a central hallway stretched out towards the middle of the big old house. Knowing these types of homes well, it occurred to him that this might be where the butler's or the maid's private rooms would have been at one time in the past. He tried the knob, letting out an audible gasp when it turned in his hand and the door opened. Holding it open just enough to get his face into the gap, he called out a loud 'hello' to the interior. Getting no response, he repeated his yell twice more, waiting and listening in between. Finally, he pulled the door closed, leaving it unlocked but making sure the latch clicked into place. He pushed the screen door closed after it, also latched but unlocked.

I need to call the police, he thought, *this is for them to deal with. Wait—no. I can't call them. The last thing I need right now is more attention from the police. But I have to do something, Don't I? Maybe there's a way I can let them know without them knowing it's me. Who was that person*

and why do I feel like I know him? This house is unheated—
has he been living in there?

With a frustrated shake of his head, Herrington walked
back to the front yard and out to his van. He got in, started
the engine, and drove away.

Who is next on my list?

16

Cutting in from Beach Avenue, Deputy Barstow paused at the stop sign before making the turn onto New Jersey. Looking down the block to the left, she recognized Frederick Herrington's white van parked in front of the row of big houses across the street. She knew that he spent part of most days making his rounds and checking on his client's properties, and she had a vague memory of having seen him checking up on the house that he was parked in front of once in the past. As she scanned past the van and along the other houses, she saw Herrington himself emerge from between two of the houses. He walked straight to the van, started it, and drove away. Barstow thought to herself that she had pulled up on the corner just as he was finishing up his inspection of the outside of the house or the yard. On a whim, and knowing that he was a person of interest in the Alaine Sawyer case, she decided to follow him. The unusually empty town streets allowed her to follow from quite far behind without losing sight of the van.

After continuing straight down New Jersey, he made a right onto Madison Avenue, and then a left one block later onto Kearney. He drove slowly along Kearney Street for a few blocks before pulling up and parking on the right. Barstow pulled over a block back and behind the only other car on the street. After a minute, Herrington got out of the van with clipboard in hand, and went up the steps of a large bed and breakfast inn that she knew to be closed for the season. She watched as he spent fifteen minutes inside the house, and then came out to spend another five minutes looking around the outside. A final two or three minutes were spent writing on his clipboard, and then he drove away again. Deciding that Herrington was making his normal rounds and that there was no need to follow him any further, Barstow turned her attention away from him and drove away to put in her last hour of routine patrolling through town.

––––––

It was almost six that evening when Dean Boudreau carefully angled the rented Dodge Charger into a space in the tight C-View parking lot. As he walked towards the entrance he saw a single woman coming towards him and the door from the opposite direction. Something about her struck him as familiar, though with the heavy winter parka she was wearing, he couldn't be sure. As they reached the door at the same time, they both had to step back as a large group of people came out. They exchanged polite smiles as the people passed, and in the glow from a nearby streetlight, Dean suddenly recognized her.

"Deputy Barstow," he said. "How nice to see you. I didn't realize who you were at first, without the uniform."

"Oh—it's nice to see you too," she said. "How about, you don't call me Deputy Barstow, and I won't call you Mr. Boudreau. It's Vic, please."

"Deal," Dean said. "As long as it's Dean for me." He saw that she was surprised to see him and also that she seemed a bit flustered at first, but had recovered very quickly.

He held the door for her and they both stepped inside. There was nobody at the host stand but they could see that there was room at the bar as well as a number of empty tables.

"Were you thinking of getting some dinner?" Dean asked.

"I was, I mean, I am," she said, "and you? I'm surprised you aren't doing something with the Chief."

"I talked to him about an hour ago," Dean said, "he was fighting a headache while trying to finish up a few things. I told him I could fend for myself for the night. Are you by yourself, or meeting anyone?"

"No, I'm by myself," She looked around at the bar and the tables. "I see a few people I know but nobody I need to hang out with."

"Well then, if you're not falling over from hunger," Dean said, "let me buy you a drink at the bar."

They took two seats at one end of the bar and the

bartender came over to drop round paperboard coasters in front of them.

"Evening Vic," she said, "nice to see you getting out on the big town for a change. What can I get you and your tall, dark, stranger friend?"

"Hey Clare," Vic said, "yeah, it was about time I came out of hibernation, don't you think?" She gestured towards Dean. "Dean is an old friend of the Chief, in town visiting. Dean, this is my friend Clare. And I'll have a Bombay martini, straight up, with a twist."

"And how about a bourbon Manhattan," Dean said, shaking the bartender's hand across the bar. "Straight up, not too sweet."

As the bartender went away to make their drinks, Barstow put a hand over her face. "I'm sorry. I wasn't sure what to say. Chief's friend—I hope that wasn't too bad."

"Don't give it another thought," Dean said, "I actually am the Chief's friend visiting town. I could be your friend too if that's okay. I hope I'm not going to cause too much trouble for you—you know, small town rumors and such."

"Oh, there will be rumors, but I can take it. I'm a big girl."

"I have no doubt," Dean said, with a laugh. "Anything new today with the case of that woman on the beach? I mean that you're comfortable telling me?"

"If the Chief think's it's okay to loop you in," she said, "that's good enough for me." Their drinks arrived and she paused to take a few sips of hers. "Nothing much new really. We're trying to talk to everyone we can find who knew her, keeping eyes and ears open. It's tough because we don't have traffic cameras in town, and there isn't anything else with a camera—like an ATM—anywhere near her apartment or the beach where she ended up. We're working on trying to list out everyone who would have been in town that night, but that's been harder than we thought."

"What do you think of all this with the mugs," Dean said. "The mugs get turned around the wrong way and suddenly the owners start dying. Coincidence?"

"It's got to be, doesn't it?" Vic said. "I mean, this isn't a movie; this is real life. Funny though, just as I say that, I'm remembering that there really are serial killers in real life. I don't know what to make of it, at least not yet."

"Yeah, that's about where I come down on it too," Dean said. "Did you and the other deputy get anywhere with the eight people on that list?"

"We did," Vic said. "Three and I. We have a few more checks to make, but we think they're all either alive or living somewhere else. We had to be a little creative because we couldn't just call them up. Facebook came in handy."

"All right then, good work," Dean said. He tapped the rim of his glass against hers. "Hopefully if there is a maniac out there, he's either all done or at least taking a break. Hey, I was just thinking—the food here is fine, but I wouldn't mind a quieter place. Maybe even with tablecloths and no TVs. As long as there's already going to be rumors, what do you think? Company for dinner is good."

"Ah…yeah, that does sound nice," Vic said. "If we can find a place still open in town, sure."

"What's your favorite place in town," Dean said, "like if you were going to really splurge."

"Well, the Merion Inn and the Washington Inn are both closed for the winter," Vic said. "So is the Harbor House. That leaves the Ascot Room at the Carolina as the ritziest place in town right now. It would probably be closed too, except that a bunch of people working on the bridge are staying in the hotel. Expensive place though."

"Sounds fantastic," Dean said, "but let's get one thing straight off the bat. Dinner is on me. My expense account is very generous."

"All right then," Vic said, "but I should warn you, I can eat and drink some expensive stuff."

After a few more sips of their cocktails, Dean paid the bill and left a tip on the bar. Relocating both their cars to two of the numerous empty spots on Jackson Street, they entered the Carolina Hotel and asked for a table for two. The elegant and softly lit dining room was mostly empty, with just a few other diners at various stages of their meal. One of the tables was occupied by a group of four men, who they both assumed to be involved in the bridge project. The rest of the customers were in parties of two, drinking wine and looking romantically inclined. Though it was a 'fancy' sort of a place, almost everyone was dressed for the weather —with substantial sweaters and sturdy footwear that would work well on snow and ice.

"Well that's a relief," Vic said, after they were seated. "I thought I was going to be underdressed, but I seem to fit right in."

"You do, and you look very nice by the way," Dean said.

"Hard to beat faded jeans and a sweater. Those are great boots too—Tory Burch, aren't they?"

"Why yes they are," Vic said. "Do you spend much time in women's shoe departments?"

"No, that's something I've missed out on," Dean said, with a laugh. "But I have been around a few women, and I know they like to break out the boots when the weather moves in. It's a great sweater too. Does an excellent job of hiding the small automatic on your left hip. Walther or Glock? Makes me feel extra safe anyway."

"Sorry about that," Vic said. "We're such a small force, the Chief wants us to be armed at all times. I suppose you know what it's like to have a boss like that, which would explain the larger automatic on your right hip. So we can both feel safe."

"Well then, now that's out of the way," Dean said, "what looks good? Are you a wine drinker? I'm thinking of the short rib special myself, though the swordfish could be a possibility."

The surroundings called for dining at a leisurely pace, and they took full advantage, with Dean opting for the short ribs and Vic finally settling on the grilled swordfish steak. A fine Washington State Pinot Noir lasted them almost all the way through to coffee and dessert, which was an embarrassingly huge—but shared—slice of black forest cake. Dean learned about Vic's degree in political science and how she had studied nursing at first before switching over to police work, eventually joining the department in Cape May. Vic learned about Dean's childhood in town before he joined the Navy and ended up getting recruited into the Special Forces for the bulk of his ten years in. That had been followed by 20 years in the corporate world, before signing up again for government service in the form of a special team within the Department of Homeland Security. She didn't push him when he gently made it clear that he couldn't say much about his work in specific terms. Nor could he be cornered into saying much about his personal life.

"I really am just here on vacation," Dean had said. "I've been all over the country for a few weeks, and I was due for a break. For some reason, Cape May started bubbling up into my thoughts, and here I am."

"Well, I'm sorry that it isn't much of a great time to visit," Vic said, "but if you like quiet, there is plenty of that to go around."

"Yeah, there sure is that," Dean said. "And, not to make light of it in any way of course, but you do have a murder mystery going on, and that is fascinating. I hope there's some way I can help. I was surprised when you told me about Tate, the Chief I mean. I either never knew or maybe I just forgot that he'd been with the State Police before this. That's an impressive gig."

"Six years, with three of them in homicide," Vic said. "Between you and me, I think that's why the mayor isn't jumping up and down this week demanding help from the state. Because he's got so much confidence in the Chief. That and Larson Finch, who's a real pro too.

"Can I ask you about, you know, when all those men broke into your house two years ago? No problem if you can't stand to talk about it."

"It's okay, I don't mind if you ask about that," Dean

said. "But let me ask you something first, because I think you work a really early shift. Do you need to run, or will you join me for an after-dinner drink in the bar?"

"Thanks for asking," Vic said, "but I'm not turning into a pumpkin just yet. We switched our shifts around for the weekend, so I don't have to get up as early as I usually do. The bar has a real fireplace, so how can I resist?"

The waiter brought the check and offered more coffee, which they both declined. Vic watched as Dean wrote briefly on the check before pushing it to the edge of the table without having added cash or a credit card.

"Are you kidding me," she said, "this is your hotel?"

"It happens to be, yes," he said. "It's not that I meant to hide it, but I didn't want you to be put off by it. I thought a friendly dinner would be nice and 'hey, there's a good restaurant at my hotel' didn't seem like a good thing to say'. Sorry. No, wait—I'm not sorry. You suggested this place."

"It's okay, it's okay," she said, laughing out loud. "I know there aren't many places to stay in town, and anyway, I can take care of myself. I've got a gun and my car's across the street. Let's go to the bar."

They left the table and walked down the short hallway to the bar, almost bumping into two men coming through the door on their way out.

"Oh, Mr. Parrish," Vic said. "I almost ran into you, excuse me."

"No, no, my fault," the man said, "I was rushing and not looking. Deputy Barstow, isn't it? Nice to see you. Ah, this is a friend of mine visiting from Europe—Doc…Mr. Dubois."

"How do you do, Mr. Dubois," Vic said, shaking the man's hand. "Vicki Barstow. I hope you're enjoying your visit."

"Thank you Miss Barstow," the man said. He spoke in excellent but heavily accented English. "A pleasure to make your acquaintance."

Dean held out his hand to Earl Parrish. "I'm just visiting town myself, Mr. Parrish, catching up with some old friends. I think we've met, but that must have been twenty years ago or more. Nice to see you again." He turned his attention to Parrish's friend. "Je suis heureux de faire votre connaissance, Monsieur Dubois. Mon nom est Dean Boudreau. J'espère aussi que vous avez une agréable visite."

The other man's face lit up as he shook Dean's hand. "Enchanté Monsieur Boudreau. Vous parlez très bien le Français."

"Well, we really need to get going," Parrish said, putting his arm on the other man's shoulder. "Good seeing you both then, have a nice evening."

Dean and Vic nodded at the other two men as they headed up the hallway towards the door to the outside. Still in the hallway, Vic gave Dean a look. "You know women's boots and now you speak French too? What's next with you? I suppose you probably know what perfume I'm wearing. What did you say to him anyway?"

"I just said that it was a pleasure to meet him and I hope that he enjoys his stay. And that was about the extent of my French. I can order a pizza and get through buying a train ticket, but not much more. And speaking of French, really now, there's no challenge in identifying Chanel No. 5—which is delightful, by the way. Let's get that drink."

The bar was cozy, with small tables and overstuffed chairs arranged to create several intimate seating areas. Several odd chairs were gathered around a marble fireplace where a wood fire crackled away, filling the room with its comforting scent. Soft piano music emanated from hidden speakers. The only other customers were a well-dressed and silver-haired couple who were nearing the bottom of their martinis. As they entered, it became immediately clear to Dean that Vic's friend Clare, back at the C-View, was not the only bartender in town that she knew.

"Hey Vic," the bartender said "what's shakin'? Are you coming in for a drink?"

"Hi Coleman," Vic said. "Oh it's nice in here. Yes, a drink. This is my friend Dean."

After introductions were completed, they ordered glasses of a dry rosé and took them over to a pair of chairs that were close together and near the fireplace.

"Was that better?" Vic said. "I upgraded you to friend for this bartender."

"I noticed that, much appreciated," Dean said. "That man in the hall, Earl Parrish—doesn't he own the Harbor House, with the fishing fleet and the different restaurants?"

"Yes, that's him," Vic said. "Probably the richest person in town. He's done a lot for Cape May though. It was him that set up the little car ferry to help us get through the bridge construction. He pays for all of it himself. He owns part of a company that's got a contract for some of the bridge repair work. I think it's called Janus Construction."

"Yeah, that's nice," Dean said. "Sounds like a good citizen. But did you notice how he was hustling his friend towards the door?"

"It did seem like that, yes," Vic said. "Like he didn't want him to be speaking with us. Maybe they were running late for something. Far as I know, Parrish and his friend aren't wanted for anything."

"Right, right. Of course not," Dean said, "something just sent my antenna up, that's all. It's interesting that he didn't want us to know that Mister Dubois was actually Doctor Dubois. People work very hard for years to be able to call themselves 'Doctor'. Odd that a friend would not use that title out of respect—deliberately. Ah, we can forget about it. How's your wine?"

"I like it. It's pleasant and light," Vic said. "Hang on a sec."

Dean watched her as she went back up to the bar to speak quietly with the bartender for a moment. When she came back to her chair she seemed to Dean to be struggling to contain a big grin.

"Doctor Pierre Dubois," Vic said. "From Paris. How do you like them apples, Columbo."

"Good work Deputy," Dean said, "good work. How did you get that?"

"I just told Coleman how we had bumped into them on our way in," she said, "and that I hadn't quite caught the man's first name. He said that he had heard Parrish call him Pierre, and also that he had heard the other man mention something about living in Paris."

"Bravo to you," Dean said. "I will file that away. Now, I

think you've earned the right to ask me questions. I think you wanted to know about that night a little over two years ago, right?"

Dean proceeded to tell a condensed but accurate version of the events of that night, about two years prior, when five armed men had broken into his house in the middle of the night in the suburbs north of Philadelphia.

"That is one hell of a story," Vic said. "And obviously your wounds healed up okay. Did that take a long time?"

"No, I was lucky there," Dean said. "Plenty of pain but no serious damage. I was fine after a few weeks. So, I was never charged, you know, because it was all justifiable. I made a lot of money from the whole thing, strangely enough. Appearances at gun shows, endorsements, a book deal."

"I'm sure you're right that you were lucky," Vic said. "And I'm glad to hear it. But you also handled a nightmare situation about as well as anyone could, during and after it seems to me. Here's to you coming through all that." She raised her glass and drained the last of her wine.

"Well, I'm just realizing how late it is," Dean said, looking at his watch. "It was a nice evening, but I wouldn't want the Chief to yell at me tomorrow for misappropriating city property."

"City property am I then?" Vic laughed as they both stood up. Dean signed the check at the bar and retrieved their coats from the rack near the door. "I had a really great time also, and I'm glad I bumped into you. Thank you for a nicer dinner than I had planned on. And wow—for that exciting story."

She led the way out into the hallway, but stopped short of the lobby, with just a foot between them, and turned back to face him. "You've been a perfect gentleman, but I have one more question for you before you send me out into the cold."

"Of course Deputy, what would you like to know?"

Her fireplace-scented hair brushed against his shoulder and he felt the warmth of her body as she leaned in close enough to whisper into his ear.

"Do you want to be alone?"

"Come to think of it…no."

17

At seven-fifteen in the morning, Deputy Vicki Barstow was halfway up the stairs to her apartment when she realized that she was 'sneaking' along as quietly as possible, hoping none of her neighbors would see her coming in so late. Or so early. *This is ridiculous*, she thought to herself, *I'm forty-two years old and here I am hoping I don't get grounded.* Later, she would laugh at herself again when she remembered that only two or three of the units in the complex were occupied at this time of year.

Ninety minutes earlier, she had been awakened by soft voices coming from the next room, followed by what sounded like a door closing. For most of a minute, she had explored the variety of feelings that enveloped her. The room was dark, but morning sunlight was peeking around the edges of the curtains that covered two windows. She was wrapped up in a luxurious comforter on a huge bed. She was naked inside a warm, soft cocoon. A news program was playing on a television in the other room and she heard someone moving about. Despite the dim light, a flushed feeling in her cheeks told her that she was blushing, as memories of the night before flooded in. *Man am I going to hear the rumors. And get the high-fives!*

"Ah, I see that somebody's awake," Dean said, setting a cup of coffee down on the night stand nearest where she lay. "Room service just delivered coffee and a muffin basket. The bathroom's all yours and here's a robe for you if you want it. I'll be in the next room." She didn't say anything as he leaned over and kissed her cheek before going out into the other room of the suite.

"Help me with something, would you?" she said, coming into the living area of the suite after a freshen-up, and leaning back against the dividing wall. She was wearing the thick, soft, hotel robe.

"Of course, what can I do?" Dean said. He got up from the sofa to come over to her.

"Just help me make this not be weird," Vic said. "Every part of last night was fantastic, and I don't want to regret any of it."

"You have my word on that," Dean said. "There will be no weirdness from me. Of course, you know, there could be a cost involved…"

Vic tilted her head and used one raised eyebrow to demand more information about the cost. Dean leaned in to kiss her neck. "I just mean that we might need to have dinner again tonight. Or maybe just late drinks."

"Or maybe we'll just go right to dessert," Vic said, feeling her face flush again even as she spoke the words.

"Now that's an idea that I can work with, Deputy."

———

By the time she was dressed and ready for the work day, Deputy Barstow had most of an hour before the beginning of her shift. Though she had delightful memories of a passionate night, she also remembered fragments of a strange dream about a big old house in a snowy yard. Thinking about the house next door to where she had seen Frederick Herrington come out of the yard the day before, she decided to drive over and take another look.

As she turned her car onto New Jersey Avenue and pulled over to park, she was startled by the loud blast of a siren, and looked up to the mirror to see that a city police car had pulled up right behind her.

Barstow stepped out of her car just as Tate got out of his cruiser, a big grin on his face.

"Chief! You scared me," she said, shaking a finger at him. She made an exaggerated shake of her head as she saw him stifling a laugh. "I had no idea you were behind me."

"Remember what they taught you in drivers-ed Vic," Tate said. "Get the big picture. Or something like that. Anyway, sorry I scared you. What are you doing out here?"

"Probably nothing Chief," Barstow said. "When I was out on patrol yesterday before the end of my shift, I came through here just as Mr. Herrington was finishing up with one of his houses, that one on the right, with the columns. I watched as he got back into his van and drove away. Only thing is, when I thought about it later, I had the feeling that he had actually come from that other house on the left there —Springside Guesthouse. Which can't be one of his houses, because you can see all the undisturbed snow on the front steps. Anyway, like I said, it's probably nothing. He was most likely just looking at the back yard, but I wanted to check it out."

"Part of being a good cop, Vic, is listening to your gut," Tate said, "so let's take a look."

Both of them pulled the zippers of their coats as high as they went, and Tate let Barstow lead the way back between the houses. They exchanged a look as they saw several sets of tracks leading from the side door of the house towards the rear and into the back yard. From the corner of the house, they could see the tracks going across the yard and off into the trees, presumably from there onward into the back yards of the homes on the next block.

They doubled back to the screen door on the side of the house, where Tate was surprised to find it unlocked. He pulled it open and looked through the glass panes of the inner door at the interior of the house. He tried the knob and found the inner door also unlocked. "Let's be careful here," he said to Barstow, as he unzipped his coat and pushed it back to rest his right hand on his holstered pistol. Barstow did the same, nodding at Tate to indicate that she was ready.

He pushed open the door and called out loudly to the inside of the house. "Hello – Cape May Police – is there anybody here?" He repeated the call several times, walking farther inside and directing his voice in different directions. "All right Vic, I doubt that anyone's here, but let's go through together and make sure." With their pistols still holstered, they started through the house, working slowly and carefully from bottom to top. They had been through four bedrooms on the second floor when they came to the last one at the end of a hallway, which put the room at the rear of the house. Tate pushed open the door to look inside for a moment before suddenly stepping back. "Somebody's been in there recently." He drew his pistol, keeping it pointed to the floor, and Barstow did the same. He pushed the door open and called out to the room, getting no response. They entered the room at the ready, finding nobody inside. Tate motioned to Barstow to stand guard while he checked the adjoining bathroom, the closet, and under the bed.

"Somebody's been using this room," Tate said. "At least off and on. Bed's been slept in."

"More than once," Barstow said, "going by how messed up the covers are. There's a pair of socks, but I don't see any other clothes. Few towels tossed around the bathroom, and the sink and toilet have been used quite a bit since the last cleaning." She was looking through the bathroom trash can. "Fast food wrappers, power bars, half a candy bar."

Tate had been poking around the rest of the room, finding some trash on top of the dresser. "Somebody likes their Wawa hash browns." Several colorful objects on the floor next to a chair caught his eye and he knelt down for a closer look. "More candy wrappers out here."

"Vic, I want you to stay here, near the door, while I go up and check the last few rooms above. It's the smallest floor so there can't be much up there. Eyes and ears open and I'll yell if I need you." He went up the stairs to the last floor while Barstow waited just inside the bedroom, where she could hear him moving around above her. He was back within a few minutes, shaking his head.

"Two more bedrooms and a small sitting room—all empty. So you think you might have seen Herrington around here yesterday?"

"I think so," Barstow said. "At least, I saw him coming from between the houses. I didn't actually see him coming out of this house."

"I don't know his address, but he lives in town some-where," Tate said. "Whoever's been in here can't really be living here though. It looks more like someone's been crashing here on occasion. Hiding out maybe. Very strange."

"I found a little ketchup in one of those fast food wrappers," Barstow said, "and it was completely dry, so at least a few days old. Course that doesn't mean that nobody's been here since then."

Tate nodded, deep in thought. He walked to the bath-room door and stood there looking around for a moment. "Okay Vic, here's what we're going to do. That door we came through downstairs is rigged up for a padlock, and I've got one in the trunk. I'll lock it up for now. You get on the horn to Doreen and get Herrington's address. Also, ask her to find out who owns this house and get in contact with them—see if they know anything. Who knows—there could be an estranged nephew or someone like that camping out inside here. Soon as you get that address for Herrington, you and I are going to pay him a visit. I'm starting to get a bad feeling about the way he keeps popping up."

Just as Barstow was about to call into Doreen, they both heard her voice come squawking out of the Chief's radio. "Chief, this is Doreen, where are you?"

Tate reached to his radio and pushed the button to transmit. "I'm up here on New Jersey Avenue with Vic, checking something out. We need you to look something up for us…"

Doreen cut him off. "Got another one Chief. A body I mean. The mailman—you know Jay Garrett—saw a door open and went to take a look, found a dead man just inside."

"Oh Christ, what the hell is going on around here, Armageddon?" Tate said. "Is Garrett sure the guy's dead?"

"Sounds like it Chief. He said he spent some time as a medic in Afghanistan, and that the guy's as dead as it gets. I'll call the ambulance soon as I get off with you. It's 221-B Washington, in-law apartment at the back of the driveway. Garrett's still there."

Tate told Doreen that they were on their way, and he and Barstow got into his cruiser. Four minutes later they slowed down as they saw a U.S. Postal Service truck pulled over on the side of the street. A uniformed man waved them into a driveway.

"You called it in Jay?" Tate said as he and Barstow got out of the car.

"Yeah Chief," the man said, "the mail's stopped for the main house, but I had something for the apartment over the garage. "I noticed the door wasn't closed all the way and I knocked and looked through the glass. He's right inside there. I took a quick look and then backed out and called."

"The ambulance should be on its way Jay," Tate said.

"Be great if you could stay here and keep an eye out for them." The mailman nodded.

Tate said, "Vic, let's take a look."

"Not expecting any trouble, but let's be on guard," Tate said, as they walked together to a door on the side of the garage building that stood ajar by about a foot. Mounted to the outside wall on the left side of the door was an old-style metal mailbox. A small rectangular frame was attached to the front of the thing, which displayed a white card with a name printed on it in faded marker. Tate shook his head from side to side before gesturing to Barstow to stand clear as he reached for the door knob. With a quick motion, he pulled the door open and stepped inside to a small foyer. Two seconds later he yelled out to Barstow. "Vic—come on in."

As Barstow stepped inside the small space, Tate shifted his body so she could see past him to the bottom of a flight of stairs, where a man's body lay face up across the first six or seven steps, with both feet on the landing. Tate moved closer and used one hand to steady himself on the steps as he used the other to check the man for a pulse. He stood up, shaking his head.

"Holy shit Chief," Barstow said. "What's that on his face?"

"A hammer," Tate said. "A framing hammer, looks like. You stay right here, or step outside if you want. I'm going to take a quick look at the apartment upstairs." He stepped carefully around the dead man, avoiding the pools of blood that had settled on several steps, and proceeded past and up the stairs, coming back down a minute later. "All clear.

Nobody up there. Dammit. All right, let me call Doreen and see if she can get Larson Finch here. He used his radio to speak with Doreen again, asking her to track down Finch and send him over. As he was about to sign off she interrupted him.

"Chief, I know you've got your hands full, but I got a message from Angela Andrews—you know, the manager over at the Ugly Mug. She said it was an emergency but you weren't answering your phone."

"Oh yeah, sorry, it's on the charger in the car. What's this emergency?"

"Here, I'll read you the note. 'Found another mug pointed the wrong way, so there's thirteen and not twelve on the list. Cody had it behind the bar for some reason, and gave it to Buddy to add to the others before he put them back up. Thought you should know ASAP.' And then she gave me a name, Chief. I guess it's the name on this thirteenth mug. She said the name is…"

Barstow had been listening also, and her eyes were locked with Tate's as they grew wider and wider. It was his turn to interrupt Doreen.

"Don't' say it—don't say it," Tate said, letting out a deep sigh. "I bet I know it. Dollars to donuts it's Frederick Herrington"

"That's right Chief," Doreen said. "How did you know that?"

"Because Vic and I are with him right now," Tate said. "And he's dead. He's our latest body. Look, I'll explain it all later in the office. See if you can get Larson Finch down here on the double. Brody too if he's available."

18

"We'll have to wait for Dr. Coyle to make the final call of course," Larson Finch said, after finding Tate upstairs in the late Mr. Herrington's living room. "But I'd say the cause of death is pretty clear."

"We're in sync on that, Larson," Tate said. "Most likely that big hammer sticking out of his face. Brody and I looked around the garage, and there's a pretty well-equipped work area along the rear wall. Some power tools, saws, levels, all that stuff. There were several different hammers hanging from hooks on the wall, with an empty spot in between. My guess is that whoever did this, popped in there looking for a weapon, passed up the screw drivers, wrenches, and the ball-peen, and grabbed the framing hammer. Hopefully the owner of the house will be able to help identify it. Unless those are Herrington's tools, which I guess is possible. His van's in there too, so he clearly had use of the garage."

"In any case, whoever owned the hammer," Finch said,

"my guess is that it was a weapon of opportunity, as hammers almost always are. Nobody plans to commit a murder with a hammer. Almost nobody."

It had been an hour since Herrington's body had been found by the mailman. After the EMTs had checked out the body, Larson Finch had gone to work while Deputy Barstow had taken pictures. Tate and Deputy Brody had canvassed the yard and the garage before moving to the upstairs apartment. With the aid of one of the EMTs, Finch was able to get a good set of the dead man's fingerprints loaded into his NikorScan 2000 fingerprint machine. As soon as the body was removed, he joined the three police officers upstairs.

"We don't see any sign of a struggle," Tate said, after Finch had been able to have his own look around. "Or of any kind of search having gone on here. The place is a little messy, but no drawers have been dumped and nothing's broken. I only knew Herrington to say hello, but I'm sure that he wasn't a wealthy man."

"His wallet's right there in that dish by the door," Brody said. "Along with his car keys and a few other things, just like many men would do. About forty bucks in the wallet. Seems like that isn't the kind of money to attract a robbery, but still, odd that it wasn't taken."

"Good point, if robbery had been any part of it," Tate said. "But I'm thinking that isn't the case at all. I'm thinking this was a deliberate murder, and whoever did it had no interest in coming up here and looking around. What do you think Larson?"

Finch was looking down to the bottom of the stairs where the body had been. He turned and scanned the room slowly, nodding repeatedly and screwing up his face before answering. "I think that you're probably spot-on with that idea Chief. I think that someone came here, to the back of this driveway, and took a look around. He either knew the door to the garage would be unlocked or just tried it, but anyway, went in, looked at the tools, and grabbed what he thought would be a good weapon. Then he came back around to Herrington's door—right down there—and knocked or rang the bell."

"And Herrington either knew the person," Barstow said, "or at least was not threatened by whoever it was."

"Precisely," Finch said. "He came down the stairs, saw the person through the glass, and opened the door. The assailant probably took a step or two inside, maybe with the hammer held out of sight, and then swung it overhand and down into Herrington's face with great force. This couldn't have been more than a few hours ago. His body isn't cold yet and very little of the blood has crusted."

"That adds up for me," Tate said. "Based on where Herrington fell down, either the killer took a few steps in, or maybe just swung the hammer from the threshold and then Herrington stumbled back a few feet before collapsing."

"We've been talking about 'him'," Brody said. "Isn't it possible that the killer could have been a woman?"

"Possible, yes, certainly that's a possibility," Finch said. "But I think it's highly unlikely. We left the hammer for the ME to remove, but it must have been buried a good three inches into his eye socket. Herrington was close to six feet tall, so his assailant was probably at least that tall and probably taller. No, I'll be really surprised if our killer isn't a powerfully built man of at least six feet in height."

"So no robbery," Tate said. "Just knock on the door, and when Herrington answers, someone takes a step in and totally surprises him with a hammer in the face. No sign of a struggle and no defensive wounds. It's hard to not see this as premeditated murder."

"It does look premeditated, doesn't it?" Finch said. "Yet crudely executed. Think about it—somebody comes over here to Herrington's apartment, planning to kill him, but also planning to scrounge around for a murder weapon before knocking on the door? That's really interesting."

"Mr. Finch, Chief," Brody said, "in the interest of not ruling anything out, however silly, isn't it possible that someone came over, someone Herrington knew, to return the hammer they had borrowed? Knocks on the door, Herrington comes down and opens it, they argue and it gets heated fast? Visitor hits him with the hammer?"

Finch directed an expressionless look at him for a full ten seconds before shrugging his shoulders. "I highly doubt that's what happened, but it isn't a silly idea. Brainstorming is good. One thought I have is, most people wouldn't stop by a friend's house to return a tool at six in the morning. But, we'll know more after the autopsy, and after we confirm that the murder weapon was taken from the rack downstairs." He looked around the small apartment again. "I doubt the assailant even came up the stairs, but, I've got Herrington's prints in my scanner now, so I'll check up here for anything recent that doesn't match. I'll also check the hammer after the ME's through with it, but I don't think that's going to tell us anything. It was a very rough, dry hardwood, probably ash or osage orange. No good for prints."

"Larson, when you're finished here," Tate said, "if you have time, there's something else I'd like you to check out. Vic and I took a look at the Springside Guesthouse up on New Jersey Avenue, in the block behind where the Admiral used to be, just before we got this call. The place is empty for the winter, and we'll be working on contacting the owners, but it looks like someone's been in and out, spending some time in one of the rooms inside. We have an idea that it might have been Herrington. Now that you have his prints in that scanner of yours, I'd like you to see if you think it's him that's been in there, and otherwise what your general impressions are. Can you do that?"

"Sure Chief," Finch said, "I don't see why not. I need about another forty minutes or so here, then I can look into that for you."

"Great, thanks Larson," Tate said. "I appreciate it. Vic, stay here with Mr. Finch please, and then you can ride back up there with him. Show him around and pick up your car. I've got a few things to do and we can compare notes later back at the station."

Finch began to work his way around the apartment with the fingerprint scanner, pausing occasionally to make notes in a little book or to take a picture with a small camera. Tate spent several minutes talking with the two deputies before leaving them to drive off in his cruiser.

19

The Ugly Mug wasn't open yet, but Tate was able to enter through the kitchen. He found Angela going over supply orders at the bar and pulled up a stool. He looked around to see if they were alone.

"It's just me and the guys in the kitchen," she said, "Cody should get here in a half hour or so. You get my message from Doreen?"

"Yeah, I did. That's why I'm here. I need you to fill me in on whatever you know about this latest mug."

"Okay, well, you know about the box I had upstairs with the twelve mugs. I found it and gave it to Buddy when he was almost done with the whole job, and along with the box, I gave him a paper where I had listed out the names and numbers—taken from the master list. I told you and your friend the other night that I would try to get an inventory done, remember? Well, it was quiet here last night, and Cody and I decided to tackle it and we went through all the mugs. Everything was pretty much what we expected, except that we found one more that we hadn't seen the other night. We probably missed it because it was hard to see up there in the corner next to the support for one of the air conditioners. When we looked at it, Cody remembered that it was one he had found behind some stuff under the bar."

"So did he hang it up, or did he give it to Buddy?"

"He gave it to Buddy. See, it was that day before we reopened, he saw Buddy with the box and asked him what he was doing. When Buddy told him, Cody gave him the additional mug. 'Here's another one Buddy, this one needs to get hung up too...' you know, something like that. Buddy did as he was told and hung up all thirteen in their proper sequence, but pointed the wrong way for whatever reason. Cody told me that he had grabbed a pencil and added it to the list I gave to Buddy, but obviously, it wasn't on my copy of the original."

"Okay, so that explains that. Buddy was given thirteen mugs to hang up, but you were only aware of the twelve that we talked about the other night."

"Initially, that's right. By the way, just in case we're being haunted by a curse or something, we fixed the remaining mugs, you know, for the living people, so they're pointing the right way now. Hopefully our karma will be in better shape going forward. But why is this such a big deal today Tate?"

"Because, Ang, thanks to your inventory, we now know that Frederick Herrington had a mug, and it got hung up wrong like the other twelve. What you don't know, is that we found his body this morning. Murdered, plain as day.

Early this morning, most likely. This whole coincidence with these mugs is looking less and less like a coincidence."

Angela's hand went up to cover her mouth as her jaw dropped.

Tate let out a quiet laugh and shook his head. "Yeah, that's how I feel about it too. This is nuts. Thirteen mugs hung up the wrong direction, and five of those people are dead within three months. I'm working on accepting that we have some kind of serial killer here in our little town and I'm having a real hard time with that. It's a lot to take in."

"You want a drink?"

"No, thanks. Sounds tempting though. I'll take you up on some coffee if you have that."

Angela went into the kitchen, coming back two minutes later with a mug of coffee for each of them, setting one down in front of Tate. "What can you tell me about Herrington? You know I won't tell anyone."

"Thanks, I know you won't Ang. Not a whole lot to tell just yet. I was out checking on something with Vic this morning when we got the call. He has—had, I guess—an apartment on Washington Street. The mailman noticed a door open and took a look, and he was right there inside. Looks like he answered the door and someone bashed him on the head. I guess now you've got to turn his mug back around to the ocean."

They sat quietly for a while, sipping coffee. They could hear pots and pans banging around in the kitchen. Angela reached one arm over to rub the back of Tate's neck. "You're going to have a busy day, but what do you say we have a drink together later? Maybe even dinner if you have time? Think of it as me doing a public service—the town needs you in tip-top shape."

"That sounds fantastic Ang, let me get back to you later though. You're right that it's going to be a busy day.

"I'm thinking about Buddy Parrish. I know he did a good job on the ceiling, and I know that he apparently had a misunderstanding when he put up those last thirteen mugs. I have to consider that somehow, somebody's watching him, or using him. Somebody learned about those mugs and is playing it somehow. Some kind of sick game maybe. I don't know—that sounds as crazy as everything else, now that I say it out loud."

Angela took a sip of her coffee, nodding. "Well, you know this place is part of the whole Harbor House complex. I'm the manager and I get a profit share. Earl Parrish is hands-off for the most part. When he asked me if there was some work Buddy could do, he didn't make any demands, but I felt like I really wanted to find something. Buddy had already helped with odds and ends, just on occasion over the past couple years, so we had a relationship. He's had tutors and been to specialists for much of his life, so he's very used to following instructions. He doesn't argue. The closest I've ever seen him to getting upset was the time I told you about—when I came in the day we were re-opening and found him about to set up a step stool in the aisle. Now I know that was probably when he had realized the error with the mugs and was trying to fix it. I come along and tell him to stop and put the stool away. Poor guy. He must have been flustered, because his father had warned him to do good here, and here I am stopping him from fixing a simple mistake. Shit, now I feel like a heel when I think about it."

"You need to let yourself off the hook about that, you were just trying to do your job and open the restaurant. Buddy might not understand how normal it is that all of us make mistakes. Have you ever seen him with anyone? Does he have friends?"

"Hmmm, I don't think so. Not like most people would anyway. I think he wanders around Harbor House a lot, you know, around the dock and the office, and stops to chat with people. He's really very outgoing, though obviously the conversation is limited. He talks to himself, but lots of people do that."

"Yeah, I do that sometimes myself. Do you know where he lives? I assume it's with Earl, but it's been so long since I've been to the house."

"He does live with Earl most of the time, but he also has a condo at Regent Beach that Earl set up for him. Far as I know he's free to go there when he wants to. Earl likes him to have as much independence as he's comfortable with."

Tate drained the last of his coffee and got up from the barstool. "I know you've got to open up. I'll be talking with Earl soon, but I appreciate your catching me up on Buddy."

"Take me up on my offer of a drink later if you can get away. Dinner too if you can squeeze me in." She leaned in to give him a kiss. "Don't forget to fit in some R & R now and then. Call me."

"That sounds really good Ang, I'll call you later. Thanks for the coffee."

Tate left the restaurant the way he had come in, through

the kitchen, and made the short drive across town to the Harbor House, where he followed his favorite scenic route along the dock and past the boats to the office.

Velma Fontaine greeted him as he entered. "Chief Saxby, what a pleasure to see you again so soon, but you look as if the weight of the world is on your shoulders."

"Some days it feels that way Velma, and this has been one of those days. What are you doing here on a Saturday? Is Earl running a sweatshop now?"

"Oh, I'm just catching up on a few things. I often do that on the weekends. Makes for an easier Monday morning. If you're here to see him, you're in luck because he's upstairs in the office. I'm sure it would be fine if you went right up."

"I'll do that, thanks Velma. I'll see you on the way out." He went up the carpeted flight of stairs that led to the second floor offices and turned down the short hallway to the large office that overlooked the fishing fleet and the harbor. He knocked lightly on the open door, seeing that Parrish was engrossed in the contents of some file at his desk.

"Tate—hello, nice to see you," Parrish said, looking up. He closed the file and came around the desk to shake hands. "Has everyone been cooperating with your investigation?"

"Everyone's been great Earl," Tate said. "The folks in the office, the Ugly Mug—no problem at all. If you have a few minutes though, I wanted to ask you about something else, kind of a family matter?"

"Oh, okay, sure Tate," Parrish said. "There isn't much family left between us. Is this about Buddy? Did he get himself in some kind of trouble?"

"No, nothing like that," Tate said. "Nothing to be alarmed about, just that I need help understanding something. Look, I want to give you some background, but I have to ask you to keep what I tell you to yourself, because it could involve an ongoing investigation."

"Sure Tate, you can count on me," Parrish said. "Let's hear it."

Tate proceeded to tell Parrish all about the work his son had done on the ceiling of the Ugly Mug, and about the apparent mistake he'd made with the positioning of the thirteen mugs. He was careful to make it clear that Buddy had done a very good job with the work overall. He talked about the five people who had died in the few months since the mugs had been placed. Parrish let out a gasp when Tate told him about Frederick Herrington.

"Herrington is the fifth, and we just found him this morning, so I really need to ask you to keep that under your hat for now. His family doesn't even know yet."

"Oh my God, it's incredible," Parrish said. "Yeah, yeah, under my hat—of course. This is a lot to process. But what do you think this has to do with Buddy? I mean, aside from him making that mistake with the mugs."

"Well, I'm just hashing it out at this point," Tate said. "I don't actually think it has anything to do with Buddy. It's more that I'm wondering who he might have talked to about it. Angela told me that she thought she might have inadvertently stopped him from fixing the mugs, so I thought he might have felt bad about that, or angry maybe, and told people about it. Then, I don't know Earl, some sicko gets inspired to start bumping people off—we're going to be looking at everything. I don't want to alarm him or scare him in any way, but I would like to be able to sit with him and talk about all of it. I mean, not the deaths of course, but just the work on the ceiling, and what he thought about those last mugs he hung up, but I decided to run it by you first as a courtesy. What do you think?"

"I appreciate that Tate," Parrish said. "I really do appreciate the courtesy, but I'm going to ask you for one more. Let me talk to him first and see what I can find out. If you need more after that we'll take it from there. He knows you, and he likes you, but, well, you know he can be sensitive, which can make him get nervous, which can make him get upset. I know I can't protect him from everything but I try to do what I can. That all okay with you?"

"That would be fine with me," Tate said. "Mostly what I want to know is, does he remember telling anyone about the mugs or has anyone asked him about it. If so, does he remember who it was or what they said? Is there anything else at all that he remembers about it? You get the idea."

"I absolutely do Tate," Parrish said. "I'll try to get with him later today and I'll see what I can find out."

20

"I'm not trying to re-open the investigations," Tate said. "Not yet anyway. I just wanted to let you know what's going on. I don't know if there's anything to this thing with the mugs, but we can't have our heads in the sand about it. It's too much to simply ignore."

Tate was aware of the mayor's habit of working on the weekend, and wasn't surprised to find him in his office. He told him what little they knew so far about Frederick Herrington's death. He had also decided to bring the mayor in on the situation with the mugs.

"Dammit Tate," Torrance said. "What did I say the other day about how we're always dealing with everyone bitching about parking in this town? Can we go back to that please? Shit. You're right, it is too much to ignore. Just tread lightly on this. Not a word to the families unless you've got something tighter than a frog's ass. Who are we talking about anyway? These accidents."

"For the moment," Tate said, "it's Gerry Fisher and Augie

Danforth that I'm interested in. They were both ruled accidental and they both had mugs turned the wrong way. There's
another accident that I've always had reservations about, but
she's never had a mug, so I'm setting that aside for now.
Forever maybe, seeing as how there's enough going on."

"Is that Mrs. Barnes?" Torrance said. "I remember that
you weren't exactly happy about that one. Her family was
on our asses to wrap that one up quick."

"That's right Jack," Tate said. "Mary Ellen Barnes.
Slipped in her bathroom and banged her head. I'm willing to
let that one go. The bathroom is a dangerous place.

"We know that the woman on the beach was murdered,
and now this morning we've got Herrington. We'll be taking
a closer look at Dan Kershaw of course too, which frankly
looks a lot like an accident."

"Good grief. What the hell is the world coming to?"
Torrance said. "Have you been in contact with Gavin Paige
at the State Police lately?"

"Yes, as a matter of fact I have," Tate said. "He has been
able to find two officers who were going to have some time
off but are willing to help us with the door to door. You
know, we're using the tax map to find out exactly who's in
town."

"Right, that's a great idea," Torrance said. "I'm glad
they were able to help out. I'll be sure to thank him next
time we talk. Oh—I almost forgot, I went up to take a look
at the bridge work, and I bumped into Earl Parrish. Apparently that was just after you had left his office."

"That's right," Tate said. "He's going to talk to Buddy to

feel him out on the thing with the mugs. I just wanted to hear what input he might have."

"Great, makes sense by all means," Torrance said. "Parrish does a lot for Cape May. I have no doubt that he'll help out however he can."

Tate stood up to go, and the mayor walked around the desk to see him out. "You're doing good Tate. Let me know if there's anything you need from me."

———

An hour later, in police headquarters, Tate finished briefing Larson Finch on the situation with the misplaced mugs, and the two of them joined Deputies Barstow and Brody around the table in the conference room. Doreen poked her head into the room. "I'm guessing Three's probably sleeping Chief, because he's not answering his phone. And I did finally get Dr. Coyle, but he isn't going to be able to dial in today. He said Mr. Finch could speak for him and could handle most questions."

Tate looked across at Finch. "That okay with you Larson?"

"That's fine," Finch said. "We talked at length just before I drove over. I think I have a grasp of it. I gather that your friend Mr. Boudreau won't be joining us either? He seemed like a very sharp fellow."

"That he is," Tate said. "That he is. I think he was headed up the ocean highway today, so I figured I'd give him the day off. I think he has a thing for exploring frozen ghost towns with a view of the ocean. I'll catch up with him later and fill him in.

"Join us please Doreen, so we're all on the same page. You can keep an eye on the emergency line from here." Doreen nodded and took a seat at the table with her notepad and pen. She pulled the phone set over towards her from its usual position near the middle of the table and punched a few of the buttons.

Tate remained standing and paced the length of the table as he talked. "Let's talk about Herrington first. The mailman, Jay Garrett, called that into Doreen this morning. What time was that Doreen?"

"I took the call at five minutes to nine Chief. I called you on the radio at exactly nine. As soon as I signed off with you, I called for the EMTs."

"And Vic and I got there about five or six minutes later. Larson, can you sum up Dr. Coyle's findings for us?"

"Glad to Chief," Finch said. "The good doctor places the likely time of death between about five and eight this morning, based primarily on body temperature and the status of blood congealment. I don't think any of us will be surprised about the cause of death, which would be the hammer blow to the upper face. The type of hammer was a framing hammer, which is very similar to your common claw hammer that can be found in half of the houses in the country, but with the sharp claw end being substantially longer and straighter. There was just one blow, but with enough force to drive the blade of the hammer three inches into Mr. Herrington's left eye socket. Doctor Coyle suggested that the blow was strong enough that the hammer would have penetrated deep into the skull even if it hit at the top of the head, but hitting at the eye socket made deep penetration all that much easier. Actual death was due to the massive and sudden trauma, along with blood loss. The doctor thought it likely that the blades of the hammer clipped the lowest part of the frontal lobe, but he is not yet able to say that for certain. He was probably unconscious immediately and dead within a minute."

"All right then," Tate said. He moved his arm several times, in an overhand arc, mimicking the action of hitting a standing person in the face with a weapon. "That confirms what seemed obvious this morning. Did the doctor agree with your theory that the killer was probably a tall, strong man?"

"He did," Finch said, "though he also conceded, as I have, that it could have been a tall and strong woman."

"The time of day is weird," Barstow said. "I mean, if somebody knocked on my door at six in the morning, I don't know if I'd answer it. Actually I'm not a good example because I'm a cop with a gun, but still."

"Remember he was just starting to make his coffee though," Brody said. "So he was awake and dressed. Barefoot, but dressed. I noticed that you could look out his kitchen window, and if someone was down there at the door, depending where they were standing, you could see them."

"Let's just say it's six o'clock then," Tate said, pacing. "You get up, pull on some pants and a sweatshirt, and go into the kitchen to start some coffee, but then you hear a knock on your door. You look at the clock and scratch your head, but then you look out the window and see someone there, 'who the hell is here at this time…oh, that's so and so…what does he want?' You go downstairs and pull the door open, but before you can say anything—bam."

"That's as good an explanation as I could put forward Chief," Finch said. "I'd be mighty surprised if that isn't just about what happened. I didn't find any sign that anyone other than Mr. Herrington had been upstairs in the living area in the recent past. I think that takes away any idea of robbery as a motive."

"Agreed," Tate said. "And while we're talking about motive, the only person that I can think of that Herrington would fight with—I think 'hate' is probably too strong a word—is Dan Kershaw, who fell off his ladder the other day. Brody, what did you find when you went through the area?"

"Nada, Chief," Brody said. "Just like the rest of the town, most of the houses on the block are empty. I did find three people at home—a single man across the street, and a husband and wife on the same side as Herrington and down a few. They didn't see or hear anything until we all started arriving. As you know it was Jay Garrett who found the body, and he came in and made his statement a few hours ago. He didn't add anything new."

"Okay, thanks Brody," Tate said. "I've spoken with Colonel Paige up at the State Police, and he has been able to free up two officers to help us with canvassing the town. They should be here tomorrow morning and can help us for at least a week. I'm putting Three in charge of them, and their main task will be to use the tax map to go door to door and get a handle on who exactly is in town now, have they been here all week, etc. When I first arranged to borrow these guys, we only had one murder. That has obviously changed today, so we'll have to take another look at just what questions we're asking the public. Probably something generic, like, 'have you seen anything strange lately', something along those lines.

"Switching to the Alaine Sawyer case," Tate said. "How are we doing with getting a look at any video from Sunday night into Monday?"

"It's slim pickins Chief," Barstow said. "There aren't a lot of cameras in town, especially now with almost everything closed. There are three ATMs that are attached to bank buildings, and we've been able to look at the footage from that timeframe for all three. There were six customers between two of them, with none for the third. We have viewed the transactions and they all look like normal cash withdrawals with nothing interesting going on in the background. As you know, if it came to it, we would need a warrant to get the bank to give us the identity of each user. Having said that, we did recognize several of them. Then there's the news and weather camera on top of the Lafayette, but that just looks out to the beach and the ocean. You can't see the cars passing below or anything else. That's about it."

"Thanks Vic," Tate said. He pointed to her and then Brody. "Can one of you give an update on interviews with people who knew her?"

"I can take that Chief," Brody said. "All three of us have worked on that, off and on. We've started with going back at least three years, talking with anyone we can find who worked with her, lived with her, or had any kind of relation-ship with her. Haven't yet found anything that doesn't fit with her being a low profile person who was well liked and was a good worker. No fights, feuds, or other drama that we can find. Nobody has been able to think of any reason that someone would want to hurt her."

"Well, somebody sure did," Tate said. "Thanks Brody, good work from all of you. We know that she wasn't broke, but certainly wasn't wealthy either. She didn't have a will that we've found or heard about, and no life insurance policy. Larson, what's the most common motive for premeditated murder?"

"Money, in some form or other," Finch said. "Hoping to steal, profit, or inherit."

"Right, so that doesn't seem to apply in Miss Sawyer's case," Tate said. "And I'm sure number two would be love, right? Or some version of that. Lust or revenge maybe. Again, no help there. Apparently no troubled relationships and everyone tells us that she was popular and well liked.

"We now have two murders inside one week. The last murder I know about—or the last that was proven to be a murder anyway, was four years ago, and that was a fight that escalated. Let's talk about the possibility of a connec-tion between Alaine Sawyer and Frederick Herrington. Maybe there is none, but we have no choice but to consider it. What are we thinking?"

After a moment of silence, it was Barstow who spoke first. "Chief, are we going to talk about the mug thing?"

"Yes, Vic, we are," Tate said. "We need to. But let's hold back on that for just a few more minutes please. By the way,

I've filled Mr. Finch in on that whole situation, so when we get to that, it's okay to talk about it."

"All right then," Barstow said, "aside from that, hmmmm. They were very different people. Female in her thirties, male late fifties. No work or social connections. She was well liked if not Miss Popular. You knew Herrington better than the rest of us I guess Chief."

"That's probably true," Tate said. "But not all that well. As far as I know he wasn't hated or shunned. He worked for a living and mostly got along with people. He may have been a bit of a curmudgeon. We know there was some baggage with Dan Kershaw, but I don't see how that could be a factor in his death."

The room was silent for long enough for everyone to hear Finch tapping the end of his pen on the conference table. He suddenly looked up and around the room, settling his gaze on Tate. "It is a good question to ask—what could be the connection between these two people. No murders for four years and then two inside a week. Any connection between those two people begs close examination. Having said that…" he raised a hand in the air before dropping it back to his notepad with an audible sigh. "I've never been a betting man, but I'm getting older and am not immune to change. I'm willing to bet that there isn't any connection between Herrington and the Sawyer woman at all. No connection between the *people*, that is. The connection is between their *deaths*. What is the connection between their deaths?"

"They both lived, and were killed, in Cape May," Barstow said "And they were both killed this week."

"Both murders appear to have been planned out in advance," Brody said. "Yet neither appears to have been for the motives that are statistically most likely—money, drugs, love, jealousy."

Doreen held up a hand. "Am I allowed to say something Chief? I have an idea."

"Of course Doreen," Tate said. "You're part of the department and we need all the help we can get."

"Well, I just made a connection in my head," Doreen said. "Both murders were committed with the means at hand. In other words, whoever the killer was, it seems like he didn't come to the scene of the crime with a weapon. Miss Sawyer was drowned in her bathtub, and if I heard it right earlier, someone found a hammer in the garage under Mr. Herrington's apartment."

"That's good Doreen," Tate said. "You're right. It appears that whoever it was went there intending to kill, but flexible about how to do it. That's actually a very interesting angle."

"That absolutely is interesting," Finch said. "We should all take a minute to think about that. These both appear to be premeditated crimes, yet the killer didn't bring a weapon. No—let me correct myself there. He may have brought a weapon, but ended up using something found at the site."

"That makes sense Mr. Finch," Brody said. "For all we know, the killer could have gone into the Sawyer woman's apartment with a gun in a shoulder holster, but then decided to do something else."

"Certainly," Finch said. "Or on the other hand, it's possible that he had checked the place out previously

—'cased the joint'—as it were, and made a plan to use the bathtub. You're deep in thought Chief. What do you think?"

"I'm thinking that anything's possible," Tate said, "but I can't see that the killer—or either killer—went there with a big plan. I think he went there with a plan to kill and some confidence that he would be able to pull it off."

"Chief, we're tap-dancing around something," Barstow said. "I get what Mr. Finch said about there being no connection between the people, and how the connection was between the deaths, but we aren't talking about the biggest connection. It's weird, but we have to talk about it, don't we?"

"Yeah Vic, I wish we didn't need to go there, but we do," Tate said. "Can't get away from those damn mugs. All right then, you first. What are you thinking?"

"Just that it's the obvious thing that they have in common," Barstow said. "I mean, aside from the other things we just said. They don't appear to have anything in common, yet, here they are, both killed this week, both in Cape May, both with available weapons. Her bathtub isn't really a weapon but you know what I mean. Are we assuming that the killer was the same person?"

"As long as we're just hashing out ideas," Finch said, "yes, for the moment I'm thinking that we have a single killer. If I'm right about that, then the fact that there isn't a clear modus operandi becomes that much more interesting. Or, another way to look at it is that the absence of a clear M.O. is in fact, his M.O."

"I'm trying to think of a way that the thing with the mugs could be a coincidence," Tate said, "but I'm having a lot of trouble getting there. Of the 326 mugs on the ceiling of the Ugly Mug, the subset that were accidentally turned around is just thirteen. What are the chances that both of our murder victims were represented in that subset? Christ, then if you add in the three accidental death folks who are also in that subset—Fisher, Danforth, and I'm including Kershaw —the odds get even slimmer. Larson?"

"Agree with you on that Chief," Finch said. "Simply sticking with the two murder victims, I'd say that odds against them both *coincidentally* showing up in that group of thirteen are stacked a mile high."

"Then if not coincidence," Brody said, "what could it be? Some kind of initiation? A game gone bad?"

"As long as we're throwing out ideas," Barstow said, "Thirteen mugs. Thirteen people at the last supper. Could this be some kind of religious thing? Not to mention all that stuff about the number thirteen."

"Which, as you just alluded to," Finch said, "has its origins in the idea that there were thirteen people present at the last supper. I think, if there's anything at all to this thing with the mugs, we shouldn't let ourselves be handicapped by looking for something that makes sense. To me it has all the hallmarks of something that doesn't make sense."

"Then, what we're looking at," Barstow said, "is either coincidence or something that doesn't make any sense. Wonderful."

"Sorry, I know that isn't very helpful," Finch said. "But it's the best contribution I have at the moment."

"All right," Tate said. "This is what I want to do. Vic and Brody, I want you to continue to work the Sawyer case as you've been doing and as we've discussed. That will go for Three too. Same for the Herrington case now. Handle them for the time being as standard investigations without adding this mug situation into it. I'm not dismissing that and I'm not trying to shut anyone up, it's just that I want to know that we've done what we can with a more conventional approach first. I'll be working on those cases with you, but I'll also be chewing on the mug thing. On Monday we start getting some help from the State Police, and hopefully we'll have more to talk about within a few days. We will assess and adjust as needed."

"Okay Chief," Barstow said. Brody nodded his agreement.

"Oh, I almost forgot," Tate said, looking at Finch. "What did you find when you and Vic went up to that guesthouse? Had Herrington been hanging out there?"

Larson shook his head. "I would say that's highly unlikely, because I didn't find his prints in any of the usual places. Doorknobs, faucets, toilet seat and flush lever. Edge of the door."

"Do you think it had been wiped down?" Tate said.

"No, there were recent prints all around the room," Finch said. "Just not Herrington's. I found a few oddballs but mostly they were from a single person, most likely an adult male, but that last part is an educated guess. I did find those in the usual places, so I would say that some unknown person had recently spent substantial time in that room. I can go back later or tomorrow to get you a good set of those prints that you can run through the system. There's something else that caught my eye that you might find interesting. That is, something that leads me to believe that two different people have spent time there. Probably at the same time. Friends, partners, lovers—that I don't know."

"Two people—really?" Tate said. "When Vic and I were there yesterday, I remember having the distinct idea that there had been some kind of loner in there."

"That was my thought too," Barstow said. "I didn't see anything that said more than one person to me."

"Oh ye of little faith," Finch said. "If you'll indulge me briefly, I'll demonstrate my theory.

"Deputy Barstow, do you remember all those power bar wrappers that we found? Some were in the trash can, but two were left on the dresser and one had fallen to the floor."

"I remember them, sure," Barstow said. "We even found the box. Somebody had bought a box of eight. I think they were chocolate peanut butter, weren't they?"

"Precisely," Finch said. "There was a box of eight, and we found all eight wrappers, the power bars having obviously been consumed." He reached down to a bag that had been sitting near his feet, his hand coming back with a small, brightly-labeled box. As he spoke, he proceeded to open the top tab of the box and dump the contents onto the table in front of him. "This is a box of eight power bars. They are a different brand than those that we found in the room, but are similarly packaged. I need you all to help me open them. He passed two bars to each of the other four people at the table. "Don't do anything until I say to. Don't completely remove the wrapper. Just open them up as if they were a banana that you planned to eat. Doreen, you first please."

Everyone watched as Doreen opened the two bars, peeling back a third of the wrapper as Finch had suggested. He then asked the other three people, one by one, to do likewise. In short order, there were eight partially unwrapped power bars on the table. Finch reached down to his bag again, producing two more loose power bars.

"Now, you may have noticed," Finch said, "that you all opened them in the same way, by performing the same steps, like almost anyone would, like this." He held one of the bars vertically, tearing the wrapper open as he narrated. "All of you held the bar something like this, and used the serrations at the end to tear into the wrapper at about a third of the way in. Once you do that, you can then pull the wrapper down to expose the bar."

"I think those serrations are probably there to give you a good place to rip the wrapper, right?" Barstow said.

"Yes, I assume that is the case," Finch said. "But now, look at this." He held up the second power bar. "And this is true by the way, for all kinds of candy bars and other products as well. You can see how the main seam of the wrapper runs the whole length here, and is folded back against the flat part of the product. If you lift the folded material at the seam—see how it expands out? Now that you have all that space, you can pull the wrapper open front to back, without any tearing. Then you push the contents up and out the end, like a…what's that thing…not a popsicle…but a…oh—a freeze pop. You push it out the end like a freeze pop."

"This is all very interesting Larson," Tate said. "But I'm still missing what you're getting at."

"Pardon me Chief, for taking so long to make my

point," Finch said. "What I'm getting at is that, five of the wrappers were opened the way you all did, by tearing at the serration, while the other three were opened like I just demonstrated. I consider it to be extremely unlikely that anyone would open some one way and some the other. No —there were two people in that room."

"Hmmm, I see," Tate said, taking a bite from one of the power bars he had opened. "But in your initial check you saw only one set of prints. What do you make of that?"

"I'm not sure yet," Finch said, nodding thoughtfully. "That is a sticking point. I may be missing something. I need to take a more thorough look."

Barstow exchanged a glance with Brody before picking up one of the power bars she had opened and taking a bite. "Mmmm, very good. Dark chocolate."

"Okay, well, thanks for all that Larson," Tate said "If you have time after this meeting, Vic can take you back over there to collect prints. Will you be able to check those wrappers for prints? To confirm your theory?"

"Yes, I will try to do that," Finch said. "The glossy paper should hold prints well."

"There we are then," Tate said. "Please let me know what you find. Everybody else, you know what to do. Meeting adjourned."

round the time that the meeting at police headquarters was finishing up, Earl Parrish reached the bottom of a stack of paperwork and decided that he'd had enough of work for the day. After spending a few minutes chatting with the small weekend staff in the offices downstairs, he left for the five-minute drive home. The house that he shared with his son Buddy was in the quiet and exclusive Harbor Cove neighborhood, where the view from several of the upstairs windows included the Harbor House complex and much of the fishing fleet across the water. Wonderful smells of dinner cooking greeted him as he came through the door into the main foyer.

"You're home early Mr. Parrish," Suzette, his live-in housekeeper and cook said. "I'm afraid dinner won't be ready for more than an hour."

"Oh that's fine Suzette," Parrish said. "Though whatever

you're working on smells so good that it won't be an easy wait. Would you know if Buddy is home?"

"He is, Mr. Parrish, up in his room," she said. "He called earlier to ask what I was making for dinner. Once he found out I was making his favorite pot roast, I don't think anything would have kept him away."

"Same goes for me Suzette," Parrish said. "Let me know when it's ready. I'll be upstairs with Buddy for a while and in my office after that."

As he climbed the stairs and started down the hallway to the bedrooms, he could hear the sound of a TV show coming from his son's room. He knocked on the door, which was slightly ajar.

"Hey Bud, can I come in?"

"Come in Pop, hi Pop," Buddy said.

Parrish pushed the door open and went in. "What are you watching? Is that Lost in Space? That used to be one of my favorite shows when I was a kid."

"Yes Pop, Lost in Space. I like the robot—'Warning, warning. That does not compute. That does not compute.' He's very funny. Dr. Smith is always up to something."

"I remember that too Bud, Dr. Smith was always sneaking around, but the robot was my favorite part of the show. I'll see if I can get you a model if you'd like."

His son's face lit up. "Oh—yes. I'd like that Pop! Maybe one that makes sounds, like in the show."

"Sure Bud, I'll work on that. Hey, can we turn the sound down so we can talk for a few minutes?"

Buddy picked up a remote from next to where he was sitting on the edge of his bed and pressed the mute button, cutting off a conversation between Will Robinson and one of his sisters. "What's up Pop?"

"Buddy, your cousin Tate came to see me today and we talked for a while. There've been some strange things happening in town recently, and he's been going all around, asking people if they might be able to help him."

Parrish had the impression that a look of fear flashed across his son's face, and that his body had suddenly tensed.

"Tate is police Pop. I didn't do anything wrong."

"Hey, hey, Bud, nobody is saying you did anything wrong. Tate is talking to people all over town asking if they can help him with a big problem. And yes, you know that he is the police chief. Do you think the police are bad? When did you start thinking that?"

Buddy pointed silently to the TV, where the Lost in Space rerun had gone to commercial.

"Oh, I see," Parrish said. "You see the police on TV. You need to remember that those are just stories, Bud. That isn't real. Your cousin Tate is a good guy, and he thought you might know about something. Do you remember last fall when you spent a few weeks working for Angela over at the Ugly Mug restaurant?"

This time, Parrish was sure that the dark look came across his son's face. He could see Buddy's lips draw tight, as though preparing to not speak.

"Buddy, I can see that you're upset about something, but there's nothing that you should be upset about. Everybody has told me that you did a really good job with the work you did there. Angela told me that she was very impressed and very thankful. She showed me one day after it was done and

I agree. Cousin Tate saw it and made a point to tell me what a good job you did."

"Thank you Pop, but I made a mistake."

"I heard about that Bud, but that's okay. We all make mistakes. Angela makes mistakes and the people that work there in the kitchen make mistakes. Your cousin Tate makes mistakes. And boy, Bud, your dad makes lots of mistakes. I made six or seven already today. We make mistakes, we apologize if we need to, or fix them if we can, then we try to learn something from it and we move on."

"I understand Pop, I've heard people say that—learn from mistakes."

"You're right Bud, it is important to try to learn from mistakes. Now, will you tell me about the mistake you made when you were finishing up the ceiling at the Ugly Mug, and hanging up all those mugs?"

"After I painted the ceiling, the paint had to dry. The next day, I started to hang up the mugs. They all had numbers on them so it was fun. Angela told me to put them in order. I worked hard to put them in order. I like numbers so it was fun. She gave me a big paper list, and she told me that they should all point in the same direction, except for some on the list with a big red mark. She told me to hang those ones up the other way."

"How many of them had the red mark, I mean on the paper?"

"I think it was thirty Pop. I can go back and count them if you want."

"No, that's okay Bud, no need for that. So you put all the mugs back up, on the little hooks, right?"

"Right Pop, I put them up, and I was almost done, when Angela came from her room upstairs and gave me a dusty box with more of the mugs. She told me that I needed to hang them up too. She gave me a paper with the names and numbers of the mugs written on it. So I knew where they should go."

"Do you remember how many mugs were in that box? The dusty box?"

"Yes, I remember there were twelve. The man from the kitchen had made me a sandwich with some french fries. I was almost finished with lunch when she came and gave me the box. I remember that there was the same number of mugs as the number of french fries that were on my plate. Twelve."

"Okay, so after you were almost finished with the work, she came and gave you twelve more mugs to hang up. What happened next?"

"I finished my sandwich, and the man who works there, with all the bottles and sodas, he took my plate away, with the four french fries that I didn't eat. He told me that the ceiling looked really good, but I told him that Angela had given me a box of some more mugs. That's when he said something like 'Oh wait Buddy', and he gave me another mug that he had down below there somewhere. He told me that Angela would want me to hang it up also. He took the paper and wrote more on it."

"Ah, so you had thirteen mugs that you needed to hang up," Parrish said.

"Yes Pop, and it didn't take me long. They all had numbers on them, so I could see where they had to go."

Parrish could see that his son's eyes were welling up. Buddy covered his face with both hands before speaking again while trying not to cry. "I hung them up facing the wrong way. I'm sorry Pop!"

Parrish reached over from the chair he had pulled up beside the bed and put a hand on Buddy's knee. "Hey Bud, remember what I said about how we all make mistakes? Don't be upset about that. You know Velma, in my office? Just this morning she told me that I needed to sign some papers, and I did, but I signed them all in the wrong place! She had to make new papers for me to sign, but she wasn't mad at me. We both laughed at it, because it was just a mistake I made. This thing with the mugs was just a mistake —that's all."

Buddy smiled at that and wiped his eyes with his sleeve. Parrish smiled back, softly patting his knee.

"I know Pop, but I heard that bad things have been happening to some people whose names are on the mugs. There was a girl who got hurt bad, right? Alaine was her name. I remember that name on one of the mugs. Is that my fault?"

"No—no Bud, none of that is your fault. And who told you about that lady?"

"It was someone down on one of the docks Pop, I don't remember who it was. You know I like to walk around and talk to the people. I heard that from one of the people I talked to."

"Well, if you think you see them again, you tell me about it, and don't listen to them anyway. I mean that—is that clear?"

Buddy's face was a blank, but he nodded right away.

"When was it Bud," Parrish continued, "that you realized you had put the mugs up the wrong way?"

"Just before I left that day, when I was putting stuff away. I looked up at a few of them, and saw that they were pointing the different way. I got sad because I remembered that Angela had told me how they should go, but Pop, it wasn't written on the paper! I had to leave then, but I thought about it all night."

"I'm sorry you had to worry about that Bud. Did you go back to try to fix it the next day?"

"Yes Pop, but I guess I got there too late, because they needed to start making food and drinks for people."

"Oh, right. That was the day that they opened up for business again."

"Right Pop, I went in and was just looking to find the mugs to fix, and Angela came up and told me to stop. 'Open' she said. She told me they needed to open. I started to tell her that I needed to fix the mugs, but she told me I had to leave. It made me sad Pop."

"I know, Bud, I know. I know I told you that you had to do exactly what she said."

"You did Pop, and I tried, but you told me something else too, before I went there to work. You told me not to make any mistakes." Buddy put his hand to his face again and started to sob. Parrish moved to sit on the bed beside him and put an arm around his shoulders.

"I know Bud, I know. And that was my mistake. Can you see that? It was my mistake to tell you that you weren't allowed to make mistakes. I was dumb when I said that to you. I make mistakes and you can too. We just try to learn from them when we can. I'm sorry that I upset you. Angela had to open the restaurant for her customers, so I'm sure she didn't mean to hurt you by not letting you fix things. Don't be upset with her for that." He sat with an arm around Buddy, rubbing his shoulder. "After that, did anyone ever ask you about the mugs? Did anyone make fun of you or complain about it?"

Buddy wiped his eyes again, thinking for a minute. "No, I don't think so. After that, she…Angela…gave me some work to do out in the storage shed, but I never did anything else with the mugs. Nobody seemed to care about it anymore. Everyone told me the ceiling looked good and told me I did a good job. I did a good job Pop, just like you told me to."

"I know you did Bud, you really did, and I'm very proud of you. That's enough talk about the mugs for now. Thanks for telling me what happened and I'll pass it on to cousin Tate. Maybe it can help him with what he's working on."

Buddy was smiling again and clearly feeling better. Parrish got up and started to walk to the door, but stopped halfway there and turned back to his son. "Buddy, have you been seeing Montel lately?"

Buddy seemed to be in deep thought for a long pause before shaking his head.

"I don't want Montel around here Buddy, I mean that. He is a bad person. I don't want him here in the house, but I also don't want him with you over in your apartment."

"I know Pop, you told me he was bad. But Pop, you know how people look at me sometimes. They don't think seriously about me. That makes me sad, and when it's like that, Montel is the only one who really listens to me."

Parrish came back to crouch down in front of his son so they were almost eye to eye.

"I'll always listen to you Bud, and I'll always take you seriously. Your Pop loves you a lot. Please remember that. Montel may say he listens to you, but he isn't good for you Bud. Remember that time up in Ocean City, when he hurt that man on the boardwalk? That man had to go to the hospital with a broken arm Bud. That isn't what a good person does. Just keep that in mind, and remember, you can always come to me and talk to me. The next time you see Montel, I want you to tell him that I said to keep away from you. Is that clear Bud?"

"But Pop, Montel thought that man was trying to hurt me—he stuck up for me."

"I know he thought that, Bud, but he was wrong. That man was reaching out to shake your hand. I was there, remember? I don't want to see Montel around here."

"Okay, okay Pop. I understand." Buddy nodded up and down several times.

"There's my boy," Parrish said, rising and patting his son on the shoulder. "How about if that's enough of that, okay? I hear Suzette is making her wonderful pot roast tonight. I can smell it from here. Will you have dinner with me tonight?"

"Oh yes Pop, I would love that," Buddy said, grinning from ear to ear as Parrish left the room.

22

After the meeting in the conference room broke up, Tate was leaning back in the chair behind his desk, taking small bites of a power bar and pondering the several puzzles at hand. The Sawyer case, the strange matter of the mugs, somebody apparently making camp inside a huge empty house, and now the Herrington murder—it all swirled around inside his head like dirty laundry banging about inside an overstuffed washer. *Are the murders connected? They can't be. Why would they be? And if they are, could there really be any connection to that crazy thing with the mugs? What about the break-in? Does that have anything to do with anything? Power bars?*

His reverie was interrupted by someone knocking on the open office door. He spun his chair around to see Doreen standing in the doorway.

"I'm sorry if I startled you Chief, Have you got a minute?"

"Of course Doreen," Tate said. "Come on in. I was just

letting all this run around in my head, you know, see if anything comes together or jumps out. What's up?"

"Chief, I think you know Velma Fontaine, don't you? She runs the Harbor House offices for Earl Parrish."

"Certainly, I've known Velma for years, you know, in a friendly way. I saw her for a minute earlier today after I left Herrington's."

"Well, she and I are old friends, and she just called me on my cell. She wanted a few minutes to talk to you about something, but didn't want anybody else to know about it."

"Hmmm, interesting. I'm guessing that means that she didn't want other people at the Harbor House to know about it. One person in particular. Is that your take on it?"

"I think that's the size of it Chief, yes. It's a small town, and you know how things get around so fast."

"Oh yes I do, like wildfire as the expression goes. Well sure then. Does she want me to meet her somewhere, or will she come into the office?"

Doreen checked her watch before answering. "She's probably closing up the office just about now, and she said she has some papers to drop off at the zoning department downstairs. Shall I call her and say you'll meet her downstairs?"

"Yes, go ahead and do that. If she wants to keep a low profile, we can duck into one of the empty offices down there to talk. Tell her to come to the side entrance as if she was going to pay a parking ticket. Let me know when she's on her way."

Fifteen minutes later, Tate opened the downstairs side door to let Velma Fontaine in.

"First of all Velma, is everything all right?"

"Yes Chief, I'm fine. No emergency. It's just that I wanted to talk to you about something and wasn't comfortable bringing it up earlier at the office."

"Okay, good then, you had me a little worried. Do you really need to drop that somewhere?" He pointed to the large manila envelope in her hand.

"Yes, this is actually a real errand. It's for Colleen in the zoning office. She told me to just slip it under the door. It's right over there."

Tate was not surprised to see that Velma knew her way around City Hall. He waited while she walked twenty feet down the main hall and knelt to push the envelope under one of the doors. As she walked back, Tate met her halfway. He took a small set of keys from his pocket and unlocked a door marked 'Department of Parking Violations'.

"The building's empty other than the police department right now. We can talk in here."

"Are you sure we're allowed to go in there?" Velma said.

"I realize that everyone's afraid of this place," Tate said, unable to suppress a small laugh, "but really now, I'll keep you safe."

Velma shrugged and followed him inside, and he closed the door behind them. He gestured to a small waiting area with an assortment of chairs positioned around a small table. They chose two that were at right angles to one another and sat down.

"So you've got your cover story," Tate said, "if anyone

spots you. And you've got me quite interested Velma. What did you want to talk about?"

Velma took a moment to gather her thoughts before answering. "It may be nothing Chief, or, there's probably some simple explanation that I'm not thinking of, but…well heck, it's about Buddy Parrish. You know, Earl's son. I think Buddy might know someone who knows something about that poor young woman you found on the beach. See, I accidentally overheard something last Thursday. Late morning it was, on Thursday, just before lunch. I've been thinking about it since then and finally decided to give it to you to think about."

Tate had leaned in closer as Velma started talking, and was listening intently. "You heard Buddy talking or you heard someone talking about Buddy?"

"I heard Buddy talking with another man. You know he has a very recognizable voice. High-pitched, like a child. But it was just snippets—a few words here and there that didn't make much sense. I was up in the storage room above the main office. We have our older copier up there that's best for certain types of jobs, and I was up there for about twenty minutes to print something out. It gets hot in that room, and then with the copier running for a long time, well, I had one of the windows cracked for a little fresh air. After a few minutes, the copier ran out of paper and it was suddenly quiet. That's when I heard voices from below. That would be the walkway between the dock and the parking lot near the fish market. Even though I couldn't make much of it out, I could tell that it was Buddy talking to some older man. Or maybe not older, but certainly another man with a deeper voice. Buddy's voice sounded almost angry, which is very unusual. He said something I couldn't really hear, and then 'don't let my father'. I'm not positive, but I think he was saying 'don't let my father see you'. Then, the other man said some things I couldn't hear, until I caught something like 'trying to help'. It could have been 'just trying to help'. I'm sorry Chief. I guess I'm a lousy witness. When the copier stopped, it was quiet for maybe twenty seconds, until a delivery truck pulled up on the other side of the building, so that was loud for a while until the driver finally switched off the engine."

"Don't worry about that Velma," Tate said. "I appreciate your telling me this, though I'm not hearing anything yet that sounds like it might be police business. Did you catch anything else?"

"Yes, there's a little more," Velma said. "That's what made me think that I needed to let you know about it. I hope you don't think less of me, but I'll admit at that point, I was parked by the window really trying to hear what they were saying. The man with the deeper voice was talking quietly, and in there somewhere I swear I heard him say 'out on the beach'. But here's the thing Chief—I really thought what he said was 'left her out on the beach'. In any case, there was a little more back and forth between the two of them. The last thing I can really say I heard was 'shouldn't have done that'. That was from Buddy. Right about then one of the trawlers fired up her engines and I couldn't hear anything more, but they must have gone their separate ways because then I saw Buddy walking away towards the parking lot. I couldn't see anything at all when they were right below me, but I saw him walk away."

"So you saw Buddy leave the area," Tate said. "Were you able to see the other man at all?"

"I did Chief," Velma said, "but not that's worth any kind of description. When I saw Buddy go one way, I rushed over to the other window that overlooks the main dock, and I could see the other man as he walked away towards one of the boats, or anyway, farther up the dock. Thing is though, that all I can say is that he was wearing a dark blue or black winter coat, with a hat like a bunch of the guys wear on the docks. I will say that he was a tall man, and probably slimmer than some."

"Hmmm, okay, so really he could have been any of several people working on one of the boats that day. Or also, he could have been somebody who had nothing to do with the conversation you heard, but was just walking by at that moment—right?"

"I'm afraid so Chief," Velma said. "Like I said, I knew it wasn't much to go on. That's all I have. I hope I did the right thing in letting you know. I went back and forth about going to Earl about it, but finally decided that you were the one to tell. I don't want you to think that I have any problem with him, because I don't. I just know how protective he is when it comes to Buddy."

"Sure Velma," Tate said, "I get why you decided to come to me and I'm really glad you did. I'll ask you to keep this to yourself for now. Another thing that I want you to bear in mind, just as I will, is that, if Buddy and the other man actually said all of those things that you thought you heard, they still didn't say anything that anyone couldn't have gotten from reading about it in the latest Star and Wave. 'Woman left out on the beach' for example. So it's interesting, and could be helpful, but we also need to keep it in perspective."

"I understand Chief," Velma said. "And I'm glad I told you all this. I couldn't hear much of what they were saying, but it's more of a feeling that I got from the whole thing. I really believe that Buddy was afraid of that other man. Or upset at him. Maybe it was both."

———

Tate had just seen Velma out and was climbing the stairs back up to the department when his phone rang. His initial dread at having to talk to anyone else at that moment faded away when he saw that it was his friend Dean calling.

"Hey, I didn't know if I'd be hearing from you today. Are you wandering around the coast?"

"I have been, yeah," Dean said. "I'm up in Margate right now. I stopped to take a few pictures of Lucy the Elephant, then I think I'll head back south. Everything's a ghost town."

"I'm not surprised," Tate said. "Were you able to find a place for lunch?"

"I was pleasantly surprised to find that the Deauville Inn was open," Dean said. "Up at the northern tip of Sea Isle. Had a pretty good burger and a Sam Adams with an icy view of the back bay. What's going on in town today?"

"Oh, you know, not much," Tate said. "Another murder early this morning, but that's about it."

"What the...," Dean exclaimed. "You're kidding me, right? You wouldn't kid about that. Are you kidding me? What happened?"

Tate took a few minutes and gave Dean the rough details of what they knew so far about Frederick Herrington, getting interrupted a few times with questions. "Same killer, different killer—we don't know yet. It hasn't even been twelve hours, so there's a shitload of unknowns. We're getting some help this week with a loan of two State Police Troopers, so we'll put them to good use going door to door. I'll tell you more about it later. Are you booked up for dinner?"

"Actually, I think I am," Dean said. "I'll check on it, but regardless, maybe we could meet up later for drinks. At the Ugly Mug or wherever you say."

"A dinner date then, hmmm," Tate said. "I was starting to worry. After all, you've been in town for two whole days. You remember Angela, from the Mug? She's been after me to get together, so maybe tonight's a good time to take her up on the idea. The four of us could meet up later, if your date isn't too shy, that is."

"She could be, but I'll work on it," Dean said. "Anyway, that sounds like a great idea. I'll call you later and let you know."

They signed off and Tate went back into the police department, running into Deputy Barstow in the small kitchen.

"How are you holding up Vic?" Tate said. "It's been a hell of a day, hasn't it?"

"I'm okay Chief," Barstow said. "I look forward to getting the image of Herrington laying there with the hammer in his face out of my mind. Got a feeling that's going to take some time." She sniffed the remains of a pot of coffee before half filling a paper cup for each of them. Tate stirred some creamer into his before taking a sip, which he followed with an exaggerated grimace.

"Yeah, I'm right there with you on that Vic," Tate said. "Something you'd only expect to see in a horror movie. Hey, how did everything go when you took Finch back up to look at that room?"

"He went all around the place with that fingerprint scanner thing of his," Barstow said. "And he bagged up those power bar wrappers and a few other things. Said he'd work on them at home and get back to you by tomorrow morning. He did a lot of scratching his head and muttering to himself. Doreen's been trying to contact the homeowners, but it turns out that they're in the middle of a month-long tour of Europe. Could be a while before we know if anyone has permission to be in the house."

"All right, well, we'll just have to proceed for the time being as though anyone in there is in there illegally," Tate said. "At least it's locked up now, but we'll have to keep an eye on it." They both sipped at the stale coffee and Tate glanced at his watch. "What do you have going on tonight? I hope you're finding a way to fit in some R & R every once in a while."

"Believe it or not, I have a dinner date," Barstow said,

trying without much success not to blush. "And same advice right back at you Chief. You need some R & R too."

"Will wonders never cease," Tate said. "I am glad to hear it, you deserve it. Is it anyone I know in this small town?"

"Oh, I don't know," Barstow said. "You might know him. You're a detective—you'll probably find out anyway."

"Hard to avoid that around here isn't it?" Tate said. "But none of my business. I'm just glad to hear that you're doing something aside from work now and then." He took a last sip of coffee, and made another face before dropping the cup into a trash can. "Well, thanks for the coffee break. I've got about another hour at my desk before I'm outta here. Maybe I'll bump into you later if you and your mystery man are out and about. I'll probably be over at the Mug later with Angela. We can get back to trying to solve the crime wave tomorrow."

23

Delaney's Irish Pub on the Washington Street Mall was about half full as the waitress cleared Tate and Angela's table after their dinner.

"That was really good," Tate said, "but now I'm stuffed like a mattress. What say you—another drink here, or would you like to go somewhere else? I hear there's a nice place called the Ugly Mug, or something like that."

"I heard about that place too," Angela said. "I also heard that the prices are good and the manager is gorgeous."

"Mmmm, yeah, I heard that too. And it's only a block away. Let's do it then," Tate said. "I talked to my friend Dean earlier, and mentioned that you and I might end up at the Mug tonight after dinner. I hope that's okay. He thought he had a dinner date for tonight, so I'm not sure what to expect."

"A dinner date? Interesting," Angela said. "After he's been in town what, two—three days? Must not believe in wasting time. Odds are that we know her, unless he ferried her across the harbor somehow."

"I'll send him a message then," Tate said. He set his credit card down on the check that had just arrived before using his phone. As they stepped from the warmth of the tavern, an icy wind whipped by and they both pulled their coat zippers up the last possible inch. They walked arm in arm to where the Ugly Mug sat on the next corner.

Entering through the side door, they walked past the restrooms and into the bar. The place was sparsely populated and there were plenty of open tables. As they looked around, Tate nodding or smiling to a few people he knew and Angela doing the same for people that she knew, Tate felt the cold air on his back as the door behind them was opened again and someone came in.

"Hey, how come there's never a cop when you need one," said a man's voice from behind them.

Tate turned around towards the voice, breaking into a wide smile and holding out his hand as he saw Dean.

"I'm glad you made it," Tate said, his face filling with surprise as he recognized the woman his friend had come in with. "What the…"

"Hi Chief," Barstow said. "Yes, it's really me."

"I really have been a lousy detective, haven't I," Tate said. "So what…I mean, when did this…"

"Oh give the girl a break Tate," Angela said, cutting in to greet the new arrivals. "Hi Dean, it's nice to see you again. And Vic—wow, okay—it's great to see you with your hair down. Let me get us a table."

Five minutes later they were all seated in one of the

larger booths and had ordered a round of drinks—white wine for Barstow, Stolichnaya and cranberry for Angela, and bourbon on the rocks for the two men.

Seated across the table from them, Tate looked back and forth between Dean and Barstow with obvious curiosity. "So…are you going to explain or do I have to interrogate you?"

"No need to get out the hot lights and the rubber hose Chief," Dean said. "Besides, it's all your fault anyway. When you bailed on me last night, I decided to get some dinner at the C-View, and ran into Vic on the way in. Almost didn't recognize her in jeans and with all this hair hanging down."

"So dinner at the C-View huh," Angela said. "That sounds nice and cozy. What happened after that?"

"Oh, so now you're in on the interrogation too," Barstow said, her face a combination of mischief and embarrassment. "I see how you guys are. Actually, it was just a drink at the C-View. Dinner was at the Carolina."

"The Carolina…" Tate said, looking across at Dean. "But that's your…"

Angela cut him off with a gentle jab in the ribs. "Okay now, that's enough questioning. Sorry Vic. We're glad to see you out, so please relax and be comfortable. You too Dean."

"And I second that," Tate said. "I'm not your boss for tonight Vic, okay? Just friends."

"Did you two just have dinner somewhere?" Dean said. "We just came from Finn's."

"Oh that's funny, we were a block apart," Tate said. "We were at Delaney's. It was very good but I ate too much."

"Well, It's good that you guys were able to take a few hours off to hang out," Dean said. He gestured to Tate and Barstow. "I know you've got your hands full. Must have been a hell of a day."

"Yeah, you said it brother," Tate said. "At least now we're getting two state troopers to help with the leg work. Maybe I can think of a way to make use of you too, while we're at it. Can't have you just driving around like a tourist all the time."

"Speaking of which," Angela said, looking at Dean. "Tate told me you took a drive up through the towns today. How was that?"

"It would have been more fun with some company," Dean said. "But it was interesting. Not much going on anywhere and not much open. Just endless rows of big empty houses waiting for the summer rentals. I had a nice lunch in Sea Isle, and after that I got as far north as Margate. Checked out Lucy the Elephant which was closed of course. Sounds like all the excitement was right here in town today."

"I've had just about enough of that kind of excitement," Tate said. "I look forward to getting back to the usual stolen bicycles and drunks pissing in people's yards after the bars close."

"I'll drink to that," Barstow said, and raised her glass in a toast. For twenty minutes the group sipped their drinks and shared old memories of coconut-scented afternoons on the beach and back yard keg parties. In a quiet moment Angela noticed Barstow looking up at the ceiling.

"We can't seem to get away from them, can we Vic?" she said. "Those damn mugs, I mean."

"I was about to say 'no, they're still hanging over us'," Barstow said. "And then I realized that would have been a bad joke."

"I was fooling around on line yesterday," Angela said, "and I spent some time reading about serial killers. Now, don't get me wrong, I know that nobody's saying that's what we have going on, but I found something really interesting. One article had a link, and that led me to another link —you know how that goes. Anyway, there was this case in Indiana—not Indianapolis but I don't remember the town right now—somebody working at the local newspaper accidentally put two obituaries in for publication when the people weren't dead yet."

"How can you accidentally publish an obituary?" Tate said. "I mean, if the person hadn't even died yet, why would there even be anything to publish?"

"Actually I believe that's pretty common at newspapers Chief," Barstow said. "It's a time saving thing. It would probably be for famous or prominent people, not just you or me."

"Right," Angela said, "like if the former mayor or some bigwig local businessman were sick, or just getting on in years, they might get a jump on their research and have an obit mostly written. Then when the person passes on, they just fill in a date and a few details. So, like I was saying, this local paper printed two obits by mistake on the same day. They had to publish a retraction of course, and apologized up and down to the families, but the thing is, within about a month, both of the people had been killed. Murdered. And they never caught the killer. What I read said that the police were never able to find a connection to the obits. Reminds me of our mugs."

"It's like somebody took the articles in the paper as some kind of order to go out and kill those people," Dean said. "Didn't that Son of Sam guy say his neighbor's dog told him to kill?"

"That's the last thing we need," Tate said, with a shake of his head. He went to take a sip of his drink and realized that his glass was empty. "Now we'll have the neighbor's dog to worry about."

Just then the waitress came by and asked if they wanted another round.

Tate held up his empty rocks glass. "I'll have another Maker's Mark."

The waitress nodded at him as Angela gave him a look and whispered something in his ear. "You know what," he said, to the waitress, "on second thought, I think a Miller Lite sounds good."

The waitress grinned and nodded again. Angela looked over at Tate, who looked across at Dean and shrugged. Barstow looked up at the mugs on the ceiling while squeezing Dean's thigh under the table. Dean pondered his own empty rocks glass for a moment before speaking to the waitress. "You know what, put me down for one of those Miller Lites also."

The waitress looked at Angela. "What'll it be boss?"

"I'll have another of these, but have Cody make it small and weak."

"I'll have another of the same," Barstow said, when it was her turn. "Small for me too. No need to waste it."

Barstow was gazing up at the mugs on the ceiling again after the waitress left. "Could somebody be trying to set Buddy Parrish up somehow? Like, frame him? I'm just trying to think if that could make sense."

"It's no secret that this Buddy guy did the ceiling work, right?" Dean said. "Far as I've heard, everyone seems to know that. Also that it was him that put the mugs up in the wrong direction. I'm just not seeing how anyone could frame him. And what possible motive would they have?"

"Problem with that question," Tate said, "is that there isn't any motive in sight. Two murders this week with no visible motive."

"Tomorrow's another day," Angela said. "And it's going to be a long day by the looks of it. How about letting it go for now. Give yourselves a break for a few."

The new round of drinks had arrived just in time to toast to her suggestion. They spent ten minutes kicking around ideas about how to solve the parking problem in town, finally giving up to fall back on talk of favorite movies and music. With Dean agreeing to drop into the station the next morning, the two couples called it a night, settled the check, and went their separate ways.

fter ten or more running tries, at last he caught a gust of warm air and suddenly was aloft. Half the height of the telephone poles at first, then level with their tops, then again as high above. He tested his turning ability by rotating his outstretched arms slightly, banking to the right to soar over the old apple orchard. The warm air flowing over him lifted him higher as he turned back to cruise over the main road, following its curves as it wound past the rows of ranch houses with their green lawns, swing sets, and back yard pools.

Looking up at the open sky ahead, he was surprised to see dark grey thunderclouds filling the horizon as far as he could see to his right and left. He moved his arms to try to turn back to the clear blue sky and the swing sets and apple orchard behind him, but his steering ability was gone. With the increasing force of the wind rushing over him, he suddenly knew that his air speed had increased and he was hurtling towards the thunderclouds, unable to turn or slow down. His breathing, easy and gentle a moment before, became strained and shallow, as the sound of the wind became a roar in his ears.

He became aware of a sound from somewhere below, faint at first, then growing louder and clearer. As the road rushed by, he looked to see a woman running along with him, pointing up to him and calling out his name. Something reached from the darkening air to grab him, arresting his flight. The voice grew clearer and louder, closer now, closer still, until suddenly the road, the clouds, and the rushing air all disappeared.

"Come on Tate, come on. Wake up. Wake up now. Bad dream." Tate's eyes opened wide as he lifted himself up onto his elbows. Angela was speaking softly to him as she shook his shoulder. "Just breathe, breathe. Are you okay? You were having a nightmare."

He nodded and fell back to the pillow, running a hand through his hair as Angela kept rubbing his shoulder. "I'm really sorry. It happens to me a lot. Dreams. Nightmares. I'm sorry I woke you. What time is it anyway?"

"It's about five, you have time. No need to get up yet."

"I don't think I'm going to sleep anymore. How about coffee in bed? Can we do that?" He looked around the room, which was slightly lit from a light coming through a crack in the door. He looked down at the comforter and the sheets. "This isn't my bed. I guess that answers the question of 'your place or mine'."

"No Chief, this isn't your bed, but you're welcome in it anytime. Give me a few minutes to get us some coffee."

She left the room and soon Tate heard the comforting

sounds of someone working in a kitchen. He went into the bathroom to rinse his mouth and wash his face, coming back to prop himself up with pillows and process the nightmare. His favorite dream of flying free, taken over and corrupted by the evil that seemed to have gotten a grip on his peaceful town and had apparently stolen into his subconscious.

Angela came back into the room with big mugs of coffee, handing one to Tate and arranging herself onto the bed next to him. "I had my own weird dreams last night you know. Not nightmares, just weird dreams. And then I was just laying here for a long time, thinking of what we talked about last night with Vic and Dean. The mugs, all of that. And I realized something. Or more like I had an idea."

"I'm sorry Ang, all that crap, and me, keeping you awake. What was the idea you had?"

She turned towards him in the bed, balancing her coffee mug on a knee. "Vic said something last night about how she was wondering if maybe somebody was trying to frame Buddy Parrish. Like, I don't know, somebody wanted to kill those people, or maybe just wanted to kill people, and was using the mug thing as cover. Well, after thinking about it for a few hours, here's the thing. I don't believe anyone's trying to frame Buddy—like, to *hurt* him—I think somebody's trying to *help* him. What do you think? I'm serious."

Tate nodded a few times and sipped his coffee.

"At this point, I can't dismiss any idea, however odd it may seem, but I also have to work with facts and evidence. Offhand, it's not jumping out at me how anybody would be helping."

"But Tate, we aren't dealing with reality here. Wait, that

isn't what I meant to say—we are dealing with reality, but not any normal reality. Weird shit is happening. That train has left the barn, or however that goes. Hear me out, think outside the box. Let's say Buddy Parrish is an innocent. We all agree that he wouldn't hurt a fly. But he has limited ability to process complicated adult situations. Think about it. From his point of view, we put him in an impossible situation. His father gave him instructions to do whatever I told him to do, but also warned him not to make mistakes. Then, because of mixed signals from me, and Cody maybe, he does end up making a mistake. Never mind that it wasn't really any kind of big deal. He makes a mistake, realizes it later, and worries about it. Just when he's trying to fix it, I come in and tell him to stop whatever he's doing, and he gets upset, but he doesn't have the ability to communicate what's happening. He goes away, the restaurant opens, and we forget about it. Only, Buddy lives in a smaller world, and he doesn't forget about it. He tells someone about it, or anyway, someone finds out, and decides to try to help. *To fix it.*"

"Okay, so what you're saying is, the mugs get hung up the wrong way—as if the owners are dead—and somebody tries to 'fix' the situation by making them be dead. Sure seems like taking the long way around, doesn't it? What kind of person could possibly do something like that?"

"A kind of person who's a bat-shit crazy psycho, obviously. You got anything better Chief? You who just had a nightmare about flying into a dark cloud of evil in your boxer shorts. I don't think you should dismiss my idea. Remember that Indiana case I told you all about last night?

That was never solved, but there was one theory that after those obits were published, somebody was trying to fix it by making them true."

"I don't dismiss your idea Ang, not at all. I'm going to think about it and see how it might fit what we know. It just throws me way off to think that somebody could do something so far out of bounds. I'm the police in this town, but between you and me in this bedroom, I can understand how some people could kill each other if the reason is strong enough. Just saying I can understand it. But this…this is a whole nother thing. No, I do not dismiss your idea Ang, and it scares the shit outta me. Like flying into a big, dark cloud."

25

T ate got into the department by seven o'clock, fortified with Angela's home-cooked breakfast and carrying a cup of Wawa coffee. He chatted for a while with Deputy Brody, who had the first shift and had already spent two hours patrolling the town, before settling in at his desk. The pre-dawn discussion with Angela had left him thinking about an old case and he was anxious to see what he could dig up in the online files. It was a solid twenty minutes before he was able to find most of what he was looking for.

It had been a warm summer evening in July of 1998 when there was an altercation on the Ocean City boardwalk involving Earl Parrish and his son Buddy. It was noted in the report that one witness had said that there had been a third person with them, but that had not been confirmed by police at the time. After reading through the file several times, Tate felt that he had a good understanding of what had transpired. *Or at least what had been recorded.*

Through circumstances that remained unclear, the Parrish family had encountered an apparent stranger—one Wayne Doyle of Philadelphia—who must have stopped to chat with them about something or other. At some point, according to Mr. Doyle's account, he had accidentally touched Buddy, at which time Buddy had reacted violently, grabbing and twisting his arm and throwing him to the ground. The boardwalk had been packed with people and there had been plenty of yelling and confusion. Mr. Parrish had rushed to calm his son down, and Doyle had been taken off to Shore Memorial Hospital where he was treated for a broken arm. In the end, after an unusually swift investigation, the decision had been made to not file any charges, and the matter had been closed. *Yeah, I think I've seen that one on TV a few times*, Tate thought to himself. *The son of a rich and powerful man hurts somebody and case closed after a few hushed meetings. No doubt there was a checkbook involved. Dammit Earl, I'm trying hard here.* Tate smiled to himself as he read the name of the police officer who'd been in charge of the case, realizing that he recognized the name and had been on friendly terms with the man for a period of some years in the past. *Pete Norris, okay then. I'll have to give him a call.*

As he finished with his reading, and sounds of activity coming from the front office increased, he stood up from his desk, stretched, and went out to meet and greet the visiting troopers. He found them in the squad room, talking with Deputies Brody and Connor, who had just arrived. He joined them for ten minutes, giving a brief outline of the two homicide investigations and their work assignments.

"Thanks for coming in. I thought it made sense to get you oriented before you start tomorrow. You'll be working with Deputy Connor as your main point of contact while you're here, but feel free to ask any one of us if you need anything. I, we, appreciate your help very much. Please make yourselves at home while you're here. Brody, Three, I know you'll make sure these gentlemen get set up with a desk and whatever else they need." He had already made it clear to the entire department that he didn't want the matter of the mugs brought up to the visitors.

Tate stayed and chatted for a few more minutes before retreating back to his office just in time for Doreen to tell him that Dean had arrived.

"So, I've been getting reports that you've been using Police Department assets in an improper manner," Tate said, after Dean had taken a seat in his office.

"Well, I don't know about improper," Dean said, "but I will say that certain of your officers sure do know how to use their assets."

"Then I'm glad to hear it," Tate said. "Hey, jokes aside, Vic and I knew each other long before we worked together —casual friends—so no issues from me. She could use a break, so I hope you'll be nice to her. Having said that, anything else is none of my business. What do you have going on for today?"

"Not much really," Dean said. "I'm coming to the end of my list of people I thought I'd look up while I was here. I'm trying out a new camera, so I thought I might take that out to the nature trail at the point. That's if the sun comes out and it's bearable outside. Let me know if you think of some way I can help."

"I will, don't worry about that," Tate said. "It might help to be able to bounce ideas off you later. We'll see what the day brings. I'll let you know."

Dean stood up and reached for his coat. "I haven't asked Vic yet, but does she get a lunch break at a certain time?"

"She's supposed to," Tate said, "but we're spread so thin that it's hard to set the time. Just ask her. She'll know when she can go to lunch. Or even if. Nobody's had a whole day off in weeks."

"Got it Chief," Dean said. "Just an idea. Let me know if I can help. And if that means buying the drinks and listening —I'm down with that."

Doreen poked her head in just as Dean was leaving. "Morning Chief. Larson Finch on line one for you."

"Okay, thanks Doreen," Tate said. "Oh Doreen, there's an Ocean City cop that I knew a long time ago—Pete Norris. I want to talk to him about a case he worked back in 1998. Could you find out what he's doing and get a number for him? I don't know if he's retired or what."

Doreen nodded and left the doorway. Tate picked up the handset of his desk phone and pressed a button. "Good morning Larson. What's going on with you this lovely winter morning?"

"Morning Tate," Finch said. "I just wanted to tell you about my return trip to that room up at the Springside house yesterday. I have to conclude at this point that I was mistaken in my thinking that there must have been two people spending time in that room. I only see the same person's prints in all the places they'd be expected."

"Is it possible," Tate said, "that someone did just a partial job of wiping the place down?"

"Mmmm…I can't say it isn't possible," Finch said, "but I don't see that being the case. No, there are prints all over —all the places you'd expect, but they're from the same person. I am surprised, primarily because of the way those power bars were torn open, but I have to go with the evidence. Those wrappers were all handled by the same pair of hands, no doubt about it. I'll have to add that one to my personal weird file."

"I hear you Larson," Tate said. "My personal weird file is getting pretty thick these days. Thanks for getting back to me on that. Anything else I should know?"

"That's all Tate," Finch said. "I've cleaned up the prints and sent them to your Deputy Barstow. She can enter them into the system and do whatever searches or compares you need."

"Good work, thanks Larson," Tate said. "Enjoy what's left of your weekend. Oh—just curious—you keep the original set yourself, correct?"

"No, that would be unethical," Finch said. "Not after I've passed them on to the proper police authority, which in this case is you. My files will purge automatically after 48 hours. If there's nothing else, Mrs. Finch has a substantial 'Honey-Do' list that I'd better get started on. Let me know if you need me."

Tate thanked him again and they ended the call. He picked up a note that Doreen had set on his desk while he'd been on the phone with Finch. On it was written 'Sgt. Pete Norris (retired)', and a phone number. Tate tried the number right away and got a recording of a vaguely-familiar voice instructing him to leave a message. He followed the instructions, leaving his direct desk number for a call-back, and had just enough time to get some hot coffee from the kitchen before his phone rang.

After pleasant greetings and a few minutes of polite catching up, the retired cop from Ocean City said "I heard about what's going on in Cape May this week, so I figure you're busier than a one-legged man in an ass-kicking contest. What can I do to help?"

"I called you because I happened to come across an old case that you worked on," Tate said. "It probably doesn't have anything to do with current events, but it's just one of those things that might help me understand where somebody's coming from or why someone sees things the way they do. You know the drill."

"I sure do," Norris said. "Background is important. What case are we talking about?"

"July of 1998, on the Ocean City boardwalk," Tate said. "There was an assault, or an altercation anyway, and a man ended up with a broken arm. Far as I can tell it was some kind of misunderstanding with a developmentally challenged young man. Ringing any bells Pete?"

"Oh yeah," Norris said, "I remember the outline anyway. That was Earl Parrish, your town bigwig, right? And his son. Guy was in his twenties I guess, but probably more like half that age mentally. The victim was Doyle something—no, something Doyle. Wayne Doyle. That's it.

See, the pet parade was happening that day, so the board-walk was even more crowded than usual. People packed in shoulder to shoulder. They were pulling little wagons with lap dogs in them, a lizard in a cage—all that kind of shit. I guess the son, Bobby Parrish I think it was, had a hard time dealing with the crowd. This guy Doyle was standing close, and he thought someone had bumped into him from behind—like, shoved him into the kid, Bobby. He overreacted and evidently grabbed Doyle's arm and yanked really hard."

"Your notes in the report mention that Doyle changed his statement," Tate said. "What do you remember about that?"

"He made a statement from the hospital on the day it happened," Norris said. "But then came into the department two or three days later to file a new one. The main differ-ence had to do with whether there was a third person in the Parrish party or not. See, he thought he was pushed, and I can understand that. Think about being in the front row at a concert. The crowd surges for whatever reason and people get shoved. He told us that it looked to him like after he bumped into a few people, an arm came out of the crowd to grab him, and he couldn't be sure if it was the Parrish kid or someone reaching around from behind him."

"It's Buddy Parrish, but it doesn't matter," Tate said. "And where did the idea of the third person come from?"

"Yeah, that," Norris said. "When it happened, a lot of people thought there was some big fight going on. You know—like a rumble. People were yelling, at least a few screaming even, and were running off in all directions. The son, Bobby, sorry, Buddy, ran away right after, but Doyle, who is now starting to go into mild shock, swears that he saw another guy running off with him, and he thought he heard the father yelling after him. My two cents—there was so much commotion, and people were running all over, there's no indication that there was a third person, but I can't say for sure. Anyway, he came into the station and made a new statement, essentially saying that he had accidentally bumped into the Parrish kid, who had reacted and yanked his arm. No mention of a third person with Earl Parrish and his son."

"That's interesting," Tate said. "How did it all shake out after that?"

"That's where it starts to smell," Norris said. "But hey, it happens every day. The County D.A. took no time flat to drop the assault charge and the whole thing went away. Guy I knew at the time was with the A. C. Press, he said that he had actually gotten this Doyle guy on the phone, you know, after, and he said it was all a misunderstanding. Something like, he had tripped on the boardwalk and the Parrish kid had tried to catch him, and it was all his own fault."

"And what was your take on that?" Tate said.

"Probably just what you're thinking," Norris said. "I think what happened is that Parrish paid all the doctor bills and wrote Doyle a big check. And the county D. A. winked at it and dropped the charges."

"Yeah, you're right about that kind of thing happening all the time," Tate said. "But I still hate it. Do you know what happened to the D. A.?"

"He went on to bigger and better things," Norris said. "As Mayor of Cape May and your boss, Jack Torrance."

"Whoo-whee," Tate said, with a short whistle through his teeth. "I didn't see that one coming, but I guess I shouldn't be surprised. He and Earl Parrish go way back."

"Right," Norris said. "That old game. But no big deal I guess, as long as Doyle was happy with whatever he got. And his arm healed. So that's that. It was really a simple deal, and wrapped up quick."

"I appreciate your time on this Pete," Tate said. "Like I said before, it probably has no bearing, but gives me some background to think about." He moved his finger to hover over the phone when he thought of something. "Oh, I think you mentioned that Doyle's first statement said that he had heard Earl Parrish yell something at the one or more people that he saw running away. Was there any indication of what Doyle thought Parrish had yelled?"

"Yes, there was," Norris said. "His son's name, 'Buddy', and then something else that he assumed was also a name. But he recanted that with the second statement."

"Got it," Tate said. "It's just interesting though. Part of the puzzle. What was the other name?"

"It was 'Montel'," Norris said. "Whatever the hell that means. Doyle thought that's what Parrish yelled, aside from his son's name. 'Montel'."

fter the call with Pete Norris, Tate leaned back in his chair and closed his eyes, staying that way for several minutes, until Deputy Barstow knocked on his door.

"You looked like you were lost in deep thought," Barstow said. "I hope I didn't interrupt anything critical."

"No Vic, it's fine," Tate said. "I just got off a long call and was taking a few to let things sink in. How are you doing? I think we all had a good time last night, didn't we?"

"I'm fine Chief," Barstow said. "And yes, I think we all had a good time. I just wanted to make sure there's nothing, you know…uncomfortable between us now."

"No, no, I don't think so," Tate said. "And lets not let it get that way, okay? If my friend Dean was some kind of jerk I'd tell you, but I don't think he is. You seem to have figured that out by yourself anyway. Who else is here, in the department?"

"Aside from us, just Doreen at her desk," Barstow said.

"Three went out with the two state troopers, and Brody's out on patrol. I just got here a half hour ago."

"Well sit down then," Tate said. "And let me fill you in on a few things that I'm going to ask you to keep to yourself for the time being."

After pushing the office door to within a few inches of closed, she pulled one of the chairs up close to the desk and sat down.

"We were kicking around ideas last night," Tate said. "Some wackier than others. Angela put forward a theory to me this morning that, well, at first I thought was one of the wacky ones, but only at first. She had the idea that it wasn't somebody trying to frame Buddy, or get him in trouble somehow, but instead it was somebody trying to help him. We talked about it for a while and it stuck in my head. One thing I kept thinking about was this thing that happened in Ocean City more than twenty years ago…"

Tate then related to her his research on the Wayne Doyle case, and the substance of his call with Pete Norris. When he finished, she nodded slowly and silently, deep in thought and appearing to ponder a spot on the wall behind Tate before speaking.

"You said something about wacky ideas. Some wackier than others. As long as we aren't dismissing them… if Angela's on to something, and maybe there's a nut out there thinking he could be helping Buddy in some way, then in that world, it would be good to know about any of his friends. I've never heard of anyone named Montel, but then I only know Buddy to say hello in the Acme. Didn't you say that you asked Earl Parrish to talk to Buddy? Has he gotten back to you yet?"

"No, he hasn't yet," Tate said. "But now I think I need to call him. Ask him about all of this. Between you and me it really isn't something I want to do."

"I get it Chief," Barstow said, "and I don't envy you, but I hope you'll let me know how it goes. Thanks for looping me in on this."

She stood up and started to go before turning back to him. "You asked me to keep this on the down-low for now. Does that include Dean? We're going to try to have lunch in a few hours if all's quiet."

"No, you can tell Dean about it," Tate said. "As a matter of fact, you know what, please make sure you tell him about it. I want the three of us to be on the same page about all this. These are strange days going on here, and I need to be able to bounce stuff around unofficially. Are you okay with being a part of that Vic?"

"Sure am Chief," Barstow said. "I'm glad to be at the table and you can count on me."

27

W hen Tate called, Earl Parrish answered on the third ring. "Hello Tate, calling you was on my list for today. How are you?"

"I'm fine Earl, thank you," Tate said. "I hope it's okay that I called you on your cell, but I had a few things to ask you about. Have you had a chance to speak with Buddy yet, about the things we discussed?"

"For Christ's sake Tate, of course you can call my cell," Parrish said. "You are family, you know. And yes, I did get to sit down with Buddy yesterday afternoon. I was going to tell you about it when I called later. But hey, I'm due for a break. Are you able to stop by? We could meet in the coffee shop. I'm just in here checking on the work."

"Sure Earl, I can meet you there," Tate said. He checked his watch. "I'm in my office now, but I can be there in about ten minutes."

The Harbor House Coffee Shop was the most casual of the eateries that fell under the Harbor House umbrella. Most locals simply called it 'the Coffee Shop', and it was a well-known spot for a quick bite in a diner-style atmosphere. Tate parked in the main lot and walked across to the entrance. A set of bells jingled as he pushed the door open. Earl Parrish was the only person in sight, and was sitting at one of the counter stools looking over a pile of papers. He looked up as Tate came in and the bells on the door played their metallic tune.

"The work's almost done in here," Parrish said. "What do you think? The counter is new, and the stools are all new. New stainless sheeting on the back wall there."

"It looks good Earl. Fresh and clean," Tate said. "Which I think is what people probably want to see when they come into a place like this."

"You hit that on the head," Parrish said. "They want fresh and clean, and they want a waitress with a big beehive hairdo. Well, at least we can give them the fresh and clean. Pull up a stool Tate. The guys all went to lunch, so it's just you and me here. What's up?"

"Well, you mentioned that you had been able to sit down with Buddy, right?"

"Right, right, of course I did. Yesterday afternoon. We talked about the work he did at the Ugly Mug, and the mistake he made when he put those last mugs up pointed the wrong way. Truth is Tate, he felt terrible about that, and I feel terrible about it because I made it worse for him. I was glad that Angela had found that work for him, and I told him not to screw it up. I mean, not in those words, but I told him. And then he made a mistake, as humans do. He tried hard to do good work Tate, and I made it worse."

"I know he did, that's a shame that it ended up with him upset. Did he say if anyone had asked him about it, kidded him about it, anything like that? Or did he volunteer it to anyone?"

"No, we talked about that, but he couldn't think of anything. I'm afraid I'm no help for you on that. I can't imagine how this thing with the mugs could have anything to do with the cases you're working on. Buddy doesn't know anything about it though."

"Okay, well, thanks for asking about it. I appreciate it." Tate looked around the empty diner before adjusting himself on the stool and spinning it back towards Parrish. "Earl, can you tell me about Buddy's friends? Are there any that are really close?"

"Tate, what are you... You asked me to talk with Buddy and I did. And I told you what I found out. You know he doesn't need this kind of attention."

"Earl, relax, please. I don't want to bother Buddy any more than you do, but I hope you understand that I have a job to do here. It goes back to what we talked about before, except now I'm considering the possibility that someone could actually think they're helping Buddy by hurting these people. Somebody sick, obviously. If Buddy has any friends that I should be talking to, well, then I need to talk to them. That's all."

"Okay, all right Tate. I'm sorry for getting a little steamed up there. I know you're just trying to do your job. He doesn't really have much in the way of friends. He talks to me, he likes my housekeeper Suzette, he talks with the people around the docks. He loves to watch TV. No real friends. At least, nobody close."

"Earl, a lot of police work is about solving puzzles. And like it is with puzzles, you lots of times get led in different directions, and you have to follow the trail wherever it goes. You look something up and it leads you to some old file, or to talk to a witness you hadn't thought of before. One case leads you to read about another. And that's why I need to ask you about something that happened a long time ago."

"Oh, I have a feeling I know what you're going to ask about. That thing on the boardwalk in Ocean City. There isn't a lot to tell really. It was very crowded up there. Some guy bumped into Buddy. It didn't mean anything, he just got shoved by the crowd I guess. Buddy must have felt threatened somehow, and grabbed the guy's arm. He didn't know his strength and the guy got hurt. His name was Wayne something or other."

"That's right. Wayne Doyle. The reason I'm asking is that, at the time, there was some confusion about if there had been another person with you that day, like a friend of Buddy's maybe. The point is, I need to know if that was an occasion that a friend of Buddy's used violence to defend him, or to somehow help him. You see what I'm getting at? Was there another person there?"

Parrish's face was a solid mask as he shook his head back and forth. "No. There was nobody else there with us. Just Buddy and me."

"Okay. So it was just you and Buddy." Tate got up off the stool and walked the few feet to the row of windows that looked out onto the parking lot. He stood close enough that his breath made a circle of fog on the glass. He reached up and drew a line through it, connecting a pair of clouds high up in the sky outside. He turned back to Parrish. "Earl, does Buddy have a friend named Montel?"

The question had an immediate and visible effect on Parrish. He sucked in a fast breath through his teeth and the muscles all across his chest and upper body tensed suddenly, as if an electric shock had caused him to stiffen up and sit straighter on the stool. Seconds later, he appeared to deflate with a great exhalation. He raised both hands to rub his temples. He looked up at Tate without speaking.

"Earl, people are dying here," Tate said. "And I need all the help I can get. If Buddy's friend Montel is in town, I need to talk to him. It's as simple as that."

"No Tate, it's not that simple. You can't talk to Montel."

"What do you mean Earl? If I need to get a warrant, you know I can do that. Why are you saying I can't talk to him?"

"Because Montel isn't real Tate. Don't you see? He's not real. Montel is Buddy's imaginary friend."

28

"But Earl, one of the witnesses on the boardwalk that day thought they heard you yell out Montel's name when people were running away. What does that mean?"

"I don't know Tate," Parrish said. "It was a madhouse up there. I can't account for what somebody thinks they heard. I was worried about my son, and worried about the man that had gotten hurt, and none of it changes the fact that there isn't any Montel. Just Buddy's made-up childhood friend."

"All right, well, no Montel then. Okay. I'm sorry Earl, but I had to ask about it. If you can think of any of Buddy's friends—an admirer maybe, I don't know—it might help. Think about it please and let me know if you come up with anything. Anything at all."

Tate couldn't think of anything else to ask along the 'Buddy's friends' angle, so he started putting on his coat to leave.

"He's not a bad kid Tate," Parrish said. "He's lived his whole life thinking—no—knowing—that he's somehow less than the rest of us. He didn't ask for all that."

"I know he didn't Earl," Tate said. "And I can hardly imagine what he's been up against. Let me know if you think of anything else."

"You're family Tate," Parrish said, when Tate was almost to the door. "But Buddy's my only son. I need you to know that I would do anything for him."

"I know you would Earl," Tate said. "You've been a good father to him. You have my number. Call me day or night when you think of something."

————

After leaving the meeting with Earl Parrish, Tate was almost to his car when Mayor Torrance pulled up and got out of his own car.

"Tate, what you are doing here?" Torrance said.

"Just my job Jack," Tate said. "Bad shit is happening in this town and I'm trying to do my job."

"Fine Tate," Torrance said. "I just hope you aren't giving Earl too much trouble, that's all."

Tate walked over to the mayor's car and stood face to face with him. "I wouldn't give Earl—or anyone for that matter—'trouble' just to give him trouble. Like I said, I'm just trying to do my job here. And I will do it, Jack. Believe it."

"Okay Tate, I get it," Torrance said. "I'm just suggesting

that some discretion might be in order for a generous man who does so much for Cape May. That's all I'm saying."

"Earl's in the Coffee Shop," Tate said, pointing to the part of the building he had just left. "You have a wonderful afternoon."

Torrance gave no answer as Tate turned and walked back to his car. He heard the cruiser start and watched it drive out of the lot and back to the main road before walking towards the Coffee Shop and his meeting with Earl Parrish.

29

As the late-afternoon sky began to darken, Tate had been in his office, alone in the police department, for several hours. The surface of his desk was littered with balled-up wads of yellow paper, and a slim stack of files and reports sat off to one side. Periods of ten or fifteen minutes of scribbling notes on a legal pad had been interspersed with equally long periods of leaning back to look at the ceiling in deep ponderment, until the notes—and the thoughts—began to read the same over and over. His silent curses to himself had increased in frequency.

As he tore up another sheet of notes, he heard someone come in through the main door and then move about the office. After a minute, Deputy Barstow appeared in the doorway.

"Hey Chief," Barstow said. "You're the only one here. Where is everybody?"

"Afternoon Vic," Tate said. "Doreen put in a few hours

and went home. Three spent a half day with the state guys and got them situated, so they should be ready for tomorrow. He and Brody must both be out on patrol. I've been here for most of the afternoon, and I guess I lost track of time. What's up with you? Did you see our friend for lunch?"

"I did Chief," Barstow said. "And there's something I need to tell you about."

Tate's face took on a pained look as he sat straighter in his chair.

"Nobody else has been hurt," Barstow said. "Least as far as I know, so don't worry about that. But there may have been a close call. We had lunch at the C-View, and Skylar waited on us. You know her, right? Skylar Park."

"Yeah, she's one of the eight people you and Three checked out to make sure they were still alive," Tate said. "Her mug was turned. Did anything happen to her?"

"No, she's fine," Barstow said. "But she told me that last night, she was cleaning up after dinner, and she saw someone outside in her back yard. She thought he had been looking in the kitchen window at her. She lives alone, but her boyfriend from Wildwood happened to be there, and he opened the back door to yell at the guy. Skylar told me that the boyfriend—Tom—saw someone running off across the back yard towards the next street."

"What description was she able to give you?" Tate asked.

"Not much, from either of them," Barstow said. "They were both sure that it was a good-sized man in dark clothes. A white man. That's all she could say. They kept the outside lights on and Tom will be staying there with her for at least a few days."

Tate rubbed his chin, unconsciously stroking a beard that hadn't been there for years. "So maybe it's all escalating. Whatever it is. Accelerating. And they didn't call the police, correct?"

"That's right," Barstow said, "and of course I asked her about that. She said that it had given her a shock, and pissed off the boyfriend, but they just thought it was some local kid wandering around and snooping. Didn't occur to her to call the police, is what she said, but then when she saw me today she decided to tell the story."

"Vic, I have a feeling that things are coming to a head," Tate said, "and I'm worried about what that could look like. I'd like to get together with you and Dean tonight. Are the two of you having dinner together again?"

"We haven't made plans yet," Barstow said, "but I assume so. Why don't we all have dinner together and we can talk then. Do you want me to see if I can get Angela?"

"No, let's leave her out of this for now," Tate said. "I want this circle to be as small as possible. Set it up, would you please? Somewhere quiet where we can talk. Any time after seven. Just let me know and I'll be there."

———

When Earl Parrish came into the house, it seemed to his housekeeper that he was hunched over, as though burdened by a great weight.

"You look like the world hasn't been good to you today Mr. Parrish," she said. "Are you all right?"

"I'm all right Suzette," Parrish said. "But you're right about the day. It has been one of those days."

"Oh, I'm sorry to hear that," she said. "What can I get for you? Can I make you a martini?"

Parrish smiled at her and allowed a little laugh to escape. "Thanks, but it's a little early for a drink. Ask me again in five minutes and I might give you a different answer. Suzette, is Buddy home?"

"No, Mr. Parrish. I saw him earlier but then he said he was going out to walk around town. He borrowed one of your coats because I hadn't finished cleaning his yet."

"That's fine," Parrish said. "What happened to his coat —do we need to get him a new one?"

"I don't think you need to," she said. "I was able to get most of it out. Just needs to dry overnight."

"I'm not following Suzette," Parrish said. "What did he get on the coat?"

"I'm sorry Mr. Parrish," she said. "I thought you knew about it. Blood. There was a lot of blood on the sleeve and around the zipper. At first I was worried that Buddy had hurt himself but he hadn't. He told me that a friend had borrowed the coat for a little while yesterday morning and had gotten a terrible nosebleed. I hung it up on the back of his door. It should be fine by tomorrow. Are you sure you're all right Mr. Parrish?"

"Ahh, I'm…yes, Suzette, sure," Parrish said. He blinked a few times and shook his head. "I'm fine, thanks. I'm sorry, I was just remembering something that I forgot at the office, but it'll wait for morning. Thanks for taking care of the coat, and I'm sure it'll be fine. Now, I've got to do a few things upstairs. When I come back down in a little bit, I think I'll be ready for that martini after all."

Upstairs in his son's room, he hadn't known what he was looking for, until ten minutes later, he found it. The single book shelf in the room held more objects that weren't books than it did books, but Parrish knew that the richly illustrated copy of Stevenson's 'Treasure Island' was one of Buddy's favorite possessions. Sticking out from around the middle of the book was a folded and well-wrinkled sheet of standard copy paper. One side was half-filled with hand-written text in the format of a numbered list. The first twelve items were written with a neat hand in blue pen. A thirteenth had clearly been added by a different writer, in a hastier style, and was in pencil. *The mugs*, Parrish thought to himself. *These are the mugs that he hung up wrong.*

He recognized several of the names. Dan Kershaw had worked for him years ago. And the one added in pencil at the bottom too—Fred Herrington. Alaine Sawyer was the woman they found on the beach a week ago. He had known Augie Danforth since forever. Milt Madden worked for him now, and there was Bo Gibbons too. As Parrish realized that five of the names on the list had a small check mark next to their number, he felt a pain well up from somewhere down the back of his neck, moving up higher to sit deep in the middle of his skull. *Checking off the dead. I think it's time for that martini.*

30

"What time did you say we're meeting Tate?" Dean asked, pouring a chilled white wine into two glasses and handing one to Vic, who was reclining on the sofa in his suite.

"Seven," she said, taking the glass and smelling the wine. "Seven o'clock at Finns, and I made sure that we could get one of the tables at the back of the porch so we'll have privacy. He said he wanted to talk. Said this whole thing was escalating. Coming to a head, I think is how he put it."

"Do you think he's coming around to the idea that this Parrish kid...man...could be doing this himself?" Dean said. "Offing these people?"

"I think he's got to be considering it," Barstow said. "I'm considering it myself, but I don't like it. Between you and me and these walls, this thing just doesn't have Buddy Parrish written on it. He's just a big dumb lunk. Sorry to put it that way, but that's the truth."

Barstow raised herself to sit up straight and sipped her wine. "Remember that French doctor we saw with Earl Parrish the other night?"

"Sure, I remember him," Dean said. "Pierre Dubois was his name. Doctor Pierre Dubois. I remember the feeling that Parrish didn't want us talking to him."

"Right, I remember that too," Barstow said. "The next day, yesterday, I tried searching him out on the internet but I couldn't find much at all. Must be some fancy doctor to the rich who doesn't advertise. Nothing I found told me what his specialty is. Don't you think that's strange?"

"Maybe his specialty is something that people don't like to talk about," Dean said. "Like, he's a leading expert on hemorrhoid surgery or something like that."

"Very funny," Barstow said. "But maybe you're right. Hey—we need to meet the Chief soon. I'm gonna pop over to my place and become a civilian. I'll be back in thirty and we can walk up to Finn's. Okay?"

Dean agreed to her plan and walked her to the door, where she paused with one hand on the knob.

"You know, I told you that I spent some time online looking for info on that doctor. What I didn't tell you is that, well, I'm not proud of it, but I also did some searching on you."

Dean grinned at her. "What did you find?"

"Nothing really," Barstow said, "which I think is odd. You're like a ghost."

"Well I guess you aren't afraid of ghosts then," Dean said. "Relax, my records are just flagged and locked down by my team's tech person. She called me five minutes after you did the first search on me the other morning."

Barstow gasped out loud and covered her mouth with one hand as her face flushed. "I am so embarrassed. I just wanted to see…"

He cut her off by leaning in to give her a kiss. "I understand. I'm a stranger who comes into town and all of a sudden I'm sitting in on your meetings. It's a small town and your department is a close group—I get it. Don't give it another thought."

"Thanks, but I still want you to know that I am sorry," Barstow said. "Your tech person must be really good."

"Oh you wouldn't believe it. Sophia is a master," Dean said. "Pick any date in your senior year of high school and she'll tell you what you had for lunch that day. You know what, that's it—I'm going to call her while you go change and see what she can find out on our friend the good Doctor Dubois."

Forty minutes later, with Barstow having changed into jeans and a sweater, they made the two-block walk over to the restaurant. Not a star could be seen in the sky, and a dry, light snow had started to fall.

"This is just the beginning. There's a storm coming our way," Barstow said. "We could get slammed."

They saw Tate's police cruiser pull up ahead of them as they turned from Jackson Street and approached the restaurant, and the three of them went in together. The seats at the bar as well as the surrounding tall tables were about half full, but the dining room itself had only a few occupied tables. As Barstow had requested, they were seated well away from any other diners. She ordered a glass of wine and the two men ordered draft beers from a local brewery. While they chatted, nobody brought up the murder cases until after they had ordered dinner.

"I've tried twenty different ways to avoid the idea," Tate said, "but I just can't any longer. Buddy Parrish has got to be in this thing. When I started to hear about this friend of his—this Montel person—it all started to fall into place. It's what Angela said to me early this morning. 'Somebody's trying to help him', she said. First I learned about Montel, and then Velma Fontaine told me about the conversation she overheard between Buddy and another man. It all started to make sense. That is, until Earl Parrish blew it all up by telling me that Montel isn't even a real person."

Their dinner arrived, and for a while, they turned the conversation towards the coming nor'easter, and how much snow it was likely to bring with it. Dean asked Tate about the conversation that Velma Fontaine had told him about, and they all talked back and forth about that for a while. Vic told Tate about how they had bumped into Earl Parrish and the French doctor in the bar at the Carolina. Dean added that he had a call in to an associate to try to get more information on the doctor.

"I almost forgot the latest," Tate said. "Earl Parrish called me about a half hour before we met up here. It sounded a lot to me like he was trying to control himself, like forcefully calm, if you know what I mean. He told me he was looking into some things and he wanted another chance to talk to his son."

"Chief, you know you're probably going to have to bring Buddy in, right?" Barstow said. "Maybe Earl too. What did you tell him?"

"I told him that time was running out," Tate said. "But to go ahead and talk to Buddy and let me know how it goes. He said he would call me again later tonight. Wonderful—and a blizzard on the way to boot."

When Tate excused himself to use the restroom, Vic leaned in closer to Dean. "You know this is complicated for him, right? He must have told you that Earl Parrish is actually a distant cousin of his."

"He did," Dean said. "That's gotta make the whole thing that much tougher."

"And he's always thought that Buddy's an innocent bystander," Barstow said. "I think he may still think that actually, even if the idea is fading fast. To top it off, the mayor's starting to pressure him about Parrish. Those two go way back."

Dean's phone vibrated in his pocket just as Tate came back to the table, and he walked over to a quiet spot near the door to take the call. When he returned a few minutes later, his expression was grim. Tate and Barstow looked at him in silence, waiting for him to speak.

"That was my associate Sophia," Dean said. "I called her earlier to see if she could dig up some background on the French doctor we met with Parrish the other night. And now it's all coming clear to me. The clouds have parted."

"What did she tell you?" Tate said. "Earl hired him to try to help Buddy somehow, right?"

"Oh, I'd say there's no doubt about that," Dean said.

"And I'll also say that Earl was lying to you when he told you that Montel was Buddy's imaginary friend. Doctor Pierre Dubois is one of the world's leading experts on Multiple Personality Disorder. Looks to me like Buddy *is* Montel."

31

"Power bars," Barstow said, breaking a moment of stunned silence. "That's what Larson Finch was trying to tell us, even though he didn't know it."

"What? I missed something," Dean said. "How do power bars fit into this?"

"It was the day you went driving up through the towns," Barstow said. "We had a meeting at the station and he went to a lot of effort to explain something he had found in that room up at the Springside Guesthouse. I'll fill in the details later, but it looked like someone had broken into the house and was spending time in one of the rooms. We found a whole box worth of power bar wrappers, and Finch was stuck on the idea that there must have been two different people eating them because of the different way that the wrappers had been torn off. He made a great case, but then he only found one set of prints all over the room."

"And just one set of prints on the wrappers," Tate said. "Now I get it. Two people with the same set of prints.

Buddy and Montel. Two peas in a bod. We are in it deep now."

"Parrish said he was going to call you tonight, right?" Barstow said. "So that could mean any minute."

"That's right," Tate said. "Could be any time. How about if we wait for that call at my place? I have a bottle of scotch and some wine, good coffee and some Oreo's that might not be stale yet. If you're up for it I could use the company, and we can hash this out."

Barstow made the executive decision to get several desserts packed up to go, and Dean paid the bill. Tate drove the cruiser down the street to his parking lot, while Dean and Barstow made the short walk. The snowfall had increased and was now blowing at a steep angle because the wind had increased as well. The cold, crisp air was refreshing, but after a few minutes of it they were both glad to arrive at Tate's condo building where he held the door to the lobby and ushered them into the elevator.

"Make yourselves comfortable," Tate said, as they shed their coats inside his foyer. "I'll put on a pot of coffee. It might be a long night."

Ten minutes later the three of them were camped out on a couch and loveseat in the small living room. On the coffee table were several plates that held the remains of slices of chocolate cake and key lime pie. Tate sipped at a steaming mug of coffee. The wind off the ocean whistled and howled outside, beating against the glass panes of the balcony door. "So, at Earl Parrish's request, Angela finds some easy work for Buddy to do at the Ugly Mug. But when Buddy makes a mistake that he isn't allowed to fix, Montel must have stepped in and said 'We'll show them Buddy, I know a way to fix this'. From that point on he must have become larger and larger until there was more Montel than there was Buddy. Is that what we're saying here?"

"That's about the size of it," Dean said. "As near as I can work out. From what you've told me, Buddy was a well-known character around town, and everyone seems to have been aware of his limitations. That helps to explain how he could move around easily, talk to someone in their yard, whatever. Nobody felt threatened by him."

"Chief, I don't remember all three of those names you had up on the chalk board," Barstow said, "the accidental deaths that you thought were sketchy. Can we look at them?"

"Let's do that," Tate said. "But only two of those three cross-referenced to the thirteen mugs on Buddy's list. Mary Ellen Barnes never had a mug, so let's set her aside for now, as probably a real accident. Next was Gerry Fisher in December, who fell down the stairs in the house he was working in. I've always thought that could easily have been a big strong man coming up behind and breaking his neck. He had a mug on the list."

"I remember the next one, because I worked it with you and it was just about six weeks ago," Barstow said. "Augie Danforth. He had a mug. He tripped and fell on that anchor."

"Right, or someone swung the anchor through the air," Tate said, "burying the blades in his chest."

"Ouch, that sounds horrible," Dean said. "What kind of anchor was it?"

"That kind with the triangular blades that hinge out," Tate said. "I don't know what it's called. Blades sunk right into him. Had to have been a lot of force. Unless he really fell on it."

"So those two," Barstow said, "until the Sawyer lady almost exactly a week ago. Drowned in a bathtub and then laid out on the beach hours later. I'm just now realizing—if it was Montel who killed her, maybe it was Buddy who came back later to try to tidy it all up somehow. Maybe he's trying to make it look like an accidental drowning? Problem with that is, that's giving Buddy more smarts than we think he has, right?"

"Maybe Vic, maybe," Dean said. "On the other hand, if it went like you say, Buddy taking her out to the beach could be the simplest thing of all. Like, 'oh, Montel drowned her, I know what, I'll put her next to the ocean, which is right over there'. Not the craziest thing I've heard so far tonight."

"Then what about Dan Kershaw?" Barstow said. "He had a mug, but that sure did look like an accident."

"It did look like an accident," Dean said, "and maybe it was, but think about this. Everyone we've just talked about, and Dan Kershaw—and we haven't even gotten to the guy that got hit with the hammer—every one of them is a brute force attack. Or an accident, but you get my point. No guns, no knives or poisons. Every one of these fits with a tall strong man using his muscles or a weapon of opportunity found at the site. Montel fits the bill."

"Maybe Buddy found that room in the guesthouse as a way to try to hide from Montel," Barstow said. "But eventually Montel showed up. I guess that's a question for this Doctor Dubois. And why has it accelerated so much in the past week?"

"Good question Vic," Tate said. "I'm thinking maybe because Montel realized the investigation was going on and his time was running out. He was rushing to 'fix' the problem for Buddy."

It was almost ten o'clock when Tate's cell phone rang. He snatched it up and looked at the display. "It's Earl." He hit the button to answer the call and walked over to look through the window at the snowstorm. The other two straightened in their seats and strained to listen. All they could hear was Tate, and he wasn't getting a chance to say much.

"Listen to me Earl…wait…don't do that…Earl, will you just listen…" and then, "shit. He hung up on me." He pressed the redial button and listened for a minute, ended the call and tried it all again. "He must have turned his phone off now. Dammit. He wants me to meet him and Buddy right now. This is not good. This is not good."

"Where Chief?" Barstow said.

"Up on the bridge. He said he's meeting Buddy where he and I met a few days ago to talk. Right up at the edge of the bridge construction, where his company's doing some of the repair work." Tate paced the room, trying the phone again with the same result. "I know what he's doing. He's going to kill Buddy. Shove him over the edge I bet. That's what he's planning to do."

"I don't buy it man," Dean said. "He's not trying to kill Buddy. He's going to try to kill you."

"I think Dean's right Chief," Barstow said. "Earl wouldn't kill Buddy."

"I don't think he would try to kill me either, but in any case, I need to get up there in a hurry," Tate said. "And try to stop him from doing whatever the hell he's got cooked up."

"All right Tate, all right," Dean said. "But we're going with you as backup. Here's the thing, so start getting your mind around it—you need to be ready to put him down. Either or both. Do you get me? There's a reason he wants to meet up on a bridge in a snowstorm, and it probably isn't for a baby shower."

"Let's go then," Tate said. "I'll take my car. You two follow in Vic's cruiser. I'll drive halfway up the bridge and walk the rest of the way up. You can pull in next to Lucky Bones. They're closed so the parking lot should be empty. Visibility is going to be about nothing, so you should be fine to follow me up a couple of hundred feet back. I'm going to start talking to him and I'll see where it goes from there. Vic —who's on duty tonight?"

"Three should have come on at eight, Chief." Barstow said. "Want me to call him?"

"Not yet, but be ready to," Tate said. "We're going to keep the circle small here, but we'll need to make it official at some point."

Minutes later, the two cars were headed swiftly but quietly towards the other end of town and the bridge with the gaping hole in it.

32

Following Tate from well behind until they entered the marina area, Barstow took the first left to go down a short hill and into the compact Back Harbor Wharf neighborhood. From there, she wound around to pull into the parking lot of a restaurant that she knew to be closed, out of sight of anyone who might be watching from the bridge or the main road. There were no other vehicles in sight. She circled the building and parked near the front in time to see the lights of Tate's cruiser rise up on the bridge and disappear into the swirling snow. She switched off the motor.

"Do you know if he's ever used his gun?" Dean said.

"I know he's had to draw it a few times," Barstow said. "He knows how to handle it, but no, he's never had to fire it at anyone."

"That's good," Dean said. "Let's hope it stays that way. Okay, I need to get up there after him. I'll stay as close as I can. I need you to stay right here and wait for us."

"Hey I'm the cop here," Barstow said. "This is my job, not yours."

"I know that Deputy," Dean said. "But you're a real cop and you have to live here in this town. You need deniability. Trust me please, and stay here? We're in my territory now."

She glared at him for a few seconds before handing over a small radio. "Take this, it's all ready. Don't make me wonder what's going on up there."

He pocketed the radio and got out of the car, going around the hood and off to the left towards the bridge at a trot.

———

Tate drove as far up the bridge as he could without running into the heavy construction equipment and piles of material that were scattered about the area. Before he got out of the car, he keyed his handset and used the car's megaphone to loudly proclaim "Earl, it's Tate. I'm on my way up."

Walking away from the car and towards the apex of the bridge, he reached to his pistol to loosen it slightly from the stiff leather of the holster. He walked quickly, but with careful steps as the ground grew slippery with the accumulating snow. The twin portable light fixtures that had been rigged up near the top of the bridge threw an eerie twilight across the scene. The gusting wind whipped the falling snow into swirl shapes, filtering the light from above, and creating strange moving patterns across the ground. As he approached the safety rope that told him he was close to the gap in the middle of the bridge, he saw a shape to his right that grew into the form of a large man as he closed the distance. The man was sitting on the edge of a machine that Tate guessed to be a portable generator, partially covered with a heavy canvas tarp. He had the impression that the man was hanging his head, which was covered by the hood of his coat, and looking down at the ground between his feet. As he moved one hand, a glint of shiny metal flashed in the intermittent light. When he spoke, Tate realized that it was Earl Parrish sitting there and not Buddy.

"He did it all Tate," Parrish said. Tate strained to hear him over the sound of the wind. "I didn't want to believe it, but I found a list in his room and there was blood on his coat. He really did it. Augie, the lady on the beach, all of them."

"Is that a gun you have Earl? You don't need that. Nobody else needs to get hurt here."

Parrish stood up suddenly and took a step closer to Tate, who backed up quickly.

"I'm not going to hurt you Tate," Parrish said. Tate saw that the gun—a large revolver—was in his right hand and pointed towards the ground. "He did it Tate, but it wasn't Buddy, don't you see? Buddy wouldn't hurt anyone. It was Montel who killed those people. You understand that, don't you? Montel has always been a bully."

Tate looked to either side of Parrish, finding strange, shadowy shapes off to both sides. "Earl, where is Buddy? Is he here?"

A high-pitched voice came from the left. "I'm here Tate. Everybody is scaring me." Tate strained to see, thinking that one of the shapes was moving closer.

A different voice came right after. It was a deeper voice, loud and forceful, more like that of a middle-aged man. It couldn't have been Earl Parrish, and it wasn't Buddy, but it came from where Tate thought Buddy had been a moment ago. "Don't listen to them. They want to hurt us both."

Earl Parrish reacted to the voice, turning quickly towards it to his right, but lost his footing on the snow-covered pavement. Trying to regain his balance, he moved backward too quickly, bumping hard into a stack of wooden pallets. His right elbow banged into a sharp corner, and the gun went off, the shot hitting Tate high in the left shoulder. As Tate staggered back with the impact of the shot, Parrish, having regained his balance, moved towards Tate with both arms outstretched. "No, no! Tate—are you all right? Oh my God, I didn't mean to…"

When Dean heard the shot, and saw his friend stagger back grasping his shoulder, he rushed up to close the distance between them, drawing his gun. Looking past Tate, he saw Parrish coming closer, still with a gun in his right hand, saying something he couldn't hear clearly enough to understand. It looked to him like Parrish was raising the gun to fire again. Dropping to one knee, he raised his arms in a two-handed grip and shot Parrish in the center of his chest.

Parrish immediately dropped his gun, grabbed at his chest with both hands, and started to walk off to the right with clumsy, shuffling steps. At the same time, Tate, holding his shoulder, turned to face Dean, in time to see Buddy Parrish emerge from the storm, screaming maniacally and barreling towards them both. Dean heard and saw the approaching figure also, and jumped to shove Tate out of the way. Passing the two men, and unable to stop himself on the slippery road surface, Buddy Parrish flew by and into his father with enough force to send them both over the edge of the bridge, tangled in the safety rope which failed to stop them.

Dean knelt next to his friend for a quick inspection, and was relieved to see that Tate's injuries were minor, with no blood immediately visible. "You're going to be fine. Looks like your radio stopped the bullet." *Radio, shit.* He grabbed the radio Barstow had given him and keyed the mic. "Vic, come on up. It's all over. We're okay but the other two are gone. No sirens and don't call anyone yet."

"On my way up," came her acknowledgement.

"I don't think that was Buddy," Tate said, moving slowly to sit up and lean against a stack of cement blocks. "That was Montel. Where are they? Did they fall?"

"Yeah, they went over the edge together," Dean said. "You have a flashlight?"

Tate pulled a flashlight from his belt and handed it over. Dean went carefully to the edge, where he lay down flat to shine the light down below, searching. Due to the partial shelter provided by the superstructure of the bridge itself, visibility below was much better than above. After a moment of moving the powerful beam around, he spotted the two bodies splayed across the ice-crusted rocks below in impossible positions. He got up and went back to where Tate was sitting.

"I see them down there on the rocks. They aren't going anywhere ever again. Do you know if the other side is over rocks too?"

Tate pointed over his shoulder in the direction of the other side of the bridge. "That side should be out over the water. For a minute there, I thought there was someone else over there, but that must have been Buddy moving around."

Dean was thinking hard and fast as Barstow appeared. "I think I heard shots. Who's hurt?"

"He took one in the radio," Dean said, pointing to Tate, "I don't see any blood so he's probably just bruised up. Parrish and his son went over the edge together, along with the bullet I put in his chest. They both hit the rocks like rag dolls."

Barstow looked at him. "You shot Parrish?"

"Just as I was coming up behind Tate," Dean said, "I saw Parrish shoot him. Then he kept coming with the gun. I had no choice."

"I know you didn't," Tate said. "But I don't think he meant to shoot me. His gun went off when he fell against that pile of stuff over there. Then Buddy charged us. Or Montel, probably."

"Right, probably Montel, but we'll never know for sure," Dean said.

"And what about you, there's blood all over your leg," Barstow said, shining her own flashlight on Dean's leg. "What happened?"

Dean looked down, seeing that his pants were ripped and his lower right leg was bleeding substantially. He used the flashlight to look around at the ground near Tate. "Shit, I thought I felt something when we fell. I must have caught one of those sharp pieces of rebar there. It'll hold for the moment."

"This is going to tear the town apart," Tate said. "Nobody's going to believe what really happened here."

"You're right Chief," Barstow said, shaking her head. "What the hell are we going to tell people?" She knelt down in the snow next to Tate to check out his shoulder. "We won't be able to prove any of this. It's all too crazy."

"Blood. That's it," Dean said, sounding to the others as though he had just stumbled upon a secret formula. "Hang on guys. This blood is the piece I've been missing. I think I know how to put a bow on this for you. Tate, you just said that you thought there might have been someone else over there on the other side, right?"

"I did for a second, but I must have been wrong," Tate said. "It had to have been Buddy."

"I know, but don't you see?" Dean said. "That's the ticket. Are you absolutely sure there wasn't someone else up here? Use your imagination. I'll give you a hint—the answer is 'no'."

"Yeah, no, I mean, yes I'm sure," Tate said. "There wasn't, right? We can't be lying to people."

"You don't have to lie," Dean said. "Just shade the truth a little bit. Or would you rather have a huge scandal without a good explanation? Look, you both just said that nobody would believe what really happened, and you're right. You'll never be able to prove that Buddy—or Montel—was the killer, but you *know it,* right? You really *know* that he was."

"I don't have any doubt about it anymore," Tate said. "Maybe if he was alive we could eventually prove it, but not now."

"So what can we do?" Barstow said. She looked at Dean. "What are you suggesting?"

"Give me a minute," Dean said. They watched as he put his leather gloves into a pocket, and pulled a pair of black latex gloves from a different pocket, pulling them on. "I'm gonna spin a yarn that nobody will be able to question. Both of you stay right here. And trust me, I know what I'm doing. Oh Vic—you can help. See if you can find my shell case. Should be right around there." He pointed to an area about six feet away. "I'll be right back. Don't be alarmed if you hear me fire a gun into the air."

He walked away from them and used the flashlight to locate the pistol Parrish had dropped, picking it up carefully. He looked around in the vicinity of the generator until he found a large rag, which he wrapped around the muzzle and body of the gun as a makeshift sound suppressor. He then crossed the roadbed to near the opposite end of the gap where he lay down in the snow to shine Tate's flashlight into the darkness below. *Perfect—black, icy water.*

Ten feet back from the edge, he found a pile of eighty-pound cement bags that had been loosely covered by another canvas tarp. He rubbed his bloody leg against the cloth a few times, making sure to leave a substantial red stain. Setting the gun down on the pile for a moment, he reached down to unlace and pull off his right boot, noting that it had plenty of blood dripped over it and inside it. His lower leg was hurting, and he cursed out loud with the pain of pulling off the boot. Pointing Parrish's gun into the air and angled out over the nearby marsh, he fired off four shots. Then, juggling the bloody boot and the rag-wrapped gun together in the air, he fired the sixth and last shot through the upper part of the boot. He then tossed the boot away to let it land near the edge of the gap. Taking his own pistol from the holster on his hip, he wrapped it quickly in the rag and fired a single shot out into the marsh, noting where the ejected shell case landed. He wiped the gun for prints and tossed it out over the edge into the dark water below.

Back on the other side of the road, he dropped Parrish's gun on the snowy pavement, near where father and son had gone over.

When they were alone together, Barstow said, "I'm not sure about this Chief. I trust him, but...what are you thinking?"

"I get you Vic," Tate said. "It's not easy, but I'm thinking that he knows how to handle this thing right now a lot more than I do. But I need to know that you're okay with it too, or we aren't doing it."

"Okay, I'm with you," Barstow said, after a moment. "If that's what you think is best. You know him a lot better than I do."

"Seems to me you're corrupting a crime scene," Tate said, as Dean was returning to them. "Convince me that we should be going along with you on this."

"I will, but hang on," Dean said. "I'm saving the day. You can thank me later."

"Here, I found your shell case," Barstow said, handing the small brass object to Dean.

"Fantastic, that'll help," Dean said. He took it from her,

wiped it on his jeans, and walked several steps away to toss it to near where he'd left the other one.

"All right," Barstow said. "What's next? Can I call this in yet—officially?"

Dean held up his hands to tell both of them to be quiet. He knelt down to tie the rag around his bootless foot. "Let's get down to Tate's car where I'll explain everything. This will work as long as you two are on the same page. The only story that comes down from this bridge will be the story you bring down to tell." The three of them made their way back through the storm to the warmth and quiet of Tate's cruiser before continuing the conversation.

"You're going to get me away from here in a minute Vic, but I need you both to listen close right now, and I'll tell you what happened here. This is the story. You're only going to guess at a lot of it because everybody here is dead, got it? Now listen. There's been a killer in town—just the two murders—lady on the beach and the guy with the hammer in his face. Forget about those accidents. The older cases are closed and it doesn't matter now anyway. Parrish somehow found out and confronted the guy. He got a gun and arranged a meeting up here. Doesn't matter why or how. Maybe he was an amateur sleuth. Maybe the guy was trying to extort money from him. We'll never know because remember, all three players are dead. Yes, I said *Three*. There was a scuffle and both the Chief and Parrish got shot by the third man. Fortunately, the Chief was only hit in the radio, but it knocked him down. Parrish managed to fire back at the guy and hit him at least in the foot, probably more. The guy then lost his boot and fell into the water on the other side, leaving the bloody boot and some blood stains across over there. They'll be easy to find. Looks like Buddy tried to help his father and they both went over the edge to die on the rocks below."

"But there's no body for the other man," Tate said. "How do we get around that?"

"I just checked, and that side is over water like you said. Where he fell, he went into the canal, and the tide took him out into the bay. His body will never be found. That's reasonable. His gun is in the water out there, so maybe the police will find it if they drag the area. It's a forty-five auto with two shots fired and no prints, so it would be okay to find. Even without it, you've got blood, a boot, and shell cases that match the slug that's probably still in Parrish."

"Okay, there was a standoff up here and they killed each other," Tate said. "The bad guy went into the water and was washed away, and Parrish is a local hero who stopped a serial killer and probably saved my life. Buddy is an unfortunate victim. What about me, why am I here?"

"You're here because Parrish called you to meet him up here at the last minute," Dean said. "That part is true, by the way. He told you that he thinks he knows who the killer is and to get here as fast as you can. You got here just in time to hear shots, and you took a bullet from somewhere over across the bridge. You think you saw the figure of a third man over there and heard the sound of his gun. You know guns, so you can say it sounded like a forty-five. You realized everyone had gone over the edge and you came back to your car to call for help. The main thing is that there was a big storm going on and you couldn't see or hear very well."

"All right," Barstow said, "but why would Parrish try to confront this guy and not just call the police until now?"

"You get to make that part up," Dean said. "Misguided but upstanding citizen maybe. Something that people will understand and forgive. It doesn't matter, everyone was killed. The crime spree is over and you have a local hero. You told me Parrish was close with the mayor, who would probably like to have the whole thing resolved neatly, so he might be of some help in that area. You know the drill, 'the tourist season starts in a few months, let's get it all out and then off the front page as soon as possible', etc.

"Looks like we're getting a break in the snow. You should call for backup now Chief, Three's on duty, right? You can help him find the gun, the bodies, and whatever else. And I hope that Vic will take me to my hotel to patch me up before my foot freezes or I bleed to death. Can we do that please?"

Tate and Barstow looked at each other for a moment until they both nodded slowly. Tate reached for the radio. Barstow and Dean got into her car, and she turned it around to head down the bridge and back into town.

33

B ack at the Carolina Hotel on Jackson Street, they walked carefully through the lobby, keeping close to the front desk so the night clerk wouldn't be able to see Dean's bloody leg. Once safely in his room, Barstow helped him out of his pants and he hung the injured leg over the edge of the bathtub so she could work on it. She rinsed the wound with alcohol from a bottle she'd brought in from the car.

"Oh yechh," she said, "that's a pretty nasty gash. We could probably wrap it up, but it really ought to get a few stitches."

"Do you know how to do that?" Dean said. "I remember you said you studied nursing for a while."

"You mean can I stitch up a cut?" She said. "It's been a while since I did it on a real person, but it's not hard. I took a refresher at the hospital last year, but anyway, it's not like we're going to call down to the front desk for a needle and thread."

"There's an aluminum case on the top shelf in the closet," Dean said. "Get that down and bring it in here please. Also, there's a bottle of scotch on the table out there. I wouldn't mind a little of that too."

Barstow went out into the suite, returning in a minute to hand a drink to Dean and set the case on the floor. "It has a little black pad on the side. Some kind of lock?"

"Yeah, it's a thumb reader," Dean said, holding out his right hand with thumb extended. She brought the case closer and positioned it so he could put his thumb on the pad. There was a slight audible click from somewhere inside and the top popped open. She set it on the floor again to open it fully. Inside was a shallow tray with a few file folders, a legal pad, and an assortment of pens and pencils.

"Lift that tray out," Dean said. "Other stuff under there."

She found small tabs at either side of the tray and used them to lift it out and set it aside, revealing a deeper compartment underneath. "Holy shi…." She said, looking down at the contents. "So, I see two automatics, spare magazines, what's this…oh…a silencer—hey, why not? Some weird kind of camera, and two different little boxes. What do you want from here?"

"The dark grey box," he said, "about the size of a paperback book. Open that up."

"Aha, now we're cooking," she said. "A suture kit, good, that'll do. Hmm, vial of morphine—don't need that. I can't imagine why you have all this, but I'll add it to the list of things you can explain later."

"Sure thing," Dean said. "There should be a little Xylocaine bottle there too, I could use a few sprays of that about now please."

"So, are you really Homeland Security?" Barstow asked, as she went to work.

"That's what it says on my paycheck, yes," Dean said. "Internal Security, is what they call us, but most people don't know that. I'm on your side here, really I am. This was my town, years ago."

"And what you did up on the bridge tonight," Barstow said, "is that the kind of thing, you know, like…is that what you do?"

"Not all the time," Dean said, "but sometimes we have to get creative. Put on a show, sort of. Look, if you want to run like hell, I'll understand and I won't blame you. No hard feelings."

"No, I'm okay," Barstow said. "No running away yet. Some more scotch?"

"That'd be good," Dean said, "and those are some of the nicest stitches I've ever had. If you're done, I need to get dressed and we've got one errand to do before the weather clears."

"Oh wonderful, I was hoping we'd get to go out into the storm again before the night is through," Barstow said, as she was taping a bandage onto his leg. "I'm listening, what is it we need to do?"

"There's a pack of disposable razors in the drawer there," Dean said. "Grab one of those and get a little blood on it before you throw all that stuff away. We'll go up to that house, where you found someone had been in the room, and leave it there. Like on the floor behind the toilet or something like that. Then you'll have physical evidence that there was a man in that room whose blood matches the bloody boot up on the bridge. Make sure you don't leave prints on it."

"Ahhh, but wait, that's your blood," Barstow said. "Are you sure that isn't going to come back to you somehow?"

"My DNA's never been sampled for anything," Dean said. "And anyway there isn't a national DNA file, so that connection will never be made. The important thing is that you can connect someone being in that room with the shooter who got washed away in the canal."

"Sheesh, I don't know," Barstow said. "Remind me not to get on your bad side. What about the prints in that room though? They must all be from Buddy Parrish."

"You guys can handle that," Dean said. "Either make sure his body doesn't get printed, or at least that they never get entered into the system for a compare. Between the police department and the mayor, respect for the late local hero and all that, you can pull it off."

At half past midnight, with Dean fully dressed again, they went back out into the snowy night, with Barstow driving Dean's car. She stopped and turned out the lights a block away from the guesthouse. "I think all the houses on this block are empty. Oh shit, I forgot—there's a lock on the door and the Chief has the key. Should I call him?"

"Hang on," Dean said. "What kind of lock is it?"

"It's a padlock," Barstow said. "Like a Master or something like that. There was a hasp on the door, like on a shed."

"Okay, no problem then," Dean said. "I have a kit with

me. Just take me a minute. You stay here and don't give me any flak this time. You've already aided and abetted me, we don't need you breaking and entering too. I want to get in and out fast. Tell me about where the room is so I don't have to search the whole place."

After she gave him directions to the side door of the house and then to the guestroom up on the second floor, Dean got out of the car and disappeared into the night. As soon as Barstow was alone in the car, her phone rang and she took a call from Tate. She filled him in on what she and Dean were doing, and then he told her about how events were unfolding on the bridge. Things were going well, and generally according to their rough plan. He told her that they should be wrapping up within the hour, and asked her to come there as soon as she finished with what she was doing. Five minutes after ending the call, Dean reappeared and got back into the car.

"That was fast," Barstow said. "Everything go okay?"

"All good," Dean said. "I dropped the razor on the floor between the trash can and the toilet, where it seemed like someone looking around casually could have missed it. Also, there was a little notepad with some pages ripped out on the dresser. I scribbled the names of the two murder victims on a sheet, and balled it up and tossed it under the bed. Now you just need to think of a reason to go back there in the morning and excitedly find those things. I suggest that you have that room thoroughly cleaned soon. The investigation's over and the city has cleaned up and secured the house—something like that. Make something up."

"Got it," Barstow said. "I will come back early in the

morning and excitedly find those things. I got a call from the Chief while you were in there, and it sounds like it's going well. Three arrived just after we left and he and the Chief checked out the whole area. He told Three about how Parrish had called him just as he was on his way to meet the mystery man and he had gotten there in time for the gunfire. They hiked down to under the bridge and found Parrish and Buddy, both dead on the rocks like we expected. The Coast Guard's sending a crew over to recover the bodies. They also found an empty revolver near where it looked like they must have fallen from. Oh, and the Chief told me that Three found a bloody boot over on the other side, and more blood where it looked like someone must have gone over into the water. They're bagging samples and getting pictures. The Chief wants me to drop you off and get back there as soon as I can."

"It looks like it all just might work then," Dean said. "And the people of Cape May can live happily ever after."

34

Mayor Jack Torrance was halfway through his press conference in the small City Hall auditorium when Tate slipped in through the rear door and stood along the wall to one side. He could see that the audience of a dozen people included members of the press from around New Jersey, along with a woman from the Philadelphia Inquirer.

"...As I was saying, I don't suppose we'll ever know why Earl Parrish took it upon himself to meet up with our John Doe, or why he took his son Buddy with him. As to the location of the meeting—up on the bridge where the repair work was being done—we don't know that either. It's been suggested that the meeting place might have been a demand from John Doe, but we can only speculate. We can take just one or two more questions please." Torrance pointed to a man in the audience who stood up to speak.

"Thank you Mr. Mayor, Jim Sampson from the Press of

Atlantic City. What can you tell us about any physical evidence?"

"Hi Jim, and thanks for the question," Torrance said. "I can't talk about all the specifics, but I'll tell you what I can. After what I'll call the 'shootout' up on the bridge, our police department, working with our crime scene expert, found quite a bit of blood and a piece of bloody clothing indicating that some unknown person—our John Doe—had been shot by Mr. Parrish and had fallen off the west side of the gap in the bridge, most certainly to his death. Chief Saxby, who as you know was injured at about the same time, apparently shot by John Doe, believes that he saw that man up on the bridge react to being shot by Mr. Parrish, and stagger out of sight towards the opening in the bridge, which of course, on that side, was over the icy water of the canal below. Now, while DNA testing takes time, we fully expect that the blood found up there, from the missing man, will match the small blood sample that was recovered from the room in the empty guesthouse that I told you about earlier. Something else that investigators found in that room was a slip of paper with the names of our recent murder victims—Alaine Sawyer and Frederick Herrington—written on it and then crossed out, like some sort of hit list. Let's see, what else…we have not yet found the pistol that we believe was used by our missing suspect to shoot the Chief and Mr. Parrish, but we have accepted an offer of assistance from the Coast Guard, and remain hopeful that they will find it in the water below the bridge. Okay, one more question. Denise?"

"Thank you Mr. Mayor. Denise Carney from the Star

and Wave. Can you address the rumors going around that there might be some connection between the two recent murders in town and a group of mugs that were accidentally turned around to face towards the ocean on the ceiling of the Ugly Mug Tavern?"

"Heaven forbid we would have gotten through this without that coming up," Torrance said, with a chuckle. "But it's okay Denise, thanks for your question. I have learned that in police work, it is good policy to not dismiss any idea out of hand, even if the idea stretches credulity. So I understand that it has been in that spirit that the police department has considered the idea very carefully. There is so much that we don't know, in fact that we will never know, about our John Doe killer. The only idea about a connection to the mugs that we believe might have some merit, is that perhaps John Doe, in his sick, twisted imagination, meant somehow to bully or threaten Buddy Parrish as part of an effort to extort money from Buddy's wealthy father. But all that would appear to fall into the 'we'll never know for sure' file.

"We have seen the best and the worst in our town this month. It seems that we have hosted an evil presence, whose motivations we can only guess at. We have lost one of our upstanding citizens in the fight against this evil, along with his innocent and defenseless son. And I have lost a dear friend. Thank you all for coming."

35

L ater that same afternoon, Mayor Torrance dropped into the police department, finding Tate at his desk. "What did you think of the news conference?"

"It was good Jack," Tate said. "I think you set the right tone. We don't want people running around wondering if there's still a killer out there in the town somewhere."

"You think we're okay with Larson then?" Torrance said.

"Larson's on board," Tate said. "I'm sure he smells a bit of politics in the air, but the fact is that we don't have any evidence to refute the official story. Anyway, I think this winter has soured him on New Jersey. He told me he and his wife are going to move closer to family in Florida."

"Oh that sounds nice," Torrance said. "Snow is the number one reason people move south. What are you doing with the two state officers now that the case is… ah…solved?"

"We've got them for two weeks," Tate said, "so I'm going to use them for routine patrols and other work. It'll give everyone else a chance to take a few days off. Everyone needs a break, including me."

"Sounds like a good plan. Hey, I don't know if you've had a minute to think about this Tate," Torrance said, "but, well…you're the only living relative of Earl Parrish."

"I figured that Jack," Tate said, "but we really weren't part of each other's lives. I doubt he left anything to me."

"You know I was an attorney long before I was the mayor, right?" Torrance said. "Years ago I was Earl's personal attorney, and even since then, I've handled a few sensitive things for him. One of those things was his will. Yes, that's right Tate. I made his will, and I can tell you that, with Buddy gone, you are the heir. I mean, there are some small bequests, and some charitable donations, but aside from that, you are going to be a very wealthy man, and one of the largest employers in Cape May County."

"Sheeesh… I don't know Jack," Tate said. "I didn't ask for all that and I'm not sure I want it. I like being Chief of Police."

"That's fine Tate," Torrance said. "That's all fine. You can still be Chief of Police. There are a lot of good people who'll help you with this. Velma's done most of the running of the fishery business for years anyway, and your friend Angela knows how to run restaurants. I'll help you any way I can."

"Oh man, this is all happening, isn't it?" Tate said, rubbing the back of his neck with one hand. "Yeah, I think I'll be needing that help."

Torrance stood up and started to move towards the door before turning back to face Tate again. "You know how I like to get ahead of things as early as I can, so I know you'll pardon me for bringing this up so soon. I'll be running for re-election in November, and then after that, I was thinking of running for state office. I lost my biggest supporter up on that bridge Sunday night. Can I count on support from the new owner of the Harbor House?"

"Yes Jack, you can count on my support," Tate said. "Because I think you've been good for Cape May and because we've mostly had a good working relationship. There's one thing though."

"Of course Tate," Torrance said. "What is it?"

"Don't ever try to tell me how to do my fucking job again."

"You've got a deal there Chief," Torrance said, with a big smile. He turned to walk to the door. "Don't forget the budget meeting was moved to this Friday."

36

That evening, after the mayor's press conference, the Savoy room at the Carolina Hotel was a warm and festive place. On one side of the restaurant, tables had been pushed together to accommodate a large party of people connected to the bridge work, celebrating the news that the project was nearing completion and the bridge should be re-opened to traffic in less than two weeks.

"Well, that dinner was fantastic," Tate said. "But once again, I've eaten too much. To good friends." He raised his wineglass to drain the last sip.

"Mmmm, me too," Dean said, patting his belly. "And I thank you all for hosting my visit. It certainly has been an interesting week."

"Come back in the summer some time," Angela said. "With luck it'll be more like eating, drinking, and sitting on the beach, with no murders."

"Oh, where's the fun in that?" Dean said, laughing.

"Now, to the immediate and important question, where shall the after dinner drinks be?"

"I know a place nearby on the mall," Angela said, "and the drinks are on the house. We can make a bet on who can avoid looking up at the ceiling the longest."

A few minutes later they were all bundled up and had started the short walk up to the Ugly Mug. Dean and Vic hung back and let the other two walk ahead.

"I've been waiting to tell you something," Barstow said, as they walked arm in arm. "We've all been wondering, why were Parrish and his son up on that bridge in a snowstorm the other night. I guess we'll never know exactly, but we did get a clue today. There was a cell phone in Buddy's pocket, and we found out from Verizon that he had called his father ten minutes before Earl called Tate. So it looks like it was Buddy who called Earl, asking him to come out to meet him on the bridge."

"No," Dean said. "Buddy wouldn't have done that. I'm betting it was Montel who called Earl, probably threatening to hurt Buddy. That's why Earl agreed to go out to meet him in a snowstorm, and that's why he took his gun."

"Ah, that's good. You're probably right," Barstow said. "So you think Earl took the gun to protect himself from Montel."

"Most likely," Dean said. "Or maybe somehow to protect Buddy from Montel, but that gets complicated. The more I think about it, I'm inclined to think that Earl might have just wanted to be done with all of it."

"The whole thing is just nuts," Barstow said. "And I'm glad it's over."

Tate held the door for them when they came up to the tavern, and they found the place to be doing a lively business with both bridge work people and local regulars. They settled into a booth near the bar.

"You gentlemen will be thrilled to know," Angela said, "that our liquor distributor dropped off a bottle of Blanton's Bourbon today. First one I've seen in ages. I thought I'd save it for special occasions and I figure this is a worthy one."

"Whoa, fancy stuff," Tate said. "And very rare indeed. Can we crack it open?"

Angela went up to the bar to give instructions and to order drinks for herself and Barstow. After they were served, the men savored the first taste of the fine whiskey, while the ladies both sampled it and made exaggerated faces. They talked about the changes that would come with the bridge opening that now appeared to be no more than a few weeks away.

"You know, the past two weeks aside," Tate said. "It's been so nice and quiet around here. It's going to be a shock to suddenly have people pouring into town again. I'm not sure I'm ready for it."

"Time marches on Chief," Barstow said. "And the town needs the business. Right Ang?"

"Yep, you're right," Angela said. "I think the shop owners and the other restaurants will be glad to have the people back after all this time. How about you Dean, what are your plans? Going to hang around for a while now that our crime wave is over?"

"I think I can stick around for a while," Dean said.

"Especially since I hear that certain, ah…city property will be getting a few days off."

"I think we can make that happen," Tate said. "I gather that you'll be taking liberties with that city property?"

"I certainly hope so," Dean said. "As much as possible."

"Oh goody-goody," Barstow said. "And Chief, I hear you're going to have a lot going on too, right? I mean won't you be taking over all the Harbor House businesses?"

"Eventually anyway," Tate said with a sigh. "I haven't gotten around to thinking about all that very much yet. What do you think Ang? Ever run a place like the Harbor House?"

"Nothing that big so far," Angela said. "Just this tavern. But I'm willing to help you with it if you like."

"I like," Tate said. "You get by with a little help from your friends."

"That sounds like a big adjustment for you," Dean said. "Are you concerned with how you're going to juggle running a business with your job as police chief?"

"I have some concerns," Tate said, with a shrug. "But what can I say? I'll cross that bridge when I come to it."

ACKNOWLEDGMENTS

I could not have completed this project without the help of several people.

For her enthusiastic assistance with the various stages of the editing process, I thank my friend, Dr. Judy Ozment, who is a scientist as well as a teacher. In both capacities, Judy helps me keep my facts straight and my writing as good as can be. Many thanks also to Joanne Sockriter-Belli (a Cape May friend from way "back in the day"), for her work on the final edit, as well as her help in promoting my books. No single person deserves more thanks than my wife and best friend, Bonnie Boumiea, who has been a priceless sounding board for me all along the way. She has been a great help with "does this make sense..." or "what if he did that..." She's also become a damn good editor!

Lastly, I would like to thank the hard working staff at Q Branch Camera in Princeton, NJ for helping me to understand the technology behind the NikorScan 2000 fingerprint reader described in the book. *Just kidding—I made that up!*

ABOUT THE AUTHOR

Miles Nelson spent thirty years with a Fortune 500 company before moving on to other pursuits. A New Jersey native who grew up in Cape May, he has traveled extensively across the U.S., as well as to Europe and to numerous Caribbean islands. When not writing or traveling, he enjoys cooking, photography, guitar playing, watching movies, and trying new wines. He lives in the Philadelphia suburbs with his wife Bonnie and their cat Starla. *Murder At Exit 0* is his third novel. For more information, go to www. milesnelsonauthor.com. You can also contact him at milesnelsonauthor@outlook.com.